"SOMETHING'S WRONG."
MALISSON PULLED OUT HER TRICORDER.
"COMMANDER DATA? ARE YOU ALL RIGHT?"

"I do not know," Data said, his voice grinding with a painful, mechanical timbre. Malisson and Muñoz both grimaced.

"Commander!" Muñoz scrambled to his feet, pointing a tricorder at him.

Data tried to push forward, but his body wouldn't move. The lieutenant, with a deepening frown, was still scanning him. "I wish I could make sense of these readings."

"My positronic brain," Data started, but the words came out garbled and indistinct. He was aware of Muñoz disappearing out of the laboratory, speaking into his combadge; he could hear Muñoz's voice even after he left the room, although his words made no sense. *You found the way home. Do you know how to speak? Do you know how to listen?*

"Do you hear that?" Data asked Malisson.

She looked up at him, her eyes wide. "I'm sorry, I can't understand you."

"But it sounds fine to me," Data said. What had changed? Why couldn't he hear the distortion anymore?

Suddenly, a jangle rose up in the room: it was the scanner and the decontamination chamber, both activating at once. The security lights blinked on and off, casting the room in flickering red light.

Malisson backed away, gazing up at the ceiling.

Data had one final moment of clarity before he opened his mouth and began to wail.

STAR TREK™

THE NEXT GENERATION

Shadows Have Offended

Cassandra Rose Clarke

Based on *Star Trek*
and
Star Trek: The Next Generation
created by
Gene Roddenberry

G

GALLERY BOOKS

New York   London   Toronto   Sydney   New Delhi

G

Gallery Books
An Imprint of Simon & Schuster, Inc.
1230 Avenue of the Americas
New York, NY 10020

First Gallery Books trade paperback edition July 2021

Library of Congress Cataloging-in-Publication Data is available.

ISBN 978-1-9821-5404-2
ISBN 978-1-9821-5418-9 (ebook)

HISTORIAN'S NOTE

The events in this book take place during the seventh season of *Star Trek: The Next Generation*, just prior to Q's pronouncement that the trial of humanity initiated during the *U.S.S. Enterprise*-D's first mission to Farpoint Station has been ongoing for the past several years ("All Good Things . . .").

1

Jean-Luc Picard was in dress uniform. Again.

The collar pressed uncomfortably against his throat as he tried to surreptitiously adjust the uniform flap in such a way that it didn't feel like it was strangling him. He was not succeeding.

"Still no word from Andor," announced Lieutenant Kociemba, who was operating the transporter controls.

Picard nodded. "It appears our guest will be keeping us waiting a bit longer," he said to Commander William Riker, who stood to his right, motionless, unbothered by the restriction of his own dress uniform.

"It would appear so," Riker responded.

Picard stared at the empty transporter pad. He was waiting on the great Andorian dancer Tirra zh'Undissa, one of the twelve guests the *Enterprise* was currently collecting on behalf of the Betazoid government for an upcoming cultural ceremony. Tirra was the first dancer, but there was also a smattering of royalty, three singers, and one Hallian sculptor who worked entirely in zutanian crystal. The route to collect them in time and in the manner they preferred was proving more complicated than most starship maneuvers Picard had studied back at the Academy.

"Sir, if I may—" Riker looked over at the captain. "I'll be happy to show Tirra to her room on your behalf. I can tell this has been a—difficult undertaking for you."

Picard smiled. "Have I been that obvious?"

Over at the transporter controls, Lieutenant Kociemba made herself very busy looking at the console.

"Not *too* bad." Riker grinned. "You never did tell me why the *Enterprise* was chosen, though."

Picard let out a long sigh. "We were personally selected to serve as a ferry by Ambassador Troi."

Riker's eyes twinkled at the mention of Troi's name. "Ah," he said. "I see."

Picard fidgeted with his collar again. Lwaxana Troi had made a compelling case for the *Enterprise* to be selected: while most of the 250 guests were being collected by Betazed ships, Lwaxana insisted that Starfleet should play a role. *We want to incorporate as much of the Federation as we possibly can!* she'd said over the comm. *And what better way to incorporate Starfleet into the ceremony than utilizing its flagship to gather guests from all across the Federation?* Apparently the gathering of guests was *itself* part of the ceremony, even if it meant sending the *Enterprise* on a rather elaborate detour for the past week.

He clearly couldn't wait for the entire affair to be over, and it was showing.

"Madam zh'Undissa is ready to beam over," Kociemba said, pulling Picard's attention back to the present.

"Very well," Picard said, dropping his hand to his side and straightening up his shoulders. "Go ahead."

The transporter beam sparkled into existence. Tirra zh'Undissa stepped icily off the transporter pad, the embroidered hem of her gown trailing behind her. "So this is the *Enterprise*," the Andorian commented, sweeping her gaze around the transporter room.

Five more, Picard thought, before stepping forward, hand extended. "It is, Madam zh'Undissa. Welcome aboard."

Tirra's antennae swiveled toward him a heartbeat before her eyes did. "And you must be the captain." She appraised him for a moment, then held out one slender hand, gloved in white gauze. "A pleasure to meet you."

Picard managed to press out a thin smile as he shook her hand. "It's my great honor to have you aboard, Madam zh'Undissa," he said, reciting the greeting he'd used on all of his guests. "Commander Will Riker will be showing you to your quarters."

Riker beamed and said, "Welcome, Madam zh'Undissa."

"Delighted," Tirra said in a tone that didn't seem delighted at all. "How long until we arrive on Betazed?"

"Two days." Riker took hold of Tirra's glittery suitcase.

"Wonderful. I was hoping to have some time to observe the effect warp speeds have on my choreography. I'm performing at the festival, you know. Two days will give me adequate time to prepare. Tell me"—she swept up beside Picard, her gown making a soft rustle like falling snow—"was a barre installed in my quarters, as requested?"

"It was indeed." Picard gestured toward the exit, hoping to move Tirra along so he could get back to the bridge. She stepped lightly, her attire drifting around her. She glided out into the hallway as if she were performing at the Intergalactic Theater on Andoria.

Picard's combadge pinged. *"Bridge to Picard."*

Tirra looked at him archly.

"My apologies," he said, tapping his combadge. "Picard. Go ahead."

"Priority One hail, sir."

"On my way." Picard offered Tirra a rueful grin. "Alas, I am needed on the bridge. Number One, see that Madam zh'Undissa is settled in at her quarters. Madam"—he gave a little bow—"I hope your practice goes well."

He was rewarded with a small smile for his efforts.

Riker stepped in smoothly, guiding Tirra down the hallway as Picard made his way to the bridge. The last few days had been a whirlwind, ever since the *Enterprise* was informed they had been selected to participate in the ceremony. Counselor Deanna Troi had explained the reason for the celebration—a lovely story about a Betazoid cultural hero named Xiomara, three ancient treasures that had never before been displayed together due to an archaic rift between the three Houses they belonged to, an entire platoon of capital-*G* Guests, and an immense amount of ceremony. *Ceremonies within ceremonies,* was how she'd put it. *I don't imagine it's your sort of event.*

He couldn't deny that.

The turbolift deposited Picard on the bridge. "Mr. Data," he said as Lieutenant Commander Data stood up from the center seat.

"It is the Federation high commissioner for refugees, sir," Data said. "She wishes to talk to you about the scientific expedition on Kota. It seems—" His executive officer hesitated. "It seems there might be an issue with the planet's suitability."

"*Merde,*" Picard whispered. Kota had been at the top of the list as a new location for the group of refugees from the Federation colony on Aratril, which was about to be uninhabitable due to an impending asteroid strike. There was currently a massive operation underway to evacuate all of the colonists before the asteroid hit, involving dozens of ships.

Picard took a deep breath. "I'll take it in my ready room."

Data nodded and slid back down into the seat. Picard stepped off the bridge, the door whispering shut behind him. He found Commissioner Fortnoy waiting for him on the viewscreen.

"*Captain Picard.*" She smiled grimly. "*I hope you're well.*"

"I am, Commissioner. I hear there's an issue on Kota?"

"*Yes. I'm not sure if you were aware of its status—*"

"The team is in the final stages of confirming suitability," Picard offered.

"*The very last round of testing, yes.*" Fortnoy's expression was steely. "*But I'm afraid there was a tragedy that occurred there yesterday. The latest expedition is set up near the shoreline, and they were hit with a dreadful thunderstorm. Unfortunately, the expedition's commander was caught in a flash flood that swept across the lowland. She was killed, along with another member of the team.*"

Picard closed his eyes at the news. Everything he'd heard about Kota had indicated it was a prime location for a colony—very little local fauna to disturb, perfect Class-M conditions. All of the previous expeditions had been textbook, from his understanding.

"I'm sorry to hear that," Picard said.

"*Yes, we all are.*" Fortnoy leaned forward. "*However, we must press on. The Aratril refugees need a home, and right now Kota is our best option.*"

"I agree," Picard said.

"*I know you're in the midst of transporting guests for the Betazed ceremony,*" Fortnoy continued, "*but the Kota team needs personnel, and you are the closest ship. Kota is so remote. Would it be possible for you to send an away team to help finalize the survey?*"

"Of course."

Fortnoy let out a long, relieved sigh. "*Oh, thank you, Captain.*"

Picard nodded. "I'll ask Commander Riker to assemble a team."

"*Wonderful.*" Fortnoy pressed a hand to her chest. "*You are truly a lifesaver, Jean-Luc. Especially for those refugees.*"

Picard smiled, but inwardly he felt a tight knot of anxiety. It was yet one more stop on their slow march toward Betazed.

2

———◆———

Kota glimmered against the inky backdrop of open space, small patches of land surrounded by a rich, jeweled purple. From up here, Doctor Beverly Crusher could see a white knot of storm clouds near the planet's equator, roiling in a slow leftward spin, and wondered if those were the storms that had led to the commander's death.

"We'll get you ready for those refugees," she murmured to herself before turning away from the viewport to collect her medkit. Commander Riker had been surprised when she asked if she could join his team for the mission—he'd already selected Ensign Josefina Rikkilä, a lab tech with field medic training, as there was no need for a doctor down on Kota.

But this week had not been an easy one for Crusher. Things were finally starting to quiet down after the *Enterprise* saw the birth of not one but three babies, including an Aurelian, whose births were notoriously dangerous to both mother and child. That was after there'd been a bout of Tanzian flu making its way through a security team. Plus, it felt like half the crew had their routine checkups scheduled at once.

With the slowdown, she thought a working shore leave would suit her. She'd been on a few missions similar to the Kota one when she first joined Starfleet, and she'd always liked fieldwork: the quiet, meditative quality of watching microscopic life wriggling in magnification, the satisfaction of running a hundred atmosphere tests and every single one coming back clean.

She could use some meditation after all the excitement. And knowing she was helping the Aratril refugees made the prospect that much more appealing.

So she'd sought out Riker and asked if she could join.

Riker had laughed. "It's going to be tedious, Doctor."

"Tedious will be welcome after the week I had." She'd flashed him a bright smile. "An Aurelian birth calls for it. And since the *Enterprise* will be in orbit around Betazed, sickbay will be covered if there is an emergency."

"You don't want to go to the ceremony?" Riker's eyes twinkled. "I hear it lasts twenty-four hours and several traditional dances are involved."

"I think I can skip it."

And so it'd been decided. Crusher would get a chance to spend some time on a Federation science station, running through planetary samples. Besides, Riker also mentioned there was a beach.

The doctor made her way to the transporter room. Commander Riker was already there with Data and Ensign Amir Muñoz, a promising young science officer from Earth who had written a very well-received paper on xenobotany in the Uskati system.

"Doctor." Data turned toward her as she stepped into the room. "Commander Riker said you would be joining us. I am . . . surprised."

"Really, Data?" Crusher smiled up at him. "I'm just looking forward to doing some good old-fashioned lab work."

"Yes," Data said. "As am I."

Crusher turned toward Muñoz to greet him just as Ensign Rikkilä came barreling through the transporter room doors, her blond ponytail swinging behind her. "Wait—please don't leave without me!" she cried, then immediately turned red and stumbled to a stop. "I'm sorry, Commanders." She straightened up her spine and hugged her tricorder to her chest. "I was delayed, and this is my first away mission—" She flicked her gaze over to Data, then Crusher, who got a crooked smile, which the doctor returned. Rikkilä wasn't always the most professional officer, but she certainly made up for it with an abundance of enthusiasm.

"Ensign Rikkilä," said Riker. "You're just in time." He stepped up to the transporter platform and the others followed. "Energize."

Beverly Crusher felt the wind first, blustery and damp. The Kotan landscape rolled out in front of her, an endless blanket of pale, silvery grass that bent sideways as the wind swept over the blades. The air smelled faintly sweet, as if flowers were blooming somewhere she couldn't see.

The doctor turned around to find a Federation science station several meters away, a compact complex of two biomass buildings that weren't so much assembled as grown. The seeds were planted around a generator with an installed computer core. When the survey was completed, the mission commander would give a self-destruct command to the computer, which would trigger an injection of an anisotropic designed to shrivel up the biomass into lightweight, three-meter-wide husks that could easily be transported offworld. The Federation took care to leave a planet just as they had found it, regardless if it was approved for settlement.

"This place is amazing," breathed Rikkilä. She whipped out her tricorder and scanned the open prairie behind them.

"Welcome to Kota!" boomed out a loud voice, and Crusher looked to find a towering Starfleet science officer strolling toward them. "Thank the *stars* that you're here. The last few days have been a nightmare." He paused, then said, "I'm Lieutenant Cecil Solanko, in charge of lab testing."

He was enormous for a human, with a barrel chest and wide, meaty arms. Solanko looked like he should be leading security teams in hand-to-hand combat. Which was rather unfair, Crusher chided herself.

"We're glad to help out," Commander Riker said, and he made the introductions.

Solanko nodded in turn. "You're all going to be lifesavers," he said. "Let's get you settled in and I'll show you around." He swept his arm toward the station and led the group forward.

"I'm so nervous," whispered Rikkilä. She was talking to Muñoz, the two of them trailing behind Crusher. "This is my first away mission, and I don't normally get sent out for fieldwork." She paused. "How about you?"

"I've been on a couple," Muñoz said. "The last one I got called on was to help identify a plant species on Hid—something was choking out the native plant life on the planet."

"Oh," Rikkilä said. "I remember hearing about that."

"Yeah, I was in the lab station the whole time, reviewing plant samples. I think that's why I got picked for this mission."

"There's tons of flora on Kota," Rikkilä said. "And hardly any fauna."

"Exactly. Just some microscopic ocean life."

The doctor picked up her pace to give them some privacy. She fell in between Riker and Data.

"The lieutenant is . . . quite formidable," Data remarked.

Riker chuckled. "Good thing he's on our side, eh? I'd hate to meet him in some Orion back alley."

"That is not what I meant," Data said. "I was referring to the fact that Lieutenant Solanko is an authority on geochronology."

Now it was Crusher's turn to laugh as Riker's cheeks pinked. "I did not know that," he admitted.

"Yes. I have read all his work. I look forward to working with him during our time on Kota." Data paused. "It is my hope we will be able to discuss the geologic history of the Nilko system at some point."

"I'm sure you will," Crusher said. "Once we've cleared the backlog and finished the survey."

Data gave her that placid almost-smile he offered whenever something pleased him.

They arrived at the entrance of the station. Solanko ducked in through the low open door and led them into a sitting room decorated with bland biomass furniture. "This is the common building," he said. "We take our meals in here, and the sleeping quarters are just down that hallway." He pointed to another low-slung doorway in the back corner of the room. "One big space for all of us, unfortunately. The laboratories are in the second building. You get to them through the hallway. Opposite direction of the sleeping quarters. The rest of the team is back there now."

"Two others on the team," Riker said.

A dark expression flickered across Solanko's face, his massive shoulders slumping. "Yes. After the loss of our commander and one of our best lieutenants . . ." His voice trailed off. "Let me say again that I'm glad you're here."

"It's our honor to help," Riker said.

"C'mon," Solanko said. "Let me show you to your quarters. Then I'll get you up to speed."

3

"What do you think of Betazed, Ms. Trigg?" Commander Deanna Troi plastered on the brightest smile she could manage. "It's my understanding you've never been here before."

Adora Trigg gazed out across the lawn of Isszon Temple, anxiety rolling off of her, all of her other emotions tight and shut off. "It's lovely," she said in a stiff voice, pulling on the strap of her overnight bag. "Is this where the ceremony is to be held?"

The word *ceremony* sent a new quake of fear radiating out of her, and Troi felt a surge of empathy. Adora Trigg rarely did public appearances. It really was special that she had agreed to the Betazed government's request to attend as a Poetry Guest.

"Partially," Troi said, guiding her forward onto the gently curving pathways that cut elegant, geometric shapes into the brilliant green of the lawn. "The opening ceremonies will take place on the lawn, as will the Iren Cotillion. But most of the ceremony will be inside the temple." She gestured toward the gleaming building, its stone walls shining in the warm sunlight.

"Aarno Roque wrote a holonovel set there, didn't he?" Trigg's anxiety seemed to disperse with the change of subject. "I experienced it years ago. I'll never forget the rendering of that temple."

Troi smiled—more genuinely this time. Adora Trigg was the fifth and final of the High Guests she had "volunteered" to bring down from the *Enterprise*, as a favor to Captain Picard. But the effort of easing their worries, appeasing their egos, and introducing them to their liaisons had been draining. The reminder of having loved Aarno Roque's holonovels since she was a teenager brought some unexpected joy.

"Yes," she said. "*The Hidden Bones*. One of my favorites."

"That's the one." Trigg nodded. The path led them into the sun garden, the blossoms bright and redolent this time of year. "I always liked his historical pieces the best. Such brilliant attention to detail."

"I couldn't agree more," Troi said. "Although I have to admit the heist plot was what drew me into *Hidden Bones*."

Trigg laughed. "Yes, when Narendra has to fight off the Taschan pirates—I always had so much fun with that. What was your weapon of choice? The sword or the axe?"

"The sword," Troi responded promptly, pleased that Adora's uneasiness had almost entirely melted away. They wove through the sun garden, moving closer to the temple entrance. It was festooned with fluttering silk banners and a holographic display of the centerpiece of the weekend's ceremony: the three treasures of Xiomara. In seven hours, the real treasures would be brought out by their respective Houses, displayed side by side for the first time in nearly five hundred years. The First House had, rather notoriously, *misplaced* their treasure, the Hallowed Urn, for two hundred years, only to uncover it in the midst of a war. The Fourth House had picked that absurd feud with the Second House and refused to allow anyone to access the Sacred Silver. And by the time *that* was resolved, the Third House had taken up its vow of isolation, blocking any outsiders from accessing the Enshrined Disk. If it wasn't one thing, it was another. The three treasures of Xiomara had therefore been kept apart for centuries.

"A woman after my own heart," Trigg said. She slowed her pace and squinted up at the temple entrance. Her trepidation rose.

"It's all so grand, isn't it?"

The commander looked up at the temple and tried to view it

from Trigg's perspective. Not just the banners and holograms, but all the sweeping gestures of beauty that Betazoids were so fond of. Two-meter statues were carved into the walls in between sconces flickering with flames that burned blue, thanks to a sprinkling of ground-up kalite stone. Once Isszon had been a religious shrine, but now it was a cultural center. The grand stone steps led up to the bronze doors, elaborately carved with scenes from mythology.

"Can I be honest?" Trigg said in a hushed voice, "I don't understand why *I* was invited."

Troi immediately felt Trigg turn sour with fear and doubt.

"I wasn't on the selection committee," Troi said, "but I'm sure it is because of *Before the Mirage*. It's immensely popular on Betazed."

Trigg seemed to blush at that. "Rather nice to hear."

They had made it to the base of the entrance stairs. Voices filtered down from the entryway, the excited chatter of the other High Guests and their Betazoid contacts.

"How much do you know about this weekend's ceremony?" Troi asked.

Trigg shook her head. "Only what was in the invitation. I spoke briefly to a gentleman—Sildar Syn—"

"The ceremony director."

"Yes, that sounds right. He told me something about needing representatives of the Five High Arts. It sounded so exciting at the time." Trigg frowned. "Now that I'm here, at the foot of the temple . . ."

The commander pressed one hand to her shoulder and immediately felt Trigg soften. "The ceremony is to honor a great Betazoid hero," she said soothingly. "Xiomara."

"Oh, I know that much," Adora replied. "I'm familiar with the story of Xiomara."

"That's wonderful." Troi laughed. "Honestly, if I had to tell it again—"

"I can understand that. It's so involved." She was calming down again, and Troi led her up the stairs.

"But there's an obscure version of the story," Troi continued. "In which losing her psychic abilities leads Xiomara to found the Five High Arts." She counted them off on her fingers. "Music, Movement, Poetry, Creation, and Dreams."

"And I'm Poetry. Even though I've never written a verse in my life."

"Your own holonovels are pure poetry. Verse or not."

Trigg gave a nervous laugh. "You're too much—thank you."

They had arrived at the top of the stairs. Troi found herself breathing a little heavier; the day was warm and it was a surprisingly good workout climbing up to the temple entrance. "Here we are," she announced, gesturing toward the open doors. Inside, the temple foyer was flooded with sunlight and the chatter of the High Guests. "Let me introduce you to your liaison. She'll make sure you get settled in the sleeping quarters."

Trigg's restlessness appeared to be back, although this time Troi felt excitement pulsing through it. Good. She didn't want to leave Trigg alone with her invasive thoughts.

The temple was a cavernous space, the ceiling soaring up more than eight meters, with huge skylights that let the sun come streaming in. The crowd inside seemed swallowed up by all that vastness, as if they could keep adding guests and still not come close to filling the space. The guests' emotions swirled around them: excitement, awe, flickers of boredom. Troi pushed them all aside in her head before they became overwhelming.

Trigg's liaison was a Betazoid artist, Andra Sai. Troi already felt her from across the way, her greetings brightening up Troi's thoughts: *Over here! To your left! Is that Trigg? I'm so excited to meet her.*

Troi turned just in time to see Andra sweeping toward them, the hem of her dress fluttering out behind her.

"Adora Trigg! I'm Andra, your liaison. I'm so *thrilled* you're here!"

Trigg's eyes were huge as she took everything in: the inside of Isszon, the other guests, and of course Andra Sai, who was decked out in traditional Betazoid finery, a floor-length ball gown with an elegant drape of sheer fabric flowing from her shoulders.

"I'm thrilled to be here," Trigg said through her nerves.

"Deanna." Andra pressed her hand to her chest. "I was so delighted to hear that you were escorting the *Enterprise*'s High Guests. I've heard *so* much about you from your mother."

"Is she here?" Troi hadn't seen her mother during her previous trips with the other guests, but she was almost certainly flitting around the premises.

"Oh, no," Andra said. "Lwaxana is meeting with the other ambassadors. But I know she's excited to have you home again!" She turned to Trigg. "How was your trip? Is the *Enterprise* grand? I've heard such wonderful things—" She was already leading Trigg over to the refreshment table. Trigg, poor thing, was rather like a bottle cast out at sea. She gave Troi a hopeless wave and a mouthed *thank you* before giving in to the requirements of being a High Guest.

Troi darted out of the reception and back down onto the lawn. She knew that the transporter blockers around the temple building had been activated, because the three treasures were already on the premises.

Troi had learned about the three treasures as a girl: the Sacred Silver of Xiomara, the Hallowed Urn of Rus'xi, and the Enshrined Disk of the Third House. Three ordinary objects that had granted a young Betazoid woman immense strength when her psychic powers failed her. Or so the story went.

She was eager to actually see them in person.

Walking far enough away from the temple to avoid the transporter blockers, she tapped her combadge. "One to beam up."

When she shimmered back onto the *Enterprise*'s transporter platform, she was pleased to note that Lieutenant Worf was waiting for her beside Lieutenant Kociemba, who was running the transporter controls. Troi and Worf had made plans to have dinner together after she delivered Adora Trigg.

"You're early," she announced, stepping off the platform.

"I am on time," Worf gravely replied.

She laughed and they walked out into the corridor together. Worf carried himself stiffly, his spine ramrod straight, and she sensed the faint brush of nervousness radiating off him—it had been like that recently with the Klingon. An imperceptible shift in his emotions toward her. She didn't quite know what to make of it, but Troi found she enjoyed his company more and more. And she always looked forward to their dinners together.

"So what will it be tonight?" she asked. "Vulcan cuisine? Or will you finally try Betazed flower stew, since we're in orbit?"

"I would not be averse to flower stew."

Troi's combadge trilled, and Captain Picard's voice filtered through. *"Picard to Troi. Are you free?"*

Troi frowned and glanced up at Worf, his brow knitted in concern. "Is there a problem, Captain? I saw Adora Trigg to her liaison."

"No problem," Picard said. *"I need your assistance with—a request."* He was quiet for a moment. *"From Betazed's ambassador to the Federation."*

Oh, no. "I was about to have dinner with Lieutenant Worf—"

"Bring him along. This won't take too long. I'm in my quarters. Picard out."

"Mother," she sighed.

Troi could tell that Worf was trying to keep his expression neutral. "I can delay our meal," he said. "If you would like me to accompany you—"

He wasn't sure, she could tell—he was giving her a graceful out. But she sensed that he didn't want her to say no.

"That would be wonderful." She turned around in the corridor and began walking in the opposite direction, toward the captain's quarters, with Worf at her side. "I suspect the captain will need all the . . . assistance he can get."

4

———•———

Jean-Luc Picard paced back and forth in front of the viewports, Betazed looming ominously against the backdrop of open space. He was already exhausted from playing cruise director to his honored guests, while navigating the endless labyrinth of social niceties that seemed to accompany every diplomatic event. When he finally dropped off opera singer Tangela Vallejo at the temple, he'd wanted nothing more than to take an hour or two for himself before preparing to beam down for the start of the festival tomorrow morning.

But a message had been waiting for him.

His door chimed. "Come," he called out, distracted. Clouds moved in pale streaks across the curve of Betazed.

He turned just as Commander Troi and Lieutenant Worf stepped into his quarters. The counselor was frowning in that very particular way she did whenever her mother was involved.

"Thank you for coming." He nodded at Worf. "Lieutenant, I'm glad you decided to join Counselor Troi. This may actually end up being of interest to you as well."

"Sir?" Worf looked over at Troi. She shrugged slightly, then turned back to Picard.

"Captain," she said. "This message—has something happened?"

"It was—" Picard cleared his throat. "An invitation."

Troi pressed her lips together. "I see."

"I'll let you listen. I hope you'll find a way to"—he waved his hand—"extricate me from the situation." He straightened up.

"Computer, play the recent message from the Betazoid ambassador."

Instantly, Lwaxana Troi's bright grin materialized on the screen. *"Jean-Luc!"* she cried, and Picard resisted the urge to slink backward. *It's a recording,* he told himself. *"Thank you so much for bringing so many High Guests to Betazoid for the ceremony this weekend! When the Federation offered Starfleet to transport the guests, I ensured the* Enterprise *was included in the list."*

Picard glanced over at his officers, their faces lit up by the screen. Troi was keeping her composure, but he thought he saw a faint gleam of panic displayed in her expression.

"And now that you're here—" Her smiled broadened, her teeth shining like the jewels set in her long dangling earrings. *"Well, let me say this first. One of the High Guests had to cancel. Something about a fire on Cuziti."* Lwaxana shook her head. *"A terrible tragedy, yes, but it leaves us one guest short."*

"Oh, no," Troi said. "She didn't—"

"She did," Picard responded grimly.

"It was E'kan Closa, the great Gartian philosopher? He was one of our Dreams Guests. There has to be precisely forty-seven of each type, and so of course the planning committee is all in a rush, trying to find a last-minute replacement."

Troi made a sympathetic noise in the back of her throat. Picard rubbed at his temple, bracing himself, as he knew the rest of Lwaxana's message.

"And I said to Casimir, the coordinator in charge of securing all the High Guests, do you know who would be absolutely marvelous *as a Dreams Guest?"*

"Jean-Luc Picard," murmured Troi, a few beats before her mother trilled, *"Captain Jean-Luc Picard!"*

"Computer, stop replay." Picard threw his hands up and

turned to Troi. "I take it I don't need to explain my conundrum to you."

"Ambassador Troi wishes you to be one of the High Guests?" Worf frowned. "It is a great honor, sir."

"Of course it is," Picard said quickly. "But an honor that belongs to an artist. A philosopher like E'kan Closa. I'm just—"

"A starship captain does fit the parameters of a Dreams Guest," Troi said.

Picard slumped down in the chair positioned behind his desk. Lwaxana Troi was frozen on the screen, her expression brimming with delight. "I know." He looked up at her. "Tell me, is there any way I can refuse? Politely, of course—"

Hesitation flickered across the commander's face, and Picard already knew the answer.

"Damn," he said softly.

"It would be considered an insult for you to turn down the invitation," Troi said gently.

Picard let out a long sigh.

"Is this an official invitation? Or did my mother simply—"

"Yes," Picard said with another heavy sigh. "Resume replay."

Lwaxana's voice again filled the room. *"And Casimir absolutely agreed, how wonderful is that? So she pushed through a request to the Ceremony Director Council and insisted on a last-minute approval, which of course they did."* Lwaxana clapped her hands together. *"As soon as you're able, all you'll need to do is beam down and I will personally present the Seal of Invitation to you."*

"Oh," Troi said, "a last-minute approval."

Picard did not like the finality of those words.

"If they rushed the invitation through—" Troi offered him a thin smile. "You will be a *last*-minute guest. I'm sure they won't expect you to do *all* of the ceremonies. Just the unveiling." She paused. "And the Welcome Celebrations. The Cotillion. Oh, I imagine the House Performances, that's terribly important—"

Picard felt himself grow heavier with each additional task. "It would be inappropriate for me to turn the invitation down."

Troi glanced at Worf, who had been watching this entire exchange with an unreadable expression. "Yes, sir."

Worf shrugged almost imperceptibly.

"I understand." Picard leaned forward, pressing his elbows onto the table. Three days. That was the length of the entire celebration. The *Enterprise* would be in orbit, waiting to return their assigned guests back to their homeworlds. Picard had intended to spend those three days on board the ship, catching up on reports.

So much for *that* plan.

"Very well." He straightened in his seat. "Mister Worf, with Commander Riker and Lieutenant Commander Data on Kota, you'll be in command of the *Enterprise* while I'm managing my"— he closed his eyes—"duties. Counselor?"

"Yes, Captain?"

"Will you accompany me down to the operations building? I would appreciate your insight."

"Of course." She nodded, and Worf turned to Picard.

"Captain, thank you for this opportunity," he said. "I will not disappoint you."

"I'm certain of that." Picard thought that he should be focusing on the positives—there were worse tasks than serving a role in a three-day Betazed ceremony. He did, however, see a glimmer of excitement behind Worf's cool facade.

• • •

"Here we are again," he muttered. Just looking at the transporter platform made Picard feel exhausted.

"Captain," Troi said, "I know this wasn't how you hoped to spend the next few days, but it really is a tremendous honor. And I think you'll do wonderfully as a Dreams Guest."

Picard suppressed the urge to scoff as he and Troi stepped onto the pads. He looked over at Lieutenant Kociemba. "You did excellent work today," he said. "Energize."

Kociemba smiled, then moved her fingers up the controls and sent Picard and Troi on their way. A few seconds later, they stood in front of a small, nondescript square building covered in vines heavy with pink and yellow blossoms. Isszon Temple rose off in the distance, its spired roof sparkling in the lemony sunlight.

"I suppose I should get this over with," Picard said, smoothing his dress uniform.

"You'll do wonderfully, Captain."

Picard felt the grim lock of inevitability clamp down on him. *It's only three days,* he told himself.

He took one step toward the building and immediately the door slid open and out swept Lwaxana Troi, her ball gown glittering in much the same way as the temple. "Jean-Luc!" she exclaimed. "Oh, I've been *waiting* for you. I am *thrilled* you'll be joining us!" She hustled over the lawn, both hands gathering up the fabric of her gown. "Deanna! Tell me you won't be wearing that to the ceremony, I hope?"

Troi sighed. "It's my uniform, Mother."

"Oh, I know." Lwaxana drew her into an embrace. *I've missed you, Little One. I requested the* Enterprise *especially for delivering guests. I had to make sure you wouldn't miss the ceremony!*

Thank you, Troi thought.

Ambassador Troi clucked her tongue and turned toward Picard. She gave him another one of her brilliant smiles. "I can't tell you how delighted I am that you've accepted the invitation," she said. "You'll be simply marvelous. Sildar and Sulel are dying to meet you." She looped her arm in Picard's and pulled him forward, and the captain felt himself slacken. No use in swimming against this current.

As serene as the building looked on the outside, Picard expected its interior to have the cool emptiness of a museum. Instead, when Lwaxana flung open the door, he was met with an onslaught of sheer chaos. The small room was cramped with tables and desks of various origins, all crammed up next to each other and piled high with fabrics, serving dishes, padds, statuary, ancient paper books, and, in the center of it all, a silent hologram of a Betazoid woman in ancient dress swinging around a large silver spoon.

Weaving between these desks were harried-looking Betazoids, most in what Picard could only call partial formal wear—a floor-length skirt with a baggy tunic, a crisp suit with bare feet. They were shouting tasks at each other, an elaborate call and response of things to be done and tasks completed that Picard couldn't follow.

Lwaxana plunged headfirst into the maelstrom and was immediately swallowed in a whirlwind of discordant glamour.

"What," said Picard softly, "is happening?"

Beside him, Troi murmured, "Organized chaos. Be grateful you only have to command a starship, and not plan a Betazoid event."

"Where are the House placards?!" someone screamed from the center of the room, only to be immediately met with, "Amalia has it! Concentrate!"

"No one is controlling their thoughts," wailed someone else. "If we would all just calm down, this would be so much *easier*—"

Picard edged closer to the door. Troi stopped him before he got trampled.

And then Lwaxana reemerged. Picard had never been so grateful to see her. This time, she was trailing two companions: an older Betazoid man dressed in a rather elaborate cape-centric ensemble and the Federation's ambassador to Betazed.

"Is this him?" asked the Betazoid man.

"It is." Lwaxana beamed. "Jean-Luc Picard, Deanna, I'm pleased to introduce you to Sildar Syn, the Ceremony Director—"

Sildar gave a quick bow.

"And this is, of course, Ambassador Sulel of Vulcan."

The Vulcan woman nodded briefly.

Sildar stepped forward, his eyes narrowed and his gaze sweeping up and down Picard's frame. Picard shot a glance at Troi, who offered the captain an apologetic smile.

"He's too small for E'kan's costume," Sildar said. "I'll have Seabert replicate a new one. Seabert!" he hollered, spinning off into the vortex of ceremony preparations.

"Costume?" Picard said weakly.

"Of course. You'll be dressed in the traditional wear of the Lakryn era, when Betazed first achieved space flight," Lwaxana said. "And you'll look *very* handsome in those pantaloons. Won't he, Sulel?"

Sulel gazed implacably at Picard. "It is not my place to say."

Picard felt his face getting hot. "Is there a Seal of Invitation you need to present me, or—"

"Of course!" Lwaxana clapped her hands and a gaunt, gray man materialized, startling Picard. "Homn, do you have the Seal?"

He nodded and produced it from a side pocket in his tunic: a rolled parchment tied with pink ribbon. He handed it to Lwaxana and she immediately turned to Picard and intoned, "In my role as representative of Betazed and daughter of the Fifth House, holder of the Sacred Chalice of Rixx and heir to the Holy Rings of Betazed, I, Lwaxana Troi, formally invite you to attend the Unveiling of the Three Treasures of Xiomara as a High Guest, a shining example of those arts we hold in glorious esteem: Dreams! Do you accept, Jean-Luc Picard?"

She had sunk down in a curtsy as she spoke, her dress pooling across the floor. Behind her, the ceremony team was still in a whirlwind, voices clattering for instructions and pleas to *use your thoughts*. The Vulcan seemed like she wanted to laugh—and *that* had to be his imagination.

He gave one last desperate look at Troi, and she only shook her head.

"I accept," he sighed.

Lwaxana pushed the scroll toward him. He took it out of her hands.

"Marvelous!" Lwaxana said. "Shall I accompany you to the reception in the temple? I'm sure it's still—"

"I can take him." Troi stepped forward. "I don't suppose there's a liaison for him, is there? I can show him to the guest quarters."

"Oh, don't be silly," Lwaxana said, pressing up to Picard's side. "It's no trouble."

"Mother, I insist. I'm sure you're needed here to help with the last-minute preparations."

"Nonsense. I can—"

"I believe your daughter may be correct, Ambassador Troi." Sulel lifted her chin, her dark eyes bright and mischievous. "It would be far more logical for us to stay and oversee the general preparations, particularly as we may be needed by Sildar."

Picard hadn't expected the ambassador to intervene on his behalf, but he certainly appreciated it.

"Ambassador Sulel is right, Mother," Troi said. "I can help Captain Picard get settled. You stay here, where you're needed."

"Very well." Lwaxana dismissively waved a hand. "It's just one more night before the opening ceremonies. And then we'll have plenty of opportunity for quality time."

Just what Picard had been hoping to avoid.

"Then it is decided," Sulel said. "Captain Picard, Commander Troi, I am sure we will be seeing each other. Come, Lwaxana. I believe the stage production team needs your help in deciding upon a drapery for the unveiling."

Picard stood very still as Sulel led Lwaxana back into the frenzy. Then he sagged, turned, and bolted outside. Troi followed him up, laughing.

"Now, that wasn't too bad, was it?" she said as they stepped back into the sunlight and the sweet-scented air.

Despite Deanna being the ship's counselor, Picard didn't want to talk about it any further.

5

Josefina Rikkilä squinted down at her tricorder. "Oh, wow," she said.

"What's that?" Doctor Crusher didn't lift her gaze from her own work.

"Kota wasn't always uninhabited, was it?" Rikkilä was examining a rock specimen, a chip off the wall of a nearby cave that had been collected a couple of weeks ago, according to the computer. "The scanners are picking up on a fossilized life-form in the rock."

"Yeah, the planet is absolutely scattered with those fossils."

Rikkilä jumped and whirled around to find one of the station officers—Lieutenant Amanda Malisson . . . or Malifoy? She was having trouble remembering everyone's names. The away team had immediately dived into the backlog. That was how she wound up with this rock/fossil.

"There's actually dozens of fossils in the rock," Malisson went on. "They're microscopic, though."

Rikkilä returned to her sample. It didn't look anything like her idea of a fossil: it was an utterly ordinary-seeming rock. Dark and smooth, the sides flattened and angular from where it had been splintered.

"We've been keeping track of how many we've managed to find," Malisson added.

"We're currently up in the five hundreds, I think." A flash of cerulean popped up from behind a stack of storage cubes. It was

Junipero Talma, a Bolian with dark stripes running across the crown of his head; like Ensign Muñoz, he was a xenobotanist.

"Got it," Rikkilä said.

"Make sure you enter it into the database. Give it the next number." Malisson turned to Crusher. "How about you, Doctor? What are you seeing?"

Crusher turned back to her station. She was running through a set of water samples taken from the beach. "The water's filled with microscopic organisms—every sample shows evidence of them. We'll need to run these all through the neutron processor, won't we?"

Malisson frowned. "Where's that sample from?"

Crusher checked her padd. "Location 2F." She shook her head, laughing apologetically. "I'm afraid that doesn't mean much to me."

Malisson's frown deepened. "2F," she murmured. "Computer, where is 2F?"

The computer's voice lilted through the cramped lab space. "Co-ordinates 34890 by 20980," it said. "Known colloquially as Bluster Beach."

"Bluster Beach?" Talma's head popped back up. "That's where we brought back the sand samples from, isn't it?"

By now everyone else had stopped their work to listen in. Rikkilä snuck a glance over at Muñoz. He'd been cataloguing plant samples and was surrounded by small floating spheres, each with a preserved snip of a grass or a flower or a few tree leaves. He was not paying any attention to the samples now.

"Yeah, it was." Malisson's brow furrowed. "But there wouldn't have been any organisms in the sand samples."

"No." Solanko's voice boomed across the room. "I tested those myself. No sign of biological life, but the samples didn't line up, remember?"

"That's right." Malisson's whole face lit up. "I knew there was something off about those sand samples, but we've tested so much the last two days—"

"Understandable," Solanko said. He stood up, towering over the station he'd been sitting at. "Doctor Crusher, do you mind if I have a look?"

"Not at all." She slid away from the microscope and stepped up beside Rikkilä. The two of them pressed together between a lab table and Riker's station. It really was a tight squeeze having seven people in the lab, but they had the converter running in the second lab, making the room far too noisy to get any work done.

Solanko peered down through the microscope. "Huh," he said, after a moment.

"What are you seeing?" Talma picked his way through the maze of tables and equipment. "Do you want me to run a scan?"

"I can do it." Solanko plucked up the slide and held it to the light. From where Rikkilä stood, it didn't look like much, just a square of glass.

"What's the significance of Bluster Beach?" Crusher asked.

Neither Malisson nor Talma answered; instead they both trailed behind Solanko as he slid the sample into one of the scanners. Blue light flared out through the lab. "Computer," Solanko barked, "is there a match?"

Rikkilä peered across the room. Muñoz and Lieutenant Commander Data were both watching the blue lights rippling across the outer shell of the scanner.

"Sample contains standard organisms for—"

The computer was drowned out by all three of the Kota scientists letting out loud, disappointed groans.

"I do not understand," Data said, eyes flicking between the scanner and the scientists. "Is that not the expected outcome for a sample of ocean water?"

"Exactly," Solanko said. "Perfectly normal. Unlike the last batch from Bluster Beach."

The lab filled with silence.

"These are the irregular testing results that were mentioned in the briefing," Doctor Crusher said. "I remember a mention of several tests needing to be redone."

Lieutenant Talma nodded. "The sand samples. We have a list of the five known microscopic organisms that live in the ocean. But in, maybe, one out of every hundred scans, they react oddly to our equipment."

"Oddly?" Muñoz tilted his head. "In what way?"

"They register as rock," Malisson sighed. "It reads to me like an error in the scanners, but I haven't been able to determine the actual problem."

"I thought it might be a new organism," Talma said, "but I couldn't find any evidence to support that."

"I don't think it is," Malisson said. "I'm telling you, we need more samples of that sand. There's something to it."

"The water's fine," Lieutenant Talma said. "We've tested dozens of sand samples—"

"Yes, but that's not water from the shore," Malisson shot back. "The computer gave the coordinates 34890 by 20980. That's farther out."

Malisson gestured at the scanner. "We need to go pull those original sand samples out of storage, and collect some water right at the shore and—"

"I'm starting to see why they're backlogged," Commander Riker said quietly. Rikkilä whipped her head over at him, surprised, and he gave her a wink.

"Will, stop," Crusher said.

The Kota science team had devolved into a full-on argument,

their raised voices blending into one another. Across the room, Data and Muñoz exchanged confused glances.

"Perhaps we should remind them that there are refugees waiting for a place to call home?" Crusher asked Riker.

Before the commander could speak, Solanko roared out, "Enough!" His voice thundered through the lab and struck Talma and Malisson silent. "We have extra hands," he said. "We'll go down to the beach and collect more samples. I'll take a big team, spread out." He looked across the room. "Commander, with your approval?"

"Yes." Riker nodded at the ensign. "Rikkilä, you and Muñoz will join them."

"Absolutely, sir," Rikkilä replied.

"Sir, with your permission, I'd like to accompany them as well." Data stood up from his station. "I'm curious about these irregularities and might be able to offer assistance in identifying their cause."

Riker grinned. "Guess it's just me and you," he said to Doctor Crusher.

"All right, team," called out Solanko. "Grab your supplies. No time to waste."

Rikkilä grabbed her tricorder and gave a final wave to Doctor Crusher. Solanko had thrown open the doors to a supply closet and was passing out sampling kits, reusable polysilk containers filled with all the tubes, stoppers, and biodegradable safety masks for each of the team.

Muñoz chuckled beside Rikkilä. "Burned through a ton of these back in the Academy."

Rikkilä gave him a quick sideways glance. "Yeah," she said, her tongue feeling heavy. "Me too."

"The beach is about a twenty-minute walk from here," Solanko said, looking over at Data, who had his sampling pack slung over his shoulder.

"Acceptable," Data said.

There was no clear-cut path to the beach, and the six of them waded into the tall, silvery grass that rolled out endlessly from the station. It came up to Rikkilä's hips and tickled against her hands, soft and feathery. She pulled out her tricorder and started scanning.

"The area is safe," Data said.

Rikkilä looked up at him. "Sir?"

He pointed at the tricorder.

Rikkilä blushed. "I just wanted to see what the readings were." She glanced over the results; they were the same as when she had first scanned the area, although the salinity in the air was increasing. "This is my first away mission," she added after a pause.

"I see." Data nodded. "You are excited."

Rikkilä smiled at him. This was the first time she got to interact with the commander. "Exactly," she said.

The wind picked up, blowing in a scent of salt and metal. The ensign turned back to her tricorder and watched the salinity and humidity levels go up and the barometric pressure go down.

They continued on, the wind sweeping around them. Eventually, Rikkilä heard a soft roaring, then a rustling noise that her friend Lorelei had once told her was the sound the stars made on long-range scans.

"Watch your step!" called out Solanko as the grass gave way to rolling sand dunes that dropped abruptly down to the beach.

Rikkilä drew in a deep breath; the beaches she had seen were nothing in comparison to this place. The water glittered a rich indigo underneath the violet sky, the waves glinting purple as they crested and broke against the shore. The sand appeared to be ground-up limestone and stretched out in either direction. Near the water was an outcropping of black rocks dotted with small, lavender tide pools that looked like jewels on a necklace.

"Wow," breathed Muñoz. "Have you ever seen anything like this?"

The ensign shook her head, the wind whipping the hair out of her regulation bun, flinging it into her eyes.

Data gazed out at the water, his expression implacable and calm.

The Kota team wasn't impressed. Lieutenants Malisson and Talma were already sliding down the gentle slope of the dunes, arms out for balance.

"That's the only way down," Solanko said. "Be careful. First time Talma took a stab at it, he went tumbling straight into the water. It was high tide."

And then Solanko took a running start at the dune slope, crouching a little as he surfed down to the waterline.

Rikkila looked over at Data. "Sir, is that, uh, safe?"

Data said, "It appears that we do not have a choice." He nodded. "I will go first."

Rikkila nodded and watched as Data skittered over the sand. He made it down safely, but he was both a superior officer and an android. She didn't have quite the same faith in herself to make her way down the dune without landing face-first in the sand.

Rikkila turned to Muñoz, but he was already sliding down the dune, his arms lifted over his head. He let out a loud *whoop* as the wind pushed his hair back from his face.

Rikkila sighed.

"All right," she said. "Here goes nothing." She closed her tricorder and eased herself over the peak of the dune. At first she tried to walk, rather than slide, but the sand was too loose and silky, and before she fully understood what was happening, gravity had grabbed ahold of her. White sand flew up around her legs, sticking to the fabric of her uniform, and the lovely glistening beach was barreling right toward her.

When she hit solid ground, she immediately fell forward, scrambling over her feet.

But then a hand grabbed her arm, pulling her upright—Muñoz. He smiled at her. "Can't wait to do that again," he said.

"Sure," Rikkilä said, who in fact hoped she never had to do it again.

Talma was already getting set up over by the tide pools, pulling out supplies from his sampling kit. Solanko waved over to Rikkilä and Muñoz. "One of you is going to grab samples of dry sand, the other wet. We need at minimum ten different samples from up and down the beach. Make sure you can get exact locations."

Touching the tricorder reassuringly, Rikkilä snuck a glance over at Muñoz. He grinned back.

"Which one of you wants to get your feet wet?" Solanko asked.

"I'll do it," said Rikkilä.

"Great. Shoreline. I've got Talma sampling the tide pools." He clapped his hands together and started walking past them. "And Commander! I'd love to have your insight . . ." His voice trailed out on the wind, as did Data's answer. But a few moments later, Data was crouched over near the outcropping of rocks, studying a tide pool.

Rikkilä smirked at Muñoz. "Race you to see who finishes first?"

"You're on." Muñoz unfolded his testing kit. "Starting now."

Rikkilä gave a shout of protest, yanked off her boots, and plunged into the lapping water. It splashed cold against her uniform as she fumbled with her testing kit, pulling out vials and stoppers. Muñoz was hunched over the dry sand.

It was easy work, gathering the samples, even though the waves sometimes splashed high as they rolled in, spritzing the ensign's face with a shivery sea spray. Up close, the water was as clear as glass and it was easy to see the rippled sand that made up the seafloor. Sand was all that Rikkilä could see. No flutters of alien seaweed, no darting flashes of ocean life.

Rikkilä knew the water contained microscopic life—but even so, the beach felt barren. The rest of the planet bloomed with plants, but not the ocean.

The ensign frowned as she waded deeper into the water, crouching down to pull another sand sample. This strange, empty beach unsettled her. On every world she'd read about, areas such as this teemed with life. The ocean was like the galaxy in that way. It only seemed vast and empty on the surface.

Muñoz shouted something from the shore, jolting Rikkilä out of her thoughts. He waved his hands wildly at her. He was halfway down the beach. Well, she lost *that* contest. Good thing they didn't wager anything.

She gave him a loser's shrug, then turned back to the empty water. It couldn't be poisonous; Solanko would never have sent her in without protection, and it supposedly contained invisible life. And yet it seemed as sterile as medical saline.

Muñoz yelled again, but when Rikkilä looked up, she couldn't see him. In fact, she realized with a low dawning of dread, she didn't see *anyone*. The beach was empty.

"Muñoz?" she called out, shoving the samples back into her kit. "Lieutenant Solanko?" She splashed back to the shore, the water cold and clammy against her skin. That was when she saw a streak of black and gold against the white expanse of the beach.

"Muñoz!" She plunged forward, her feet sinking into the sand. Muñoz had collapsed, his testing kit propped up beside him. He stirred, then rolled over, his eyes glossy.

"You were the only one I could see," he mumbled.

Rikkilä knelt beside him, immediately pulled out her tricorder, and scanned him. His temperature was a little high, as was his blood pressure. "What happened? Talk to me, Muñoz."

"I don't know." He pushed himself up to a sitting position and dug his palms into his forehead. "I was taking the samples, and then Lieutenant Talma ran by and said Lieutenant Solanko was sick. I didn't think I'd heard him correctly."

Rikkilä frowned down at the tricorder readings. None of her scans were picking up a source for Muñoz's fever or elevated blood pressure.

"Where's Commander Data?" Rikkilä asked.

"Talma said something about him going farther down the beach. He was hailing me—" Muñoz dropped his hand and squinted out at the water. "Then I started to feel dizzy. Everything was spinning—I couldn't stand up straight. That's when I called for you, the second time. You ignored me the first."

Rikkilä jerked her head up. "I thought you were telling me you were done!"

Muñoz shook his head. "I'm . . ." He squeezed his eyes shut and lay down on the sand. "I don't even know where they are."

Rikkilä laid her hand on his shoulder. "We need to get you back to the station. All of us. Which direction did—"

Fatigue slammed into her, almost knocking the breath out of her lungs. She slumped, dropping the tricorder into the sand. Her limbs felt as if they weighed five hundred kilograms.

"Oh," she said, bracing herself against the sand. "Oh, I feel—"

The beach was moving like ocean water, rippling up and down. Rikkilä pressed her hands into the sand, trying to steady herself.

"You feel it too," Muñoz muttered.

Rikkilä dug her fingers deeper into the sand, as if she could push the beach into staying still. Her muscles ached. Distantly, she knew she needed to follow the medical procedures she had learned. Diagnose, make the patient comfortable and secure.

But she didn't have a diagnosis. The tricorder couldn't find anything wrong with Muñoz.

Rikkilä's head hit the sand, the grains cool against her cheek. How did she get down here? She blinked and pushed herself back up. The effort exhausted her.

She slapped her combadge. "Rikkilä to Doctor Crusher. We have a medical emergency."

Even that action was too much. As Doctor Crusher's voice trickled out over the combadge, Rikkilä dropped back down in the sand, her eyes fixed on the purple waves crashing against the shore.

6

—•—

Deanna Troi rapped on the door to the captain's guest quarters. It was early morning, the sun sending up strata of pink and orange over the horizon. The commander had to beam down at this time if she wanted to fetch Picard before her mother.

The door to the quarters swung open. Picard sagged with relief when he saw her, leaning his weight into the door.

"I told you I'd be here first thing," she said.

"You did, and I must say I appreciate it." Picard held the door open so that Troi could step inside. The room was small but lushly decorated in a style associated with the Third House: great swaths of silk hanging from the ceiling, a twinkling solar-powered chandelier, and plants. Lots and lots of plants, spilling out of stone pots carved with swirling, abstract designs.

Troi had to stifle a laugh; Picard, still dressed in his pajamas, looked out of place among all this finery.

"The opening ceremonies are scheduled to begin in an hour, sir," Troi said casually.

Picard gave her a dark look. "I suspect you know the horror that awaits me in that closet."

Troi smiled. "I'm sure it's not that bad."

She could tell, from the waves of discomfort rippling off Picard, that he did not agree.

"Come now, Captain." She strode across the room, batting aside the flimsy, billowing silk. "It's only for a few days. And remember. It *is* a great honor."

She slid aside the closet door and found a froth of shimmery fabric waiting inside.

"Do you understand now?" Picard asked.

Troi pulled out the first item: a traditional First House–style gentleman's tunic, the fabric a rich, jeweled blue that, when it caught the light, let off a rainbow sheen. The tunic paired with a set of white pantaloons and stockings, both dangling from their own hanger. White, high-lacing boots sat neatly at the bottom of the closet.

"It could be worse," Troi offered. "You could be going to a Betazoid wedding."

As Picard scowled, the commander could sense that annoyance wasn't the only emotion roiling around in him. The captain was anxious. Maybe even frightened—the emotions shifted so rapidly that she couldn't quite get a handle on them.

"Captain," she said, laying the tunic out on the bed. "I can sense your anxiety. But remember that you aren't going into the ceremony alone. I'm here to help you through it. And most of the *Enterprise* crew will be attending the ceremonies as well."

Picard ran his hands down over his face. "I really could do without this particular honor."

"Relax," Troi told him. "Try to enjoy yourself . . . sir."

This earned her another scowl, but at least when she offered the tunic to him, he took it with one hand.

She left his quarters so he could change, stepping out into the sunny, breezy day. The guests' quarters were all grouped together, a tangle of rooms that blended into the surroundings. Troi could see glimpses of Isszon Temple in the curving gaps between the buildings, its white stone draped in colorful House flags.

Footsteps sounded on the path behind her, and she turned around to find the captain, his tunic buttoned up high to his throat, the long bell sleeves grazing the tops of his knuckles. His combadge gleamed on his right chest.

"You could take that off," Troi said, "and treat this as a vacation."

"This," Picard said, "is *not* a vacation."

"I'm sure you'll wind up enjoying yourself."

Picard made a strangled noise in the back of his throat.

"Shall we?" She gestured toward the temple over the tops of the guest quarters.

Troi started down the path, and Picard followed her, tugging anxiously on his tunic hem. Other guests made their way toward the temple, all dressed in costumes from various periods of Betazed history. A Benzite in a slinky cape dress laughed uproariously with her Betazoid escort. There were four Rigelians whispering among themselves, their excitement rolling off them like jasmine-scented perfume. Picard seemed to be the only guest who *wasn't* thrilled.

The path curved around the last of the guest quarters and Troi found herself gazing upon a riotous ocean of colored fabric. The lawn of Isszon Temple had transformed overnight, bright-colored food stalls and billowing tents blossoming like hothouse flowers. Visitors streamed across the lawn, many draped in traditional Betazed clothing. Vendors called out singsong merchants' chants, imploring guests to try their grilled sea slugs or their blackened honeycake. When a streak of light soared overhead, voices clattered with excitement.

"Oh, they have a bird-soar!" Troi cried. "I haven't seen one of those since I was a little girl."

Picard pressed his mouth into a thin line.

Her own excitement bubbled up, drowning out Picard's mood. Troi told herself there would be plenty of time to explore later that evening. Worf had promised to beam down once he was off duty. She couldn't wait to see how he reacted to the bird-soar.

"My mother sent over your itinerary last night." Troi noticed Picard's ever-deepening scowl. "I'm to take you into a side chamber in the temple so you can prepare for the opening ceremony."

Picard let out a deep and world-weary sigh. "Let's get this over with."

"*That* is not the right attitude to have, sir," she chided him.

They walked toward the temple, keeping to one side of the celebrations. The scent of flower cakes and honey swirled on the wind, plunging Troi back to the midwinter festivals her parents would take her to when she was a child. Those had been much smaller, but the scent was the same, and it made her mouth water for the syrupy cakes.

The steps to the temple were roped off with long silk scarves. Betazed Security officers stood at evenly spaced intervals, checking guests and their handlers before letting them in the building. The Starfleet officers fell into line behind a Bzzit Khaht that had shimmering stones draped over its tunic.

"Would you mind sharing what exactly will be expected of me?" Picard asked. "It never was fully explained."

"I didn't want to overwhelm you."

"I'll manage."

A swell of music, jangly and bright, rose up behind them, eliciting cheers from the crowd.

"All Betazoid ceremonies incorporate the Five High Arts," Troi said. "So as a High Guest, your presence is key to ensuring the ceremony goes off exactly as it should."

Picard pressed her. "What am I going to have to actually *do*?"

The line moved closer to the last security check.

"Walk onstage and parade through the crowd," Troi said, "and wear the right clothing." She smiled, gesturing at his tunic and pantaloons. "Don't worry, it's all choreographed ahead of time. You'll just have to do whatever the person in front of you does."

"And how *much* of this am I going to have to do?"

They stepped up to the security officer, who immediately put the thought *Name?* in Troi's head.

"Jean-Luc Picard," she said, a bit of heat tingeing her cheeks. She really wasn't fond of the traditional mode of Betazoid communication. "I'm his handler. Deanna Troi."

The security officer was still skimming along the surface of her thoughts. *You're Ambassador Troi's daughter!*

She gave him a stern look.

"Sorry," he mumbled before running his tricorder over them. "You can go on in."

They joined the rest of the guests making the long trek up the glittering stairs. Troi took a deep breath, steadying herself—it had been a while since she'd last spent any time on Betazed, and the differences in communication always took some getting used to. As a half-Betazoid, her skills were empathic: she could read emotions of most species, but she couldn't read *thoughts* unless those belonged to another Betazoid who would share them with her.

She sensed more discomfort from Picard, drawing her out of her reverie. He was frowning deeply up at the doors, which were flung open and draped in garlands of Catarian gems that caught the light the same way his robes did.

"I never answered your questions," Troi said. "It's only three days."

"I know." Picard shook his head. "I take it I can expect a lot of this pomp and circumstance, then?"

"Betazoids do place an emphasis on ritual," Troi said after a pause.

They filed in through the doors, the inside of the temple swirling with guests in their extravagant costumes. The room had been transformed; the shutters that covered the stained-glass windows had been removed, and fragments of rainbowed light spilled across the polished stone floors. A massive platform was set up against the far wall, draped with colorful curtains as well as hovering stage lamps that sent rays of light crisscrossing each other.

At the center of the platform was an empty display case, a force field around the simple black base.

"There," Troi told Picard, "is where the artifacts will be displayed."

Immediately, Picard's curiosity rose, overcoming the low-grade dread that had been flowing off him all morning. "It will be remarkable," he said, "to see them brought together after all this time. These items reflect so much of Betazed's history."

"Betazed's history certainly kept them apart for long enough. By the way, you'll be onstage when they're revealed." She grinned at him. "One of the perks of being a High Guest."

"Really."

A horn sounded through the temple, the rich sound amplifying off the walls. Troi resisted the urge to clamp her hands over her ears.

There were a few moments of confusion as the guests spun around, trying to find the source. A voice rippled through Troi's thoughts: *Upper balcony, please.*

All of the Betazoids looked up, and the rest of the High Guests followed, quiet eventually settling over the room. Sildar Syn stood next to the balcony's edge, clutching a silver horn in one hand. "Welcome to the Unveiling of the Three Treasures!" he said, his voice reverberating through a speaker and a burst of telepathy. "On behalf of the Betazed Cultural Committee, it pleases me to see Isszon Temple filled with guests from across the Federation. So many testaments to the creativity and ingenuity of life in the known universe all to help us celebrate this important moment in Betazed's history!"

Polite applause rippled through the room.

"We will be starting our opening ceremonies shortly," Syn continued. "High Guests, I ask that you join your assigned choreography coordinator!" He pointed toward the stage, and the entire room turned around to find that the five ceremony staff members, each dressed in the corresponding costume style of the five guest categories, had stepped out from the billowing curtains.

The room was a riot of emotions, but Picard's discomfort managed to stand out.

"You've been through worse," Troi said to him.

"Yes," Picard said. "I was stabbed through the heart, and nearly died."

Troi laughed. He gave her one last pained look before making his way toward the stage. The commander watched the guests gather, the choreography coordinators all waving their hands around wildly as they attempted to corral them into some semblance of a position. She kept her eye on the captain, who was hanging back, looking utterly put out. Mother really shouldn't have put him in this position. But perhaps it would be good for him; she had been encouraging the captain to step outside his comfort zone.

The Dreams coordinator was pulling her guests into a tight huddle, and Picard's reticence had not escaped her. She had the haughtiness of Betazoid royalty, her demeanor lofty as she pulled Picard into the group.

This was going to be a long three days.

"Betazoid ceremonies are . . . interesting," Worf said.

Troi looked at him over the tower of whipped cream atop her uttaberry cloud pudding. She had been eating it for the last thirty minutes without making a dent in the thing. "And what do you mean by that?" she teased.

He frowned. "I didn't expect so much dancing."

Troi grinned. "The Third House is known for its dancing. Would you like some of my pudding?"

Worf's frown deepened.

"There are uttaberries in there somewhere." Troi winked. "I promise."

It was early evening and they were out on the lawn of the temple, two Starfleet officers watching a performance of a troupe of *taitath* dancers accompanied by a thirty-piece band. The banner of the Third House of Betazed flapped overhead as the dancers swirled and shimmied in elaborate formations across the lawn.

"I will try it," Worf finally said.

For a moment, Troi considered spooning some up and feeding it to him. She handed him the spoon, her cheeks hot. *Inappropriate*. Both of them were in uniform, for goodness' sake.

Worf took a bit of the pudding. "Acceptable."

"High praise." Troi laughed.

The music swelled to a crescendo and the dancers whipped themselves up into a bigger frenzy. From what Troi had gathered after a rather exhausting lunchtime conversation with her mother, this performance was an ante-ceremony, the first in a trio. Each ante-ceremony was developed and presented by one of the Houses that held the three treasures. When the three ante-ceremonies concluded at midnight, the artifacts would be unveiled in the temple.

"Do you know the whereabouts of the captain?" Worf asked.

Troi ate another bite of pudding. It was as sweet and thick as the perfumed evening settling around them, and she was sure she would not be able to consume any more. "I believe the guests will be introducing the second ante-ceremony," she said. "They're probably preparing in the temple."

Worf nodded, but she could sense he wasn't completely satisfied with the answer. The security officer wasn't watching the dancers; his gaze was shifting around the crowd.

"Worf," Troi said, "Captain Picard will be fine."

The music ended with a crash of cymbals and the dancers froze into place, drone lights flickering around them.

"Look," Troi said. "His part in the ceremony is about to begin. You'll see, he's just fine."

"I'm not worried about the captain," Worf said. "There are just—quite a lot of people here."

"It's a major cultural event!" Troi resisted the urge to roll her eyes. "Here. Eat the rest of my pudding. It's supposed to put you in the celebratory spirit."

The Klingon stared down at the luxurious dessert, then, begrudgingly, took another bite.

"That wasn't so hard, was it?" she asked, smiling.

Worf grunted.

The Third House dancers dissolved their formation and spilled out into the crowd, connecting with friends and admirers. Joy roiled off the press of people, a heady sweetness that reminded Troi of jasmine blossoms. Feeling light-headed from the festivities, she rested her hand on Worf's arm and felt the jolt of his surprise. She found it sweet, the way he always seemed startled—and not at all displeased—whenever she made these small overtures.

"Let's walk," she said.

"As you wish." Worf tossed the remains of the cloud pudding into a composting receptacle and together they drifted into the labyrinth of tents.

"I'm glad the captain gave the okay to let Geordi watch the bridge so you could see the ceremony," Troi said. "It really is something remarkable."

Worf said nothing, and Troi suspected he would have preferred to stay aboard the *Enterprise*. But the captain had agreed Worf could take two hours' leave that evening, as an apology for interrupting their previously scheduled dinner.

"So how was it being in command of the *Enterprise*?" Troi asked.

"Uneventful," Worf said. "We're running a skeleton crew. I have allowed many of the crew to attend the ceremony." He stared toward Isszon Temple.

"Hoping to catch a glimpse of the captain?"

"Yes." There was a muffled amusement to his voice.

They walked in front of a tent filled with cut flowers, their scent wafting out on the air. Worf stopped and sniffed. "They have *raw'bah* flowers in there."

"Oh?" Troi glanced up at the sign glowing above the tent: *Flowers for the Unveiling*. Guests were asked to toss them into the air at the end of the pageant, before the unveiling of the three artifacts. The flowers were to represent the return of Xiomara's telepathic abilities.

"They're native to Qo'noS." Worf ducked inside and Troi trailed after him. The tent was warm and hazy. Worf pulled out a long, thorned stem topped with a knot of dark gray petals curling around a brilliant red stamen. "They're notoriously difficult to grow offworld. I could never get them to survive in my quarters."

He gave Troi a small, shy smile and handed her the flower. "Careful, they're thorned."

"As befitting a flower that is native to Qo'noS." She took it from him, gingerly, and then returned his smile, suddenly feeling shy herself.

A horn blasted across the lawn.

"The second ante-ceremony is starting," Troi said, glad to have something to distract from their closeness in the tent. "We should go in and support Captain Picard."

"Yes." For a moment, though, they just looked at each other, surrounded by flowers.

"I'll save this for the unveiling," she said.

The High Guests were parading down the steps of the temple, lights illuminating their path in the falling light.

"He's in a blue tunic from the late antiquity period." The commander pulled Worf through the crowd. The guests streamed down onto the lawn, their appearance met with cheers and applause as they split off into five streams, forming the shape of a star, the sign of the Fourth House of Betazed. The lights brightened, casting the shadows of the guests into stark relief on the grass. Suddenly, music played from the foot of the temple: another group, this time led by Jarkko Sentis, son of the First House and Keeper of the Hallowed Urn of Rus'xi, one of the three treasures.

"I see the captain," Worf murmured. "He—does not look pleased."

She swept her gaze over the guests until she found Picard standing with his arms crossed, wedged between an astonishingly beautiful Bolian man and Marta Gilbert, the famed Earth astrobotanist.

"He's been doing this all day."

Worf looked down at her. "The captain is doing his duty."

"I *know*." Troi swatted at him with the *raw'bah* flower. "Plainly, he's not enjoying it."

The horn sounded and the guests immediately broke apart, scattering off into the crowd just as a troupe of acrobats tumbled into place.

"He's free," Troi said. "Let's go talk to him. See if we can boost his morale."

"A good idea," Worf agreed. He led the way through the crowd, a path clearing. A Klingon in a Starfleet uniform was an unexpected sight at a Betazoid cultural festival.

They were almost to the knot of Dreams Guests when Troi felt it. A connection stronger than any she was likely to feel, even here on Betazed. A familiar, slight ringing in the back of her head.

She whispered to Worf, "My mother's on her way."

"The ambassador?" He sounded surprised.

Troi jogged up to the guests just as her mother swept into view.

She had changed since their last meeting, into full Fifth House regalia, with the long, trailing cape and the classic floor-length skirt and the ruffled sleeves. That she could move so quickly in such an outfit was a testament to her Betazoid strength.

"Jean-Luc!" she sang out, throwing her arms wide. Picard whirled around, an expression of terror momentarily flashing across his features. "Oh, you did *wonderfully*. I knew you'd make an excellent High Guest!"

She threw her arms around Picard just as Troi skittered to a stop beside them. "Ambassador Troi," Picard said in a voice of quiet desperation.

"Mother, please let him go. I'm sure the captain is exhausted."

"Exhausted?" Lwaxana peered at Picard. "How is that possible? The evening's just beginning!" She threw her arm out toward the acrobat troupe, who were tumbling and leaping over each other in time to the steady beat of a *brimet* drum. "We haven't even gotten to the most important piece yet—"

"*Mother*." Troi stepped in between her mother and Picard and brandished the *raw'bah* flower in her direction. "Please. Let him rest before he has to reconvene for the next ceremony."

Lwaxana's gaze zeroed in on the flower. "What is that thing?"

Troi sighed. "It's a *raw'bah*, for the unveiling later."

"It looks like a weapon." Lwaxana frowned. "They're supposed to be passing out sand lilies for the Rain of Blossoms. I've never—" She stopped, her face lighting up. "Mister Worf! I didn't expect to see you here." She lifted up her skirts and glided over to him. "How's my little warrior?"

"Alexander is doing very well," Worf said gravely. "Keeping busy with his studies."

"He beamed down for the ceremony earlier today with a group from the school," Troi said. "I'm sure he's around here somewhere."

Lwaxana laughed. "Oh, he doesn't want to see *me*. There's a girl he has his eye on, and he's planning to woo her this weekend." She winked.

"What?" Worf said. "What girl?"

"Nothing you need to concern yourself about, Mister Worf. Just young love."

"He is too young!" Worf started. "And when did he tell you—"

"He sends me messages on occasion." The ambassador flapped her hand. "It's all quite innocent. Right, Deanna?"

"You knew about this?" Worf turned to her.

"He asked me not to say anything." Troi pressed the *raw'bah* flower to her chest. "Mother's right—it's completely innocent. Just a schoolboy crush. It's quite sweet, really."

Worf narrowed his eyes. "Sweet."

"You'll approve of the girl," Troi added, sensing his anger at Alexander for keeping it a secret from him. "It's Rosamund Beshtimt, Lieutenant Beshtimt's daughter."

Worf's expression softened. "She could be a good influence on him, yes."

"See?" Troi smiled at him. "You shouldn't worry so much. Not about something as simple as growing up."

Worf returned the smile and Troi felt his anger melt into a soft warmth toward her. Toward the idea of young love.

She felt the heat rise in her cheeks and wondered if he saw the blush.

"Jean-Luc! Where are you going?"

"Mother!" she hissed, looking up in time to see Picard vanishing into the crowd. Lwaxana turned back to her.

"That man!" the ambassador said. "He doesn't know how to have fun."

Worse, though, was the telepathic whisper of her voice inside Troi's head: *Are you and Mister Worf together?*

Mother! Troi thought back.

So that's a yes.

"We should follow the captain," Worf said. "I want to speak with him."

"Of course," Troi said, embarrassment strangling her voice. "Mother, *please* stay here."

Lwaxana tittered. "Oh, fine. I'll have plenty of time to speak with Jean-Luc at the House dinner tomorrow." She waved her hand toward the crowd. "Make sure he's back at the temple in time for the unveiling." Her eyes twinkled. *There's a lovers' garden on the other side of the lawn. I'm sure Mister Worf would find it most amenable.*

Troi's cheeks flushed, and she whirled around, plunging into the crowd, trying very, very hard not to think about Worf, a Betazoid lovers' garden, or anything at all.

7

Doctor Crusher's fingers flew across the transporter controls. She hadn't done this in ages, but the station's transporter was an older model, similar to the one she had trained on at the Academy.

It helped that none of her targets were moving.

"I've got a lock on Ensigns Rikkilä and Muñoz," she said. "Beaming over now."

She moved her fingers up the controls and immediately light shimmered on the platform.

"I can help you!" Riker shouted through the door. Crusher had locked the door leading into the hallway to serve as a quarantine barrier. Imperfect, but better than nothing, and if this was communicable, she'd be the only other one infected.

"Will," Crusher replied as Muñoz and Rikkilä materialized on the platform. "I can't risk further infection, if that's what we're dealing with."

She checked both of the ensigns, their uniforms streaked with white sand, the scent of the sea still clinging to them, and scanned them with her tricorder. Temperatures normal. Slightly elevated blood pressure. No signs of infections.

"Josefina," she said, brushing Rikkilä's cheek with a gloved hand. The station's medkit had been mostly empty, its supplies all utilized during the storm that had killed the team's original commander. Fortunately, she had brought a medkit with her—although most of the items it contained were basic. "Can you hear me?"

Rikkilä's eyes fluttered. "Doctor Crusher?" she mumbled. "I feel so— Everything's *cloudy*."

"Riker to Crusher." He was contacting her through her combadge. *"We've got a problem."*

Crusher gently opened Rikkilä's eyelids. Her pupils contracted in the light.

"Data informs me Solanko, Malisson, and Talma collapsed as well. He says that he is unaffected."

Crusher took a deep breath. "I'll beam them out next." The doctor shifted over to Muñoz. "Ensign Muñoz?"

He turned his head toward her, his eyes moving beneath his eyelids. "Am I still on the beach?"

"No. You're back at the station. I need you to move off the platform."

Muñoz stirred, pushing himself up on wobbling arms. Even though she knew the risks of transmission, she helped him up, looping her arm around his waist, then half guiding, half dragging him over to the corner. His boots clattered against the floor, so she wasn't pulling dead weight. He could hold himself up.

"There you go." She set him back on the floor and turned to find Rikkilä crawling off the platform on hands and knees, leaving a trail of seawater in her wake.

"I've got it," she murmured when Crusher knelt to help her. "I heard Commander Riker. Beam over the others."

Crusher nodded, wondering what was affecting them.

She studied the transporter controls. Solanko, Malisson, and Talma were scattered across the beach. She had a lock on them, but not Data.

"Will, where's Data?"

"He's making his way back on foot," Riker answered. *"He's almost here. He was away from the rest of the team when the others collapsed."*

"Got 'em!" she said as the three remaining members of the team materialized on the pad. They were also stunned. Solanko groaned and looked up at her. "What happened?"

"That's what I'm trying to figure out." Crusher studied the readings. Normal. "How are you feeling?"

"Bit roughed up." Solanko struggled up to sitting. "Like I went a few rounds with a Klingon. How are the others?"

Crusher moved to Talma. Temperature was forty degrees, normal for a Bolian. Blood pressure, heart rate, breathing—all normal.

"Better," answered Muñoz.

Both Rikkilä and Muñoz were standing up, Rikkilä wobbling a little. "Let me help."

"Sit back down." Crusher turned to Malisson. "I don't know what's wrong with any of you."

Malisson was trying to sit up. "That came out of *nowhere*." She rubbed her head. Her scans were normal.

"You should not exert yourselves," Crusher said.

"Doctor, did you beam over the samples?" Solanko asked.

"Of course not." Crusher returned her attention to Talma. He was the only one of the five who was still affected. "There's nothing in the Federation database to explain—"

Talma shot up with a loud gasp, "Huh!" he cried. Then, blinking: "Where's the beach? How'd I get here?"

"I beamed you back." Crusher frowned down at him. "Do you remember what happened?"

Talma shook his head. "I was speaking with Commander Data by the tide pools. Then he went farther down the beach to gather some samples, and—" Talma let out a long breath. "Everything's a haze after that."

"I see," Crusher said. "Thank you." His scans weren't showing anything out of the ordinary. And just like the others, he seemed to be recovering quickly. Already he was sitting up and making his way off the transporter pad.

"We need to look at those samples." Crusher sighed. "None of us can leave this room until I have a better sense of what we're dealing with. I don't know what caused the episode on the beach, and all six of us are now potentially infected, maybe even Commander Data." She tapped her combadge. "Crusher to Riker."

"I'm here." Riker was still watching through the window. *"What's the plan?"*

"Is it possible to remotely operate any of the scanners in the lab?" Crusher looked over at Solanko, who nodded sharply. He and Malisson were both standing, and Rikkilä was up on her feet, pacing barefoot around the room. *How* did everyone recover so quickly?

"Perfect," Crusher said. "Solanko? If you could beam the samples over to it? I don't want to risk exposing myself any more than I have to."

"On it," Solanko said, moving his hands over the transporter controls.

"Computer," Talma said. "Ready the decontamination chamber in lab B."

Crusher leaned up against the wall and watched as the planet's survey team jumped into action. There was no evidence that any of them had been unconscious less than ten minutes ago.

"Ensign Rikkilä," Crusher said. Rikkilä turned away from a conversation she'd been having with Muñoz and Malisson. Crusher gestured for her to join her.

"I was getting their histories," said the ensign. "Before the team was beamed down for the mission, they did comprehensive scans of the surface." She shrugged. "There was no sign of any kind of harmful life-forms or viruses."

Standard operating procedure. "What exactly do you remember?" she asked Rikkilä. "When did the dizzy spell come on?"

The ensign began to speak in a nervous, rapid-fire cadence. She had been in the water and then noticed that Muñoz had collapsed on the beach. Crusher recorded her account into the tricorder; she needed to hear from everyone. Without any kind of clear-cut cause, the next step was to understand what had happened.

"Ensign," Crusher said when Rikkilä had finished, "I want you to get statements from everyone. Get as many details as you can."

"Yes, sir." Rikkilä paused. "What are the scans showing? I feel fine now."

"Your scans were all normal." Crusher studied the team. "The recovery was so fast. I'd say there was something on the beach." Perhaps a strange microorganism the scans hadn't discovered. No, that didn't make any sense. The survey team had already gathered samples from the beach without any adverse reaction.

Crusher tried not to think about the refugees currently strewn across Federation starships. Kota was supposed to be for them. This last remaining survey was intended to be just a formality.

The station didn't have a proper medical lab. Even the replicator wasn't rated for medical material.

"Riker to Crusher."

Riker's voice jerked Crusher out of her thoughts. She was aware the team was listening in, even if they were trying to be surreptitious about it.

"Report," Riker said.

"They appear to be okay, Will." Crusher flicked her gaze across the team. "But something clearly happened."

"Do you have any reason to keep them in quarantine?"

Crusher curled her hand, pressing her fingers into her palm. She had been hoping to delay breaking quarantine until she finished talking to the others.

"I feel fine," Solanko offered, and the others nodded in agreement.

"Doctor Crusher?" Riker asked.

"Nothing is showing up in my scans," Crusher said with a defeated sigh. "Will, this is an unfamiliar planet—"

"That's been cleared by Starfleet. You know the high commissioner wants answers. We have to examine those samples."

Crusher looked at the team. All of them appeared to be healthy and vibrant. It would be so much easier to deal with a mystery like this in her lab.

"Let me do one more round of tests."

The tests found nothing.

Crusher had reluctantly let the rest of the crew out of quarantine so they could return to their duties. She had stayed behind to examine Data, who had been isolating himself outside after walking back from the beach. Once the space was cleared, she called him in to see if he might be able to provide any answers.

"How do you feel?" she asked him, running her tricorder over him for the third time, looking for any hint of an irregularity. Although she usually had Lieutenant La Forge's help when examining Data, he'd been her patient long enough that she knew what his readings should look like.

"I did not experience any symptoms as did the others," Data said. "Likely due to my being an android."

"Weren't you also separated from the others?"

"Yes. I had moved farther up the beach when I received the call from Lieutenant Talma that Lieutenant Solanko had collapsed. But I was not any farther from Lieutenants Talma and Solanko than the two ensigns."

Crusher frowned as her tricorder reported normal readings. They had been spread equidistant across the beach. Data was the only one apparently unaffected and did not appear to be carrying the contagion on his person, as all of the others had recovered. A localized toxin seemed the most likely suspect. Something on the beach . . .

"While you were collecting samples," she asked Data, "did you notice anything unusual about the beach? The air? The water?"

"Everything was as expected based on the Federation reports." He looked at Crusher, his head tilted. "I am sorry I could not be of more use."

"It's not your fault, Data." Crusher smiled thinly at him. "I can't find any reason to keep you in isolation. Or myself." She told herself that the station was isolation enough; she would need to keep an eye on Commander Riker. Given what she'd seen so far, he wasn't likely to start showing symptoms.

"Let's meet that deadline," she said as she pushed the door open.

The following morning, Crusher was the only one awake; she'd had trouble sleeping. The bed in the station's sleeping quarters was hard and unfamiliar. The doctor couldn't shake the feeling that she had made the wrong decision in breaking quarantine. Something *had* happened. *Damn the high commissioner and her deadline.*

But there was nothing in their systems. No sign of infection or foreign antibodies. Just normal, healthy Starfleet officers.

Pulling a cup of coffee out of the replicator, Crusher slipped outside of the station. The horizon was limned in pale orange light that deepened into the rich purple of the Kotan dawn sky. The stars had faded into pale freckles across the expanse.

She sipped the beverage, its heat warming her face; mornings were apparently chilly here. For the millionth time since yesterday afternoon, she studied her tricorder. They had all said the same thing: a sudden onslaught of dizziness and then collapse, their thoughts racing. The effect immediately faded when they were transported back to the station.

"Doctor Crusher?"

She jumped. Data was standing in the station's entrance.

"You are up early."

"I had some trouble sleeping."

"You were not the only one. I heard several members of the team get up during the night. I was in the laboratory, working through the backlog."

Data had been the only member of the sampling team who hadn't been affected, which only cemented her belief that they were dealing with something biological. Something that wasn't in the Federation databases and did not show up on any scan.

Crusher leaned against the wall, her coffee cooling in its cup. "You know, Data, I requested to come on this away team because I thought it would be some enjoyable downtime."

"It is fortunate that you are here, Doctor," Data countered.

"Fortunate?" Crusher sipped her coffee and gazed out at the rustling grass, moving like the ocean in the dim morning light.

Her combadge chirped.

"Riker to Crusher. Report to sleeping quarters."

"You said you heard people getting up last night?" she asked Data as she darted back into the station. Riker was waiting for her outside the sleeping quarters.

"What's wrong?" she asked, already running her scanner over Riker.

"I'm fine," he said as the tricorder confirmed it. "It's the others, the ones who went to the beach. Probably nothing—"

Crusher frowned and pushed her way into the sleeping quarters. No one was in bed, which was *something*. Solanko and Malisson were already dressed, and Talma was pacing around in a draping Bolian robe.

Rikkilä was gripping her tricorder. "Ensign Muñoz has a slightly elevated temperature. Thirty-seven point five degrees."

Muñoz gave a wave from the corner of the room, his hair still mussed from sleeping.

"What is the problem?"

"Dreams," Rikkilä said.

Riker stood in the doorway, and once again Crusher considered that the entire station was a quarantine zone. She and Riker had to be contaminated.

But Crusher didn't remember dreaming. "I'm not following." She turned to Riker, who shook his head.

"We all woke up last night around the same time," Solanko began. "Me and Amanda ran into each other out by the replicator. We talked."

"We'd had the same dream," Malisson added.

"Now, I wouldn't go that far," Solanko said. "Not *identical*."

"They were close enough." Talma stopped his pacing and turned toward the doctor. "I had it too. I heard the two of them talking."

Crusher turned to Rikkilä, who had perched herself on the edge of Muñoz's bed. Both of them nodded.

Crusher considered all this. She hadn't heard them stir, but it was probably during those few hours she had managed to fall asleep.

"What was the dream *about?*" she asked.

"The beach," Rikkilä said.

"But it wasn't the same," Muñoz said. "Everything was brighter."

Rikkilä shrugged. "Yes. But I was in the water, getting thrown around by the waves, and then I got tossed up into the dunes and sank into the sand."

The others murmured in agreement. Solanko said, "I got pulled down into the sand. A common theme, right?"

Everyone nodded.

"It was what was under the sand," Rikkilä said. "People I've known throughout my life, all talking to me at once. I couldn't make out anything."

Muñoz said, "People I haven't seen in years. Others I didn't recognize."

More murmurs of agreement.

If this is contagious, Crusher thought, *it hasn't jumped.* It had only affected the beach team, so it couldn't have a long incubation period. And that was assuming it even *was* an infection. The shared dream suggested some kind of psychic bond. Despite being on the beach, Data was unaffected—clearly it was bio-based.

"Ensign Rikkilä," she said. "I'm pulling you off the lab work. You're going to help me get to the bottom of this."

Rikkilä rose, clutching her tricorder.

"Collect a second blood sample from the beach team," Crusher continued. "And load your scans from this morning into the station computer. No one is going out to collect new samples until I have a clearer picture of what happened." *What's still happening,* she corrected herself.

"That's fair," Riker agreed.

"One other thing." Crusher turned to Solanko. "Those irregular sand samples you mentioned yesterday. I need one."

8

The air thrummed, and Troi felt dizzy from the excitement of the crowd. Hundreds of people were pressed into Isszon Temple, their voices low, but there was a constant murmur in the back of her head. The *Enterprise* officers had managed to slip into seats to the right of the stage. Her mother had offered her a place in the Fifth House's balcony, but she wanted to sit with the guests.

"Will there be more dancing?" Worf asked, his voice jolting her out of her reverie.

"What?" Troi laughed. "Oh, Lieutenant, there's an entire pageant involved."

Worf nodded an acknowledgment as the lights dimmed throughout the temple, bringing everyone's voices to a soft hush. A single circle of light appeared on the stage, illuminating the softly billowing curtains.

"Five thousand years ago," a melodic female voice rang out through the temple, "in late antiquity, a lyre player, a *taitath* dancer, a poet, a sculptor, and a ship's captain met at a crossroads—"

Troi sank into her chair. When her mother told her about the pageant preceding the unveiling, she'd failed to mention that they were starting with the story of the founding of the five Houses. This was going to last all night.

She tried not to think about the captain, having to sit through all this onstage. At least the High Guests were tucked away behind the curtains.

"They made a pact," the voice continued as the circle of light widened to show five actors, each representing one of the five Houses. The story continued in a slow, graceful pantomime. Mother had told it to her when she was a girl and it came back to her in pieces. The journey through the haunted forest, the great battle at Mount Alain, the masquerade ball where the five founders met again many years later.

She could feel Worf shifting beside her. "I do not understand what this has to do with the three treasures," he whispered.

"Just wait," Troi said.

Eventually, the Houses were founded, which was marked by a burst of music, a flood of stage lights, and the reveal of the guests, all lined up beside their corresponding founder. The audience politely applauded.

"And from the first of these Houses," the narrator said, her voice swelling through the temple, "a hero was born: Xiomara, daughter of the First House, She Who Lost the Way, Keeper of the Three Treasures!"

This brought a louder round of applause.

"Finally," Worf mumbled.

Troi smothered a laugh. "I wouldn't be so sure." She glanced at him sideways and found him looking back at her, affection radiating off him.

The stage light changed, turning softer and murkier, and an actress dressed in a green gown and towering headdress, the traditional depiction of Xiomara, stepped out. "All the thoughts have gone silent!" she cried. "The First House is in grave danger!"

The pageant continued, moving through the story. Xiomara, her lost telepathic ability, the impending threat of the invaders from the stars, the Daor, the group making their way to the mountains where the First House was founded. The actress playing Xiomara flung herself about the stage in delight, weaving around the guests as they stood stiffly in their costumes, blending into the backdrop of the stage. Eventually, she fetched glittering reproductions of the three treasures, each House leader stepping forward and hoisting it above their head as they recited lines from the Xiomaran epic.

"Too much dancing," Worf said.

"It's not like *you* have to be up there."

He studied the captain.

"Xiomara defeated the Daor invaders with three everyday objects," the narrator said as the actress dodged holographic Daor and swung the oversized Enshrined Disk at their bulbous heads. Eventually, the Daor flickered away, leaving a victorious Xiomara surrounded by the replicas of the three treasures.

The actress took a deep bow as the crowd erupted into cheers and tossed flowers filled the air. Blossoms showered down around her onstage, drifting like snow. Many of the older Betazoids in the crowd stood and sang out the final lines of the Xiomaran epic, the melody flooding through the temple.

"We still have not seen anything," Worf grumbled. "No Klingon would take so long to get to the point."

"Betazoids are all about the journey," Troi told him, even though she agreed. She caught the *raw'bah* flower she had tossed up lightly—she'd rather take it back to the *Enterprise* than fling it at the stage.

The actress playing Xiomara stepped forward, and a circle of light surrounded her, blacking out the rest of the stage. The audience quieted and she began to speak, her voice clear and bright.

"On that day," the actress said, "Xiomara turned down the marriage proposal of Anton Rus'xi of the Fourth House. As a gift of lament, she gave him the urn she used to capture the Daor captain."

A rather nervous-looking Benzite in the Early Restoration robes of Create stepped into the light and accepted the prop urn. The light was bright and Troi was close enough to see the trembling tendrils above his breathing apparatus.

"Xiomara accepted the marriage proposal of Rohana Ahmo of the Third House, on the condition that she would leave her home and accompany Xiomara on all of her adventures across Betazed. As a dowry, she gave to Rohana's parents the disk she used to behead a Daor warrior in ritual battle, preventing further slaughter on both sides."

A human woman in the same Early Restoration robes stepped forward. She had the air of a holodeck star and she shot a bright smile out to the crowd as she accepted the prop disk.

"As for the spoon Xiomara used to dismantle the Daor's communications, those she left with her nephew, Harshod of the First House, who took on the mantle of House leader in her absence."

The actress handed off an oversized prop spoon to a Vulcan in a floor-length green tunic.

"For the next five thousand years," the actress said, her voice soaring, "these three treasures were kept in the Houses. Never brought together as they were in the Battle of Cataria."

The actress paused and Troi sensed the anticipation of every single audience member. She felt the prickle of the hairs on her arm, a strange and unfamiliar surge of Betazoid pride.

"Until tonight," the actress said, to a hushed and reverent room.

She stepped back as the light widened and the layers of fluttering curtains dropped away, one by one. Troi leaned forward on her seat, her heart thudding. She could just make out the outline of the display case behind a shimmery gold curtain.

"For the first time in five hundred years," the actress said, grabbing hold of that final curtain, "the Keepers of these artifacts have brought them out of their ancestral homes to Isszon Temple." Her smile widened, she sent out her thoughts, and there was that strange reverberating effect of mind and tongue.

"Tonight, we bring together the Hallowed Urn of Rus'xi."

Murmurs of excitement rose up from the crowd.

"The Enshrined Disk of the Third House."

Someone up on the balcony let out a gasp of delight.

"The Sacred Silver of Xiomara!"

The actress yanked down the curtain. For a moment all Troi could see was flowing, rippling gold. The fabric drifted down to the stage, revealing the display case, glowing faintly behind its force field.

Empty.

At first, Troi couldn't register what she was seeing.

She felt the first swell of confusion. Of panic. Of anger.

The actress felt it too. Her smile became manic, plastered on. She seemed terrified to turn to the display case and confirm what the audience was telling her.

Baffled Betazoid voices rose up in Troi's head, followed a heartbeat later by physical voices, shrieks and wails of despair. People surged toward the stage and the actress raced off into the wings, leaving the High Guests still standing in their formations, confused.

"Please remain calm." A different voice boomed out through the temple. "Stay in your seats. We are locking down Isszon Temple. Repeat, we are locking down Isszon Temple."

A Betazoid woman in traditional dress barreled onstage, flinging herself toward the display case. "Where is it!" she shrieked. "You promised it would be secure!"

Worf was up on his feet, his hand at his hip—but of course he didn't have his phaser. Only Betazed Security were allowed to have weapons in the temple. "I have to get to the captain."

"Wait!" Troi cried as he pushed his way toward the aisle. She tried to follow him but was blocked in by the crowd.

"Remain in your seats," the voice boomed out again. "Isszon Temple is now locked down. No one is allowed in or out."

Betazed Security officers came spilling into the temple, corralling the audience back to their seats. Troi looked onstage, where the guests were being cleared off and the display case was now ringed with high-ranking security officers in white-and-gray uniforms.

She took a deep, shuddery breath and braced herself against her chair. The voices swirling around inside her head were almost too much, but she squeezed her eyes shut and reached out with every ounce of strength she could muster.

Mother? she called out. *Mother, what the hell is going on?!*

9

—◆—

Jean-Luc Picard was swept up in a tidal wave of confusion. He and the rest of the guests were being corralled offstage by a trio of Betazoids wearing stiff-necked white-and-gray uniforms and carrying phasers, their faces hidden behind dark masks that projected down from their helmets. "Stay together," one of them ordered.

"What's going on?" whispered Sh'yan, her voice tight with fear. She had scurried up beside Picard, blinking at him with large, damp eyes. Sh'yan was another Dreams Guest, a diminutive Hekaran ship designer who had, much to Picard's surprise, studied his command of the *Stargazer* during her time at university. She'd proven a comforting ally as they'd made their way through the exhausting litany of ceremonies, ritual dances, and other assorted nonsense.

"I don't know." Picard twisted around and caught a final glimpse of the empty display case. *Empty.* How was that possible? Every second of these ceremonies had clearly been planned, rehearsed, and backed up by every conceivable contingency.

"Dreams Guests!" Eliana, the Dreams coordinator, sent up a shimmery blue energy flare, which had been her primary mode of communication all day. "This way, please!"

She kept up a facade of brightness, but Picard heard the tremor in her voice.

"This way," she repeated as the Dreams Guests flowed around her, peppering her with questions. Her smile was desperate as she offered clipped answers. "I don't know, they haven't— Mr. Sasek, please don't wander off, it's imperative we stay in a group— No, the temple is on lockdown—"

Sh'yan looked over at Picard. "Lockdown!" she said. "Were the artifacts *stolen*?"

"I don't think anyone knows what's happened," Picard said. "But that would be my guess."

"But *how*?" Sh'yan shook her head in disbelief. "We saw the Keepers bring them in. And backstage was *swarming* with security, someone would have seen—"

They stepped through a curtain and out into the temple proper, which was currently storming with the onslaught of hundreds of angry, confused Betazoids. Picard swept his gaze around, immediately taking stock of the situation. Betazed Security forces were spaced out at equal intervals; all the entrances and exits were blocked with force fields. The crowd was still in their areas; the din of questions was ringing out through the temple.

The stage had also been blocked with a force field, the display case reflecting the soft glow of the field's energy.

"Attention! Dreams Guests! Attention!"

Eliana flapped her hand, trying to catch everyone's eye. She had to shout to be heard over the noise. When she seemed satisfied that the guests were paying attention to her, and not the pandemonium around them, she threw out another one of those frantic smiles.

"I have been informed that security would like to speak to each of you individually. As witnesses." She added that last part quickly. "Because we were all backstage prior to the unveiling—"

"Captain!"

A very familiar voice cut through the cacophony. Picard whirled around to find Worf making his way through the crowd, a look of fierce Klingon determination on his face.

"Mister Worf," Picard said, surprised.

"Sir, are you all right?"

"I'm fine." Picard offered a wry grin. "I'm glad you're still here."

"Yes, sir. De— Counselor Troi asked me to join her for the unveiling while I was off duty. Commander La Forge has command of the *Enterprise*." Worf leaned in close. "Sir, with all due respect, I don't think it's safe for you to be—"

"Captain Picard?" Eliana materialized beside Picard and Worf, her smile fighting its inevitable progression into a scowl. "Would you care to introduce me to your"—she took in Worf—"officer?"

"I am head of security for the *Starship Enterprise*. I'm here to ensure my captain's safety."

Eliana's pleasant expression wavered. "Oh, of course. I—" She closed her eyes, took a deep breath. "I'm just a bit *overwhelmed*—"

"Eliana," Picard said, "please, tend to the others. I will speak to Betazed Security before the night is out. They will have my full cooperation." He tried to offer a reassuring countenance. "All of us want to see the artifacts returned as quickly as possible."

Eliana's eyelashes fluttered. "Of course," she said, pressing her hand to her forehead. "It's just so—oh, there are so *many* voices telling me what to do, and—"

"Sh'yan, see if you can get Eliana a glass of water."

"We have to stay in a group!" Eliana said.

"I'll be right back," Sh'yan said quickly. "You don't have to worry about me." And then she disappeared into the crowd. Marta, the astrobotanist, guided Eliana over to a nearby seat. "Here, you just need to rest," she said. "You don't need to worry about any of us."

Picard turned back to Worf. "Do you have any insight into what's happening?"

"No, sir. The counselor and I were watching the"—Picard noticed the slight hesitation in his voice—"*performance*. I saw nothing unusual."

"Neither did I," Picard replied. "We were backstage when the three Keepers brought the treasures and placed them in the case—but they were all covered with black cloths. I didn't see them."

A flash of sequined glitter caught Picard's eye. "Oh no," he breathed. "Not now."

"Captain?" Worf frowned and turned around. "Oh."

It was Ambassador Lwaxana Troi, in a frothy dress draped in crystals. She was weaving her way through the crowd with her own Klingon-like determination, and when she saw that Picard had spotted her, she hiked her skirts up higher and plunged forward.

"Mister Woof!" she cried.

Worf closed his eyes and sighed.

"I've been looking everywhere for you." She bustled up to them, a little breathless. Curls of hair had loosed themselves from her elaborate up-do. "Deanna said you had wanted to find Jean-Luc." She flashed Picard a quick smile.

Several paces away, Troi was sidling through the crowd, trying not to get caught in some wayward eddy that would send her off to the other side of the temple.

"Ambassador Troi." Worf frowned. "May I ask—"

"Come, come." Lwaxana scooped her arms in Worf's and dragged him forward. Worf shot a confused look back at his captain. "We don't have much time."

"Mother," Troi asked, "did you even *explain*?"

"There's no time!" Lwaxana tugged on Worf's arm. "Commander Rusina needs all the help he can get if we're to stop the thief!"

Picard glanced back at Eliana, who was still draped across a chair, surrounded by a trio of Dreams Guests. He turned his attention to his officers to find Worf glowering at the two Troi women. Picard wondered if he could escape from his guest duties.

Finally, Troi said, "Voices, Mother."

". . . help with the investigation."

This caught Picard's interest. "What?"

Troi took a deep breath. "Betazed Security forces are slightly overwhelmed. And Mother—"

Lwaxana pulled once more on Worf's arm. "Come *now*," she insisted.

"Mother has convinced the commander that Worf would be able to discover what happened." She sighed, looking unhappy. "Something about Klingon intimidation measures."

"That is absolutely not what I said!" Lwaxana dropped Worf's arm and peered up at him. "I told Commander Rusina that we had the very *best* Starfleet security officer in attendance. He could be *instrumental* in—"

Picard held up one hand. "I understand," he said. "Mister Worf, go with Ambassador Troi. Offer any aid they might need."

"Oh, thank you, Jean-Luc!" Lwaxana cried, and Picard took a reflexive step backward. To her credit, she made no move to embrace him, but went into the crowd. Worf glanced back at Picard and gave him a quick nod, then followed Lwaxana into the fray.

"Sir," Troi said, "Worf was scheduled to go back on duty at zero three hundred."

"None of us will be beaming back until this matter is solved." Picard tugged at his tunic, wishing he could pull it off, along with the ridiculous pantaloons. "Believe me, the sooner we can find this thief, the better it will be for all of us."

10

———

Data deposited the last slide of plant fibers into the storage chamber with one hand and input his observational data into the station computer with the other. At the same time, he was aware of the actions of the two others in the lab: Ensign Muñoz was running soil samples through the scanner, the *click-whir* of the scanner's processor a quiet, soothing white noise. Lieutenant Malisson was examining the comparisons on a selection of readings of Kota's atmosphere, and every now and then she let out a soft *hmm* underneath her breath, punctuating the rhythm of the scanner.

"I have cleared out your backlog," Data announced, turning away from the storage chamber.

"Already?" Malisson jerked her gaze up from her padd. "Thank you, Commander. Ensign Muñoz, any progress?"

"I'm coming along." Muñoz didn't lift his gaze from the scanner. The refracted light of the main apparatus slid across his features, momentarily staining his face red. "Rock samples?"

Malisson snapped her fingers. "Of course! From the cave system. Stack C, row 390."

"I will get them." Data turned toward the cabinets that filled an entire wall of laboratory A, the larger of the two labs. Laboratory A was where the samples from Bluster Beach were being kept. They were still in the decontamination chamber, running through every cycle that was programmed into the machine.

Data slid out of his chair and walked over to the cabinet. When he tilted his head to read the labels, they seemed to zoom all the way up through the ceiling. He lowered his gaze. Curious. He normally did not experience visual impairments.

He straightened his head and everything looked normal.

Data pulled open the C cabinet. He was hyperaware of the grinding of the hinges in the cabinet's doors, which scraped unnaturally loudly.

The scanner hummed.

Data keyed in the code and watched as the shelves revolved and settled to a stop. He reached out to the spot, but instead of finding a box of stone samples, there was a case of microscope slides.

He checked the number plate above the keypad. *Correct sequence.*

Data dropped his hand. "Lieutenant Malisson?" he said, and his voice came out distorted, as if it were being fed through a broken comm system.

"Whoa," Malisson said. "What happened to your voice?"

"I do not—" Data's internal thermometer alerted him to the fact that the temperature in the room had dropped to 2.3 degrees Celsius. Nearly freezing.

"The scanner's jammed," Muñoz said. "I've got a sample stuck half in."

Data turned around. Neither Muñoz nor Malisson appeared to be suffering from the cold. Malisson was frowning at her padd, and Muñoz thumped the side of the scanner.

"It was just working!" he said, frustrated. "I'm so close to being done and it just—stopped."

"Something's wrong." Malisson pulled out her tricorder. "Commander Data? Are you all right?"

"I do not know," Data said, his voice grinding with a painful, mechanical timbre. Malisson and Muñoz both grimaced.

"Commander!" Muñoz scrambled to his feet, pointing a tricorder at him.

Data tried to push forward, but his body wouldn't move. The lieutenant, with a deepening frown, was still scanning him. "I wish I could make sense of these readings."

"My positronic brain," Data started, but the words came out garbled and indistinct. He was aware of Muñoz disappearing out of the laboratory, speaking into his combadge; he could hear Muñoz's voice even after he left the room, although his words made no sense. *You found the way home. Do you know how to speak? Do you know how to listen?*

"Do you hear that?" Data asked Malisson.

She looked up at him, her eyes wide. "I'm sorry, I can't understand you."

"But it sounds fine to me," Data said. What had changed? Why couldn't he hear the distortion anymore?

Suddenly, a jangle rose up in the room: it was the scanner and the decontamination chamber, both activating at once. The security lights blinked on and off, casting the room in flickering red light.

Malisson backed away, gazing up at the ceiling.

Data had one final moment of clarity before he opened his mouth and began to wail.

Beverly Crusher careened into the laboratory, Will Riker right behind her. The pair immediately clapped their hands over their ears. It did not drown out the racket filling the room.

"Data!" Riker could barely make himself heard over the cacophony. He rushed past the doctor and said something to Data that she couldn't hear.

Data didn't respond. He just sat with his mouth hanging open, screaming what Crusher could only describe as an alert siren.

"Something's affecting him!" Malisson yelled into Crusher's ear. "And every machine has gone haywire!"

A mysterious disease was bad enough, but Crusher knew how to approach that. Data, though?

She wasn't an engineer. When she examined him aboard the *Enterprise*, it was always with Commander La Forge at her side. They worked together, interpreting the readings. But La Forge was back on the *Enterprise*, and the Starfleet team on Kota was made up of botanists and biologists. Malisson was a scanner engineer, not a cyberneticist.

Riker looked over at Crusher, his face stricken with confusion. "What do we do?" he shouted.

Data kept screaming, his expression blank, his hands stiff by his sides. The mechanical systems in the room had descended into chaos, their lights flickering and their engines humming and emitting their own painful, high-pitched screeching. Every system alert signal was shrieking in an arrhythmic syncopation, and the scanner was letting out a loud, grinding noise that made Crusher's teeth ache.

"Can you help him walk? Let's get him to the sleeping quarters!" Crusher shouted back at Riker, wondering if she should ask Riker to deactivate Data. She didn't want to unless it was absolutely necessary.

Riker picked up Data's arm and draped it over his shoulder. Data, still open-mouthed and screeching, went along stiffly, but he did move. The doctor put her shoulder under Data's other arm and led him out into the hallway. His screams hurt her eardrums.

As they passed the threshold into the common room, the screaming suddenly stopped.

The rest of the Kota team were in the room; Crusher had been with them when the noise started. She'd thought it was an alarm at first, but then Muñoz had hailed her.

The *Enterprise* officers helped ease Data down onto the sofa tucked into the corner. "Data, can you hear me?"

Data turned toward her. His face was blank, expressionless. *Truly* expressionless. An emptiness to him that made Crusher feel uneasy. "Data?" she whispered.

He spoke, the words garbled.

"He was doing that before," Malisson said. "Before he started— screaming."

Data spoke again, and this time Crusher was able to make out some of the words: "*Confusion. Safe.*"

"Data, we still can't quite understand you." Crusher could feel the weight of the others' gazes, their frightened curiosity. She twisted around. "Please," she said. "Give us privacy. Muñoz, please give me your tricorder."

He handed it over, and Crusher slaved it to her medical tricorder. "Thank you." Crusher turned back to Data as the others left, their voices a low murmur. "Will, if you could stay."

"Of course," Riker said. Data looked at Riker, his gaze unfocused. He said something, the words again slow and garbled. Crusher could make out that he was asking about his cat, Spot.

"Your speech is becoming a little clearer," Crusher said to him. Riker nodded in agreement.

"I am better." The last syllable sharpened and Data shook his head, the life burning in his face again. "Better," he said, with no distortion. "I am much better."

Crusher let out a long breath.

"What happened?" Riker said.

"I am running a diagnostic now." Data's eyes flickered slightly. "But I am not detecting anything out of the ordinary. This episode was . . ." Data stopped. "I do not have the words to properly describe it. I have experienced nothing like it before."

"Tell me about it." Crusher knelt down beside him. She was scanning him, watching as her tricorder compiled the data.

"I hesitate to call it a malfunction," Data said. "Although it—"

He stopped again. "However, it felt like one. I was not in danger of shutting down, and my sensory receptors were providing me with inaccurate data." He looked toward Riker. "I was hearing voices."

"Voices?" Riker asked. "What did they say?"

"'You found the way home.'" Data's voice took on an airy quality. "'Do you know how to speak? Do you know how to listen?'"

Crusher rolled the words around in her head. The others had not heard voices, but then, their recollections had been hazier.

"I ran the words through my database," Data said. "I have found nothing that matches them exactly."

"Any other hallucinations?" Crusher asked.

"My internal sensors registered the air as much colder than it was. Only two point three degrees above freezing."

Crusher got up to sit beside her patient. Data gave her more details: he had not been able to control the siren wail, and his movements had felt mechanical, not fluid.

"It was almost as if," he said, "I had become a primitive form of an android."

A primitive form. "Data, tell me more about that feeling."

"I am not certain if there is more to say." Data sat thoughtfully for a moment. "I did not . . . feel like myself."

As a physician, she found his observation fascinating. He was speaking in the way a biological life-form might speak about an illness.

"My sensory inputs were muffled," Data continued. "I felt limited in the ways I could express myself."

"Data, all I have available to treat you is your baselines from past exams . . ."

"Doctor Crusher," he said. "I believe you will uncover the cause. With my help."

Crusher smiled, touched by his confidence. "Thank you for your trust."

"Doctor, perhaps I should examine the other affected items," Data said. "There may be answers there."

"I agree. And we have to examine those samples again."

Riker frowned. "I was afraid you were about to suggest that." He looked her in the eye. "You're our only doctor."

Crusher set her mouth into a firm line. "Ensign Rikkilä is a trained field medic."

Riker shook his head. "There's got to be some other way."

"I will not put anyone else in danger," Crusher said—more defensively than she intended. "I wasn't on the beach, and I'll take care to limit my exposure."

"At least let me help—" Riker started.

"No. Absolutely not. You have not been exposed. Let's keep it that way."

Riker opened his mouth as if he was going to protest further, but Crusher shot him a severe expression.

"Fine," Riker replied. "Then I want this lab work to be as limited as you can make it."

"Understood," Beverly said.

"Doctor, you have twenty-four hours. If you cannot find what is causing this, I'm shutting this mission down, and getting us off world."

11

—◆—

Deanna Troi followed the flash of her mother's dress as she and Worf made their way through the crowd. Emotions crashed over her, leaving her feeling suffocated and breathless like the room was slowly losing air.

"Counselor," Worf said as the Klingon dodged a woman in a towering glass headdress who was arguing with a security officer. "I have concerns about this."

Troi forced herself to concentrate. The entire room was thick with anxiety, but his felt different: there was a professional distress, a swirl of quiet bafflement. It was the sort of emotional distress she was *used* to dealing with aboard the *Enterprise*.

She asked, "What exactly are you—"

A group of Betazoid teenagers careened between them.

"   worried about?"

Worf looked at her sideways. "I'm being asked to conduct an investigation." Lwaxana Troi was just on the other side of a crush of Arcadian dignitaries, waving her hand wildly at them. Worf led Troi over to a relatively clear path past the dignitaries.

"You've done this countless times," Troi said.

"I am unfamiliar with"—Worf took in a Betazoid woman wearing an enormous hoop skirt as she squeezed through the crowd—"Betazoid culture."

"I can help you," Troi replied. "If you don't mind me being your partner."

Worf looked down at her, his dark eyes serious. "You would do me a great honor."

"Hurry, hurry!" Lwaxana swooped in, shattering the moment. "Commander Rusina is waiting."

The ambassador led them up to a door being guarded by a pair of Betazed Security officers who stepped aside as soon as they saw who it was. Going through the door into the room beyond was like taking a deep breath; everything fell audibly quiet, and the air was cooler. Troi could feel Worf's tension decrease.

But an audible quiet wasn't the same as a telepathic one. Troi's thoughts were filled with whispers. The place was awash with tension. A tall Betazoid man with streaks of gray at his temples stepped forward. He wore the gold-and-black uniform of Betazed Security. "You must be Lieutenant Worf," he said. "Welcome to my command center."

"I appreciate the opportunity." The Klingon studied the room. Troi watched as he took it all in: three high-ranking security officers and a massive viewscreen showing the stage, littered with fallen curtains and the empty display case.

"Mister Worf will prove indispensable, I'm certain of it." Lwaxana flashed Commander Rusina a dazzling smile. Troi wondered if her mother had put in the request for Worf's help *because* she thought they were together. They weren't. They were just *friends*.

Lwaxana looked over at Troi, her eyes twinkling.

"I'll be assisting the lieutenant," Troi said, forcing herself to concentrate.

"What?! You need to stay with Jean-Luc. It's too dangerous out there." Lwaxana gestured toward the stage door.

"Mother, the captain will be fine. This sort of thing is my *job*. My literal job." She turned to Commander Rusina. "I serve as ship's counselor aboard the *Enterprise*. I can help Lieutenant Worf navigate the Betazoid customs he might be unfamiliar with."

I knew it! You are *seeing Mister Worf!*

"Mother!" Troi snapped back, her cheeks hot. She glanced over to see Commander Rusina and the other two security officers staring at them. At least Worf wasn't telepathic.

Lwaxana looked pleased with herself.

Worf cleared his throat. "Have you spoken with anyone?"

"Not in any detail," Commander Rusina replied. "I have the three Keepers and their entourages backstage—they were in hysterics, as you can imagine. We need to question them. The guests and front-row audience members might also have some insights."

"The Keepers," Worf said. "We should start with them."

"Of course." Commander Rusina gestured to the security officers. "I'll send my men to assist you. I hope a pair of Starfleet officers will have better luck than we did."

"Why would we have better luck?" Troi asked.

Commander Rusina shook his head. "You are not as . . . *involved.*"

Troi could feel her mother trying to wedge into her thoughts. She ignored her as best she could, focusing her attention on Worf. He caught her eye and she gave him a quick, encouraging smile.

"Officer Andra will take you to the Keepers," Commander Rusina said.

A slim woman peeled away from the group that had just come into the room. She nodded briskly at her superior. "They've been in our custody since the unveiling. We—"

"Custody?" Lwaxana asked. "You don't think a Keeper is responsible?"

"The Keepers and the guests are the most likely to have witnessed what happened," Officer Andra said. "The Keepers most of all."

"Should I come along?" Lwaxana turned toward Troi. "Perhaps I can offer—"

"Mother, you should see to Mr. Syn," Troi said quickly. "I'm sure he's going to want to discuss how to salvage the ceremonies."

"I agree," Commander Rusina said, and Troi felt an inward sigh of relief. He put his hand on Lwaxana's back and guided her toward the exit. "I appreciate you bringing Mister Worf to us, Ambassador. We can take it from here."

Troi ignored the sound of her mother's faint protest, while Officer Andra offered, "We've set the Keepers up backstage. Easiest way to get there is to go out in the crowd again. Come on."

Andra led them past the main exit, where Lwaxana was still speaking with Commander Rusina about *something*. Troi couldn't worry about it right now. They went out through a smaller door that deposited them, just as Andra promised, back in the crowd, in the front of the stage.

Stay close to the wall, Andra said. *Let the lieutenant know.*

Troi shouted Andra's instructions over the din to Worf, who nodded in acknowledgment. He stepped around Troi so that he was between her and the crush of people. The force field was still up, protecting nothing.

Eventually, they arrived at the left side of the stage. Security officers, who kept their eyes on the crowd, opened a portal in the force field and waved them through when Andra said, "Keepers."

Stairs had been set up, giving easy access to the stage. Worf let the commander go first behind Andra. Being onstage was disorienting. The curtains were piled up in messy lumps around the empty display. Andra strode right past it.

"We have some of our most psi-sensitive officers on duty. None of them sensed anything out of the ordinary." Andra shrugged. "Whoever did this knew Betazoid limitations. And exploited them."

"Agreed," Worf said.

They slipped backstage, into a forest of old props and racks hung with costumes, then into a narrow hallway. To Troi, the air was stuffy and thick with alarm. She realized she was feeling the emotions from the officer standing in front of a closed door at the end of the hallway—and the Keepers behind the door.

"Panic," Troi observed.

Andra grinned. "Overwhelming. At least they've calmed down some." She paused. "Most of it was from Jarkko Sentis. He's First House, Xiomara's direct descendant and all that." Andra hesitated. "By the way, the commander allowed them to bring in family and friends."

"A mistake," Worf muttered.

"Perhaps, but I needed something to settle them down," Andra explained.

The Betazoid security officer swung open the door, revealing a dressing room crammed with people. Some of them were speaking verbally, others psychically. All conversations stopped when the Starfleet officers stepped into the room.

Then, instantly, a flurry of voices, in Troi's head. *Who are you? Who is* that? *Do you know anything about the robbery? Starfleet?!*

"Quiet!" commanded Andra. "This is Lieutenant Worf and Commander Deanna Troi of the *Starship Enterprise.* They're here to ask some questions—"

"No more questions!" shouted Onora Opeila, her small, bird-like features buried beneath a towering floral headdress. "Haven't we suffered enough?"

One of her attendants patted her arm, murmured softly in her ear.

"I will not be quiet!" Opeila cried. "The Sacred Silver has been *stolen.*"

Her words were met with angry stares.

"We do not have time for questions!" she continued. "We have to catch this thief."

"Madam, I agree." Worf stepped forward, his posture straight and self-assured. "Which is why we're both here. You were all backstage when the objects were taken—"

The room erupted.

Calm down! Andra said. *And verbally answer Lieutenant Worf's questions. The more you protest, the longer this is going to take.*

While Andra pleaded with the Keepers and their various attendants, Troi swept her gaze around, trying to find Aviana Virox, daughter of the Third House. Three women in the corner were all wearing Third House regalia, layered dresses that looked like froths of steamed milk, but Troi didn't know which one was Aviana.

"We don't need to be calm," snapped Jarkko. "We need to find our treasures!"

Shouts of agreement. Worf gave Troi an exasperated look, and Andra stepped forward, holding up her hands. "For the final time, that is why Starfleet is *here*," she said. "The entire temple is secured with a force field to ensure no one gets in or out. Security is doing everything they can."

"Why haven't you found them?" one of the Third House women demanded. *Aviana?* Troi didn't know much about her, but she had gathered, from various conversations with her mother, that Aviana adhered to the Third House tradition of being reclusive.

"The resources of Starfleet's flagship are being put at the disposal of Betazed to aid in the recovery of the artifacts," Troi announced. Had she just done that? Promised the resources of the *Enterprise*, without the captain's approval? The panic, the despair, was overwhelming. But the objects needed to be found.

She glanced sideways at Worf, and he gave her a little nod. She added, "We are here to talk with *you*. To listen."

"I am Onora Opeila, daughter of the Fourth House, Keeper of the Sacred Silver and protector of Xiomara's legacy." Onora's voice quavered with indignation. "I have already made it clear to Officer Andra that I know nothing about the robbery."

"Madam," Worf said, "it is entirely possible that you know something without *realizing* you know something."

Onora blinked in surprise. "I'm sorry?"

Worf stepped up to her, his eyes level with the top of her head-dress. She craned her head back to glare up at him. "Every detail is important, and the key to catching a thief is the details."

Troi stepped up beside him. "We're here to uncover the facts. We just want to talk."

Onora's heavy eyelashes fluttered. *It's just so distressing,* she cried, and Troi took Onora's gloved hand and pressed it between her own. Immediately Onora's emotions flooded into her, anger and fear being the strongest. Woven through them both was a faint, pulsing shame. Not strong enough to call guilt.

"This was not your fault," Troi said quietly.

"The Silver had never been taken out of our holdings in five hundred years." Onora dabbed delicately at her eyes. "When I received word that the Historical Council was planning a viewing, I was so *excited*—"

"Of course you were." Troi guided her over to the sofa where her three attendants were sitting, wearing less ostentatious versions of Onora's dress. Very traditional.

A young woman threw her arms around Onora's neck. "It'll be all right, Mother," she whispered.

Onora sniffled. "I wanted you to keep the Silver." She looked over at Troi. "I was so thrilled, I had to find people to serve as my attendants. My family did away with this years ago, but I wanted to uphold the tradition for the ceremony."

Worf lowered himself to Onora's eye level. "There is great honor in keeping tradition."

"I never in my wildest dreams—" Onora started verbally, and then there was a flood of telepathic agreement from the others in the room. —*thought this would happen*. Her sentence was finished inside Troi's head by a dozen different voices.

Officer Andra was standing in the corner, her arms crossed, watching; Troi felt her approval.

"Did everyone feel that way?" Troi asked the room. "The excitement at being part of something so momentous."

"How could we not?" said Jarkko. "This was meant to be a celebration of Xiomara, of Betazed history."

Betazed wasn't foreign to Troi, but it wasn't home. She knew the history, the rituals, the costumes, the elaborate system of Houses— none of it had any appeal to her. But she knew the importance of Xiomara's treasures to the Keepers and their Houses.

To hold one of the three treasures was to hold a piece of Betazed. Someone had snatched it away.

Troi offered, "Perhaps we can see this . . . *difficulty* as a chance to embody the principles that Xiomara taught us."

Jarkko scowled. "Whoever stole the treasures wasn't embodying any of the principles."

"Of course not." One of Jarkko's party stood up, wound her arm through his. "Because certainly a Betazoid didn't do this—"

A bolt of fear sparked in the back of Troi's head. She could tell the others felt it too. A sense of discomfort filled the room, and Officer Andra stepped forward, her body tense.

"Who was that?" she demanded.

"What was—" Worf looked at Andra, then at Troi. "What is happening?"

The Betazoids in the room were all turning toward the women in the Third House regalia, still standing together in a tight knot in the corner. Immediately, Troi understood the fear was coming from all three of them.

"It's them!" shrieked Onora. She leaped up and grabbed Worf's arm, yanking him toward the Third House women. "They did it!"

"We don't know that." Officer Andra stepped closer. "Madam Virox? What are you afraid of?"

Aviana Virox turned toward Andra, her face stricken. Emotions roiled off her, a bizarre, confusing mélange that made Troi's head ache. It didn't help that it was blending in with the onslaught from the others in the room: confusion, panic, concern.

"Commander," Worf said in a low voice, "could you explain what is happening?"

"They're afraid," Troi whispered back. "All of the Third House women are afraid."

Worf frowned as one of Aviana's attendants stepped toward her. But Madam Virox shook her head, tears streaming down her face. Her emotions swelled, thick and overpowering. Her attendants looked utterly terrified, their eyes wide. And Troi felt a thrum from them.

They were communicating, speaking telepathically. But they were cutting their conversation off from the rest of the room. A rare skill, and a taboo at that.

"They're talking to each other," she whispered to Worf. "But not letting any of the other Betazoids hear. That's not—"

Care to share what you're discussing? Officer Andra asked the Third House women, her emotion cold.

Madam Virox wrung her skirt in her hands. She closed her eyes. Troi could feel the others in the room pressing forward; she could feel the weight of their questions.

"I'm not Aviana Virox!"

Troi froze, bracing herself against the onslaught of reactions. The slam of a dozen shocked Betazoids was followed a few milliseconds later by audible gasps and at least one fiercely hissed, "She wouldn't!"

The woman collapsed on the floor, sobbing.

"Everyone out!" Officer Andra shouted. "Except for Starfleet officers and the Third House."

"Where are they?" Jarkko demanded. "Where are the treasures?"

Worf acted quickly, catching Jarkko before he could move any closer. "There is no need for this."

"She stole the treasures!" Jarkko bellowed.

"We don't know that," Troi said.

Worf loosened his grip on Jarkko, who made another attempt to reach the sobbing woman. Worf stepped in front of him, blocking his path.

"Let me *through*!" Jarkko's face had turned a vivid shade of red. "She didn't steal them, but Aviana did! The real Aviana Virox!" He shoved at Worf. "Isn't that what she's saying? Why else would Aviana have a—a *stand-in*." He spat the word. "I always knew the Third House was shifty."

"Mr. Sentis, please." Officer Andra put a hand on Jarkko's shoulder. "Allow the professionals to get to the bottom of this."

"Jarkko." Troi sent over a pulse of gentleness, trying to soothe him. "Go outside with the others. We will find out what's going on."

"Don't try that on me!" Jarkko tried to get past Worf, who squeezed harder. He glared back at the woman, still weeping on the floor.

"She used a double," he snarled. "I'd heard the rumors but didn't think it was true."

"Mister Worf will find out what's going on," Troi said firmly, and sent another wave of calm in Jarkko's direction. It did little to cool his anger, but at least she was able to corral him toward the door. Outside, the poor security officer who had been keeping watch looked at them with an expression of resigned confusion.

"What's going on in there?" he said. "Do you need backup?"

"No." Troi deposited a still-seething Jarkko along with the others and shut the door behind her.

"They will only speak telepathically," Worf said.

"Even then, they aren't saying much." Andra sighed. "All I can get from her is that she's a double and her real name is Loriana Virox. She's terrified. They all are."

Troi looked at the three women in their traditional dresses.

"Was the real Aviana Virox *here*?" Troi asked. "At the ceremony?"

A surge of affirmation from Loriana, who lifted her gaze up at Troi. *She wanted to deliver the Disk herself.*

It was very unusual, thought one of the other attendants—Troi couldn't tell which one. *Aviana never leaves her estate.*

Troi knelt down beside Loriana, took her hand, and sent a surge of comfort in her direction. The Third House woman softened a little, but her fear and guilt were overwhelming. How had Betazed Security missed this?

"Tell me about Aviana," Troi said softly; she also thought her question, as these women were clearly very traditional. "When was the last time you saw her?"

Hesitation wafted up in a cloud. Loriana glanced back at the others, but whatever passed between them, Troi could neither hear nor feel.

Before the ceremony, Loriana thought. *We helped her remove the Enshrined Disk from its traveling case.*

She was so excited! one of the attendants added. *She's so proud of the Disk, she would never—*

An overwhelming grief washed out of her and then, abruptly, vanished.

How are you doing that? Officer Andra demanded, the question riding in on a wave of aggression. *Locking your emotions down. Hiding your thoughts.*

It's a skill of the Third House. The second attendant lifted her chin. *Developed by Brice Virox five generations ago, when he was facing constant assassination attempts due to his role in the Tanton War.*

Officer Andra's aggression turned to unease. "That's—" Her lip curled. "Why would the Third House do such a thing for so long?" She looked over at Worf. "They're lying," she said, the words breathy with disbelief. "What sort of Betazoid lies?"

Not a lie! Loriana's voice rang out in Troi's thoughts. *A tradition! A safety measure! Aviana would never, ever steal the treasures.*

The earnestness in Loriana's thoughts was overwhelming, and Troi sent back, *I believe you.*

"Where is she now?" Troi asked. "You said you saw her before the ceremony. Did she instruct you to take her place afterward?"

Loriana Virox hesitated.

"She could be in danger," Troi added.

I don't know, Loriana said, and then sent a flood of impressions through Troi's thoughts. Aviana Virox, looking identical to Loriana in a frothy dress and a tumble of curled silver hair, placing the Enshrined Disk in a case. The four of them walking into the temple. Aviana placing the Disk in the display case while Jarkko and Onora looked on, smiling. Then—the attendants climbing the spiral staircase up to balcony seating to watch the ceremony. Aviana wasn't with them; she had opted to stay behind and watch from the wings.

And that was the last time we saw her, Loriana said. Deanna could sense agreement from the others.

Officer Andra was describing the thoughts to Worf. "Officers have confirmed that they saw Aviana Virox backstage during the ceremony," she told him. "And so did the other two Keepers." Her frown deepened. *Unless that was you,* she thought to Loriana.

Indignation flooded out of Loriana.

"You still haven't explained why you chose to take her place," Troi said gently. "Was it after the display case was revealed to be empty?"

Loriana nodded. One of the other attendants pressed her head onto Loriana's shoulder and Troi knew, from the way Loriana's head tilted ever so slightly toward the attendant, that they were speaking privately.

"They're doing it again," Andra said to Worf. "Talking without letting us hear."

"I cannot hear any of these conversations," Worf said. "It is very difficult to discover the truth if the suspects won't speak."

The attendants gave him a dark look, but Loriana sent out a burst of terror. Troi realized, after a few seconds of disorientation, it was Loriana's reaction to seeing the display case empty. Images started to flash through Troi's head: Loriana and the attendants grabbing at each other in shock, one of them gasping audibly. A frantic search for Aviana and not finding her. A frantic telepathic conversation where it was decided Loriana would go backstage as Aviana, hoping to find her.

Troi could sense Andra's disbelief, but Loriana's actions made sense to her; it was the only way she would have gotten backstage while the temple was going into lockdown.

Exactly, Loriana said. *I had no other choice. But I was swept up by security and escorted to this room.* Images accompanied her words: security officers swarming around her, believing her to be Aviana Virox and insisting that she had to be secured for her own safety.

Andra sighed and raked a hand through her cropped hair. "We need to find the real Aviana Virox," she said to Worf. She then glared at Loriana. "You should have informed us of who you were immediately."

Loriana stared back, her emotions, her thoughts, completely shut down.

"It's not natural," Andra said. "What you're doing."

"Officer Andra," Troi said as she rose to her feet, "I don't get the sense that Loriana is lying."

"Neither do I, but that doesn't mean much, does it?" Officer Andra tapped her combadge. "Andra to Rusina. Aviana Virox is missing. We need to find her immediately."

12

———

Jean-Luc Picard pressed his fingers into his forehead, trying to massage away the beginnings of a headache. The frenzy on the temple floor was palpable even for a non-psychic.

"I want to make sure I have this right," said the Betazed Security officer sitting across from him. They were at a makeshift interrogation station that had been set up at the base of the stage. Behind the captain, Betazed Security was sweeping the space for clues. "You didn't have a direct line of sight to the treasures while you were backstage?"

Picard replied, "No. I was too far back in my group to see anything. The Keepers paraded past us after they had placed the items in the display case."

"So they were empty-handed." The security officer furrowed his brow. He was young, probably a recent graduate, and Picard could sense that he was in over his head.

"You're doing fine," Picard said. "And that's right, they were empty-handed at that point." He paused. "I'm sorry I don't have anything more useful."

The officer nodded. "I understand. The other Dreams Guests said the same thing . . . I'm just worried I'm *missing* something." He scrolled through his padd. "There were *dozens* of people backstage—"

"Which means someone has the answers," Picard said. "If I think of anything else, or if I hear anything, I'll let you know."

"Thank you, Captain Picard. If you could send over the next person—"

"Of course." Picard stood up and made his way back to the section of seating where the Dreams Guests had been sequestered. Eliana had calmed down: she was no longer pacing frantically back and forth. She had draped herself sideways over three seats, a hand laid dramatically over her forehead. One of the Betazoid guests, a ship captain whose name Picard couldn't recall, was speaking to her in soft murmurs.

"You're up next," Picard said to Aurelius Ardid, a rather queasy-looking human cyberneticist.

"How was it?" Ardid asked, his eyes wide. Not Starfleet, but he had done excellent work for the Daystrom Institute.

"You have nothing to worry about," Picard said gently. "We aren't under suspicion. They just want to know what we saw."

"But I didn't see anything."

"Neither did I. And that's useful for them to know."

Ardid made his way over to the interrogation station. Picard sank down into a chair. The last hour had been like this—the captain trying to help his fellow guests stay calm and focused.

"Jean-Luc!" trilled a bright, grating voice.

That burgeoning headache flared out behind Picard's eyes.

"How's the investigation coming along?" Lwaxana Troi breezed up to him, Ambassador Sulel at her side.

"Betazed Security forces are doing what they can," Picard said stiffly.

"I'm very glad to hear that," said Sulel, sweeping her gaze across the Dreams Guests. "Your group seems calmer than the others."

"Does it now?"

"Yes. Most of the guests are in an utter state of panic."

"The pageant actors are too," Lwaxana added. "Poor things. They all feel like they should have *known*."

Picard caught a flash of blue through the crowd: it was Sh'yan, bringing a tray of steaming hot tea from the replicator.

"If we're calm, you can thank Sh'yan," Picard said as she walked up to them. She smiled at both the ambassadors.

"Would you like tea?" she said. "I've been bringing cups of it back for anyone who needs it." Her smile deepened. "It was the captain's idea."

Picard's cheeks burned. "I wouldn't go that far," he said. "Sh'yan's the one who found the replicator—"

"It was backstage," she said. "Hidden behind some props. But Jean-Luc suggested I fix tea for the security officers and the guests. Anything to help distract them, isn't that what you said?"

"Logical," Sulel said.

"It was just tea," Picard muttered.

"It was more than that," Lwaxana said. "Sh'yan, dear, do you think you and the captain could see to the other guests?"

Picard felt a slow-coiling knot of dread rising within.

"An excellent suggestion," said Sulel. "If the other guest groups were as calm as the Dreams Guests—"

"The security officers would have a much easier time," Lwaxana finished. "Exactly what I was thinking. Sulel, are you sure you're not a psychic?"

Sh'yan looked over at Picard with an expression of mild alarm. She had not mentioned that his suggestion of tea was to keep the others distracted so they would stop pestering him with questions; they all seemed to believe that, being a Starfleet officer, he had to know about the current situation. No one would accept his answer that he simply didn't. When Sh'yan told him about the replicator, he figured a beverage would be the perfect distraction.

"Please, Jean-Luc," Lwaxana said, pressing her hand against her chest. "The calmer the other guests are, the faster we can get through the questioning."

"Yes," said Sulel; somehow, her easy, unemotional voice was

more insistent than Lwaxana's. "And the sooner we can have answers. And a possible solution."

"Perhaps," Picard said. The captain didn't think he was the person who should be doing this now, but he had to admit it sounded better than sitting with the other Dreams Guests, waiting for news from security. And Sh'yan was hesitant about being out on the floor with nothing to do. The replicator had been a lucky find.

"The Poetry Guests seem to be the most anxious," Sulel was saying. "You could start with them. Our goal is to keep them relaxed and happy."

Picard wanted to say that he was not a ship's counselor. But Sulel and Lwaxana were watching him so hopefully, and for the first time, he noticed the dark rings under Lwaxana's eyes . . . faint but just visible. The captain realized how difficult this was for all concerned.

"Very well," Picard said. "Sh'yan?"

She hoisted the tray of teas. "I think we found our calling."

Picard resisted the urge to comment.

"This way to Poetry," sang out Lwaxana, gesturing with one hand. "If we can successfully calm down the guests before Deanna and Mister Worf have finished speaking with the Keepers, I'll consider it a success."

The Keepers. Picard could imagine what they'd be like. He supposed delivering tea and kind words to the rest of the guests was the easiest duty in this sudden diplomatic crisis.

He sorely hoped the treasures were recovered, and damned well soon.

13

—◆—

"A Keeper would never do this." Ambassador Lwaxana Troi appeared furious at the thought. "Never. It's impossible."

Troi exchanged quick glances with Worf. They were both sitting in the conference room on one of the temple balconies, with silk-covered chairs around a huge table. The Federation ambassador to Betazed, Sulel, was there, along with Commander Rusina and Officer Andra. Sildar Syn paced around behind them, occasionally flinging out impressions of anger and frustration.

Right now, he was in total agreement with Lwaxana Troi.

"Aviana Virox's disappearance is our only lead," Commander Rusina said patiently. "It's not a matter of guilt or innocence. Perhaps she saw someone. Perhaps it wasn't a robbery." He reached across the table and pressed his hand on top of Lwaxana's. "Our goal is to find the three treasures, Ambassador Troi."

Lwaxana sniffled rather dramatically, and Troi resisted the urge to roll her eyes.

"I agree," said Ambassador Sulel. "Commander Rusina, your people should have located Aviana Virox by now."

Commander Rusina sat back. "We're dealing with numerous Betazoids and limited equipment due to the lockdown." He tapped his combadge and asked for a status update.

A hesitation from the officer on the other end, then a thin, unsure voice: *"We are, ahh, not finding her."*

Silence.

"Say again." Commander Rusina's dismay was evident.

"We haven't been able to locate Aviana Virox, sir. There's no sign of her anywhere in the temple complex." Another pause. *"And her personal ship appears to be missing."*

Rusina sighed. "Thank you."

Lwaxana let out a low wail of despair.

"Mother!" Troi hissed.

"I thought you locked this place down? How could she—"

"Ambassador Troi, you don't think it was one of our own?" snapped Sildar.

"I don't!" Lwaxana cried. "How could she be missing?"

"How quickly was the force field put into place?" The Vulcan's calm voice cut through Lwaxana's quiet sniffling.

"Almost instantly," Commander Rusina said. "The disappearance of the treasures was a"—he hesitated, glancing sideways at Lwaxana—"contingency that my team had planned for."

"Really?" Any hint of weepiness fled from Lwaxana's voice. "Sildar, did you know about this?"

"I knew they were planning for many contingencies, but—"

Ambassador Sulel held up her hand, cutting Sildar off. "Aviana Virox left the temple before the reveal. It is logical to assume she is connected with the thief or thieves. It may also be assumed that *she* could be the thief." Before Lwaxana could protest, she continued, "Or perhaps she is a hostage. She could be in danger. Regardless, she must be located immediately."

"If she is even still onworld," Worf said. "The temple was locked down immediately. But it took two hours for Betazed Space Control to secure the planet. Are Betazed's forces prepared for a deep-space search?"

Rusina shifted uncomfortably. "I wouldn't exactly say that."

Lwaxana glared at him. "And what *would* you say, Commander?"

"Most of the forces were deployed for the ceremony's finale,"

Sildar said. "It was going to be grand, all the best ships in our fleet, streaking—"

"The entire force?" Worf said.

"There were some ships . . . that's why it took two hours. Maybe the *Enterprise*?" Rusina looked over at Ambassador Sulel. "They have more powerful sensors." He smiled. "Plus her captain is right here in the temple."

"We should easily be able to locate Aviana," Worf said. "Assuming you can provide us with a bioprint."

"She's a Keeper," Lwaxana said. "Of course we can. I think this is a *brilliant* idea."

Troi felt hopeful for the first time since the empty display case was unveiled. "Even if she has gone offworld, the *Enterprise* should still be able to track her."

"You make a compelling argument." Sulel nodded at Worf. "If this plan is acceptable to the *Enterprise*'s captain, I would very much like to proceed."

Worf tapped his combadge. "Worf to Captain Picard," he said.

Picard's voice crackled through the badge. *"Go ahead."*

"Requesting permission to initiate the *Enterprise*'s scanners to help in the search for a potential subject."

"Of course," Picard responded. *"The* Enterprise *will help any way we can. Make it so."*

"Worf," Troi said. "I'd like to accompany you. I'll be better equipped to communicate with Aviana Virox once we've located her."

"I would appreciate that, Counselor."

"A good idea," said Rusina. "Commander Troi, Lieutenant Worf—beam aboard when ready."

Geordi La Forge stood as Worf and Troi walked down into the command well. "The data is loaded into the ship's computer." He took the first officer's seat and activated the controls on the console to his right. "Is the captain all right?"

"Yes," Troi assured him. "But to lose Xiomara's treasures is a devastating blow to all of Betazed."

"Initiating scanners," announced Ensign Challinor from the back of the bridge.

Worf stepped up and watched the ensign work, as the *Enterprise*'s scanners searched the planet for Aviana Virox.

"No match, sir." Challinor twisted around in his chair. "I don't think she's on Betazed."

"Wait." La Forge was checking his screen. "I'm reading an anomaly in the temple."

"What sort of anomaly?" Worf asked.

La Forge moved up to the security station, adjusting the sensors. "I'm not sure. It appears to be an issue with one of the force fields. I'm seeing something—"

"Put it on main screen," Worf ordered.

As he made the adjustment, the viewscreen displayed an overlay of Isszon Temple. A tiny dot of light appeared right in the middle of the space where the stage was set up.

"That's where the display case is." Troi moved closer to the viewscreen, trying to make sense of the images. "What is that?"

"Uncertain," La Forge said. "But it's suspicious." His frown deepened as he made further adjustments on the scans. "Oh, I see it now. That one force field has a power cycling flaw."

Troi frowned. "But surely the Betazed Security team would have picked up on that?" Troi asked.

"Maybe not," La Forge said. "This disruption is barely there, and they might not have had the technology to detect it."

Worf made a snorting noise in the back of his throat. "I see they were not prepared for *everything*."

Troi asked, "What's causing the flaw?"

"That's what I'm trying to figure out. It's just so *slight*—" La Forge snapped his fingers. "It was a hole!"

"Explain," Worf said.

La Forge gestured toward the viewscreen. "It was a hole in the force field. It's closed now, but there's just enough residual weakness for it to show up on our scans. Although the hole was a tiny one. Barely half a meter across."

"Too small for a person," Worf said.

"But not for the three treasures," Troi said, alarmed. "That's how the thief did it. Somehow they tore a hole in the force field—"

"Micro–transporter enhancers," La Forge said. "After getting them out of the display case, *that's* how the items were stolen. They were small enough that if the thief used an enhancer to teleport them, it could have overpowered the ceremony's transporter dampeners."

Troi stared at the image on the viewscreen, at the small hole where the treasures had been pulled through. "How did Betazed Security not notice this when it happened?"

"Likely some kind of sensor dampener," La Forge said, still studying the screen. "It would likely have registered as a quick glitch in the power logs."

Troi nodded. "And if our thief had timed it for the middle of the ceremony, security forces might not have noticed with all the excitement onstage."

"Exactly. Then the enhancers self-destructed once the treasures were transported away. Without the *Enterprise's* technology, Betazed forces wouldn't have noticed the residual reading."

Troi nodded grimly. "I doubt whoever did this was expecting the incident to be investigated by a *Galaxy*-class starship."

"We can assume that our thief is not in the temple," Worf noted.

"Most likely not, no." La Forge offered a wry smile.

"And we already know Aviana Virox isn't on Betazed." Troi felt dizzy. Had a Keeper actually stolen all of the treasures? She tried to imagine her mother doing such a thing, and the idea was so absurd she almost laughed out loud.

"Aviana Virox is our prime suspect," Worf said, and Troi felt the regret of his words.

"Yes, I agree," Troi said. "What other answer is there?"

14

—•—

Beverly Crusher pushed her chair away from the laboratory computer, irritated. The last sample collected from the beach—a few grains of sand from the tide pools—had traces of those microbial fossils like all of the other samples. The scans said they were inert, no threat to biological life, and Muñoz and Talma, the two botanists, agreed.

The doctor reviewed the collection of notes. The sample collection had been handled by the members of the Kota team and in larger quantities than what Crusher was looking at in her own samples. None of them had experienced any of the symptoms like they did recently on Bluster Beach.

Reading into her tricorder, she noted, "I have completed examination of the final sample, number"—Crusher checked the label—"309D. Nothing to account for the hallucinations experienced by the beach team, including Lieutenant Commander Data."

The last few grains of sand glittered on the slide. *Was it because they had been in the decon chamber?* Data had been affected, and the equipment in the lab.

It just didn't make any *sense.*

Someone knocked on the door—Crusher spun around and found Will Riker peering in through the window. *"Ten hours left. We're about to have dinner. Decon yourself and come join us."*

"I still haven't figured out—"

"Stop. That's an order."

Could she remember the last time she ate? Will's mention of dinner set her stomach grumbling. She put away the final sample and ran the decontamination wand over herself. The doctor wasn't sure if leaving this room was the right thing to do, but she also didn't have any real evidence otherwise.

"You didn't have to wait for me," Crusher said.

"Didn't have to. Wanted to." Riker peeled himself off the wall and sauntered toward the common room. "I thought a communal dinner would boost morale."

They stepped into the common room. It had been transformed, the chairs all pushed up around a big table that folded out of the wall. A few of the team had already replicated their meals and were sitting down, the food letting off wisps of steam.

"Doctor Crusher!" Rikkilä bounded up to Crusher. "I'm so glad to see you. I was worried about you."

"I'm fine, although I appreciate the concern. Unfortunately, I couldn't find anything." Crusher shrugged. "I guess we'll have to take another approach." She didn't add that she had no idea what that could be.

"Hmm." The ensign and Crusher walked over to the replicator, where Muñoz was pulling out a big bowl of mujadara. The scent of cumin and fried onions filled the room.

"That smells *amazing*." Rikkilä joined Muñoz. "Would you be mad if I replicated the same thing?"

"No." Muñoz laughed. "Why would I be?"

"I don't know. People are weird." Rikkilä ordered her dinner. "Doctor, what are you thinking we should try next?"

"To be frank, I'm at a loss," Crusher said. "With ten hours left, I want to monitor the crew. Gather all the data I can."

"Those poor refugees. I guess this place won't be hosting a colony. I hope they find someplace for them." Rikkilä pulled out her own mujadara and breathed in the scent. "I am *starving*."

Crusher stepped up to the replicator. She didn't know what she wanted to eat; she was hungry, but really wasn't in the mood to sit down for a morale-boosting dinner. Her mind was completely preoccupied.

She asked the replicator for her old standby, a ham and cheese sandwich with a side of fruit, and joined the others at the table.

"The good doctor!" boomed Solanko as she slid beside Riker. "Glad you could join us. And you, Mister Data, our miracle man." Solanko lifted up a shot glass of synthehol. "In fact, I'd like to toast the entire away team from the *Enterprise*." He waited for a moment, grinning, then cried, "*Za vstrechu!*" He knocked back his synthehol, and the rest of the table took a long drink, even though most were just having water.

"Kota might not have shown us the warmest welcome," Riker said. "But the Kota science team certainly has."

His words were met with cheers, and then everyone dove into their food. Conversations kicked up around the table: Talma, Muñoz, and Rikkilä debating the merits of a Bolian musician who Crusher gathered was immensely popular and vaguely controversial. Solanko and Malisson laughing together over a shared joke and their synthehol while Riker offered something that had them all in fits.

None of them seemed ill. But something *had* happened to them.

"Are you not hungry, Doctor?" Data's question broke her musings.

"Starving," she said.

"You have not touched your food."

It was true; her sandwich sat just as it had been replicated, a blob of cheese congealing into a rubbery mass. She picked it up and took a big bite. "I'm just distracted," she said. "I just—"

Solanko's laughter rumbled down the table. If Crusher didn't know better, she'd think there was actual vodka in his glass. Malisson joined in, her voice rising.

"Those two are certainly enjoying themselves," Crusher murmured.

Data said something that Crusher couldn't make out.

"Data?" She turned away from her sandwich and found him sitting with his mouth hanging open.

"Data!" Crusher scrambled over to him. Solanko was still laughing. She shook Data's shoulder but got no reaction from him.

The scent of fried onions wafted through the room. She looked up and saw two bowls of mujadara sitting in the replicator. As she watched, a third appeared, knocking one of the others to the ground, spilling lentils and rice across the floor.

"Doctor, we need you over here!"

Riker was leaning over the table, pulling Solanko up; he had fallen face-first into his plate of dumplings. Malisson was stumbling backward away from the table, her eyes fixed on some point in the air. "What do you want!" she screamed, pulling her hair loose from its tightly woven braid. "Leave us alone!"

"Something's wrong with Data as well." Crusher looked around for her tricorder.

A shriek tore through the room. It was Talma, launching himself at the wall, waving his arms as if swinging an invisible sword. Rikkilä moved her hands wildly, clawing through the air—*swimming*, Crusher thought distantly. *She's swimming upward.*

Muñoz was gone.

"Ensign Muñoz," she said to Riker, who had crawled across the table and was feeling for Solanko's pulse. "He's vanished."

"Solanko's still breathing. I'll look for Muñoz." Riker leaped over his chair and raced out of the room. Malisson's screams had melted into soft, frightened muttering.

Crusher found her tricorder and started scanning Solanko.

A crash slammed through the room: another bowl of mujadara spilled onto the floor.

"What is wrong with that damned replicator?" Crusher said, exasperated.

The doctor concentrated on Solanko. The replicator was an engineer's concern, not hers. She looked down at the tricorder readings.

A temperature of eleven degrees? Blood pressure *zero*?

Crusher put the tricorder aside. She pressed two fingers on Solanko's neck. He was warm to the touch, heart rate normal, breathing normal.

Scrambling to her feet, Crusher grabbed another tricorder. Everything in the supply closet was alight, blinking in rapid, random patterns. The doctor stopped short, studying them.

"Found him!" Riker pulled in a stumbling, shouting Muñoz. "He was in the sleeping quarters stripping the blankets off the beds."

"We surrender!" Muñoz screamed. "Don't you understand? We *surrender!*"

Malisson began to howl again, and she lunged at Muñoz. Riker yanked him away, but she kept running, right out the door.

"No!" Riker guided Muñoz to the nearest sofa. "I'll go get—"

All the lights in the station flickered off, plunging them into complete darkness. The computer's voice trilled out: *"Initiating shutdown of all unnecessary systems."*

"*What?!*" asked Riker. "Computer, no one ordered—"

"Initiating." The safety lights blinked on, casting the room in an eerie, amber glow. Rikkilä and Talma were both collapsed in a heap on the floor; Muñoz's head lolled back against the sofa. For a moment, Riker and Crusher stared at each other from across the room.

"Computer, this is Commander William Riker—"

The lights flickered back on. Cool air from the environmental system blew across the back of Crusher's neck, chilling her sweating skin.

"Computer?" Riker said uncertainly.

Another bowl of mujadara crashed to the floor, adding to the mountain of lentils and rice piled up there. But with that bowl, the replicator let out the soft chime that indicated it was powering down.

"Computer, run a diagnostic of the replicator," Riker said.

"Running diagnostic."

The *Enterprise* officers waited.

"Diagnostic complete. Replicator functioning within parameters. No malfunctioning systems."

Crusher knelt down by Talma and Rikkilä and felt for their pulses. She did the same to Solanko.

"Normal." Gingerly, she turned on her medical tricorder. All life signs normal. "It's like before. There is nothing wrong with any of them.

"Will, please locate Lieutenant Malisson."

"On it."

Crusher moved over to Data. He was still unmoving, although he had shut his jaw. "Data?" she whispered.

His eyes blinked. He looked at her.

"Doctor Crusher." His voice carried that same strange metallic timbre as before, but it flattened out and disappeared as he spoke. "I fear I may have lost time. I cannot recall the last seven minutes and thirty-nine seconds."

Seven and a half minutes. The attack lasted seven and a half minutes.

"How do you feel?" Crusher asked.

"I am fine." Data shook his head. "I feel no different than before."

Crusher suspected when the others woke up, they would be fine as well.

• • •

"What are you seeing?" Riker asked.

They were outside, standing in a circle several paces away from the station, its windows lit up with light. Crusher had linked another tricorder to her own and was scanning the team. Both tricorders appeared to be working properly; everyone's signs were normal, including Data's.

"Nothing." She stared down at the readings. "According to the equipment, there's nothing *wrong*." She looked up at the others. "According to my own eyes, right now, there's nothing wrong."

"I feel fine," Rikkilä offered, and the others let out a round of agreement.

"You *feel* fine," Crusher said. "But you clearly aren't fine. Something's obviously not right here."

For a moment, everyone was quiet while the wind whistled around them. In the darkness, the station didn't look like a beacon, even though it was wreathed in warm light. It felt as if something was lurking inside, keeping itself hidden.

"Dammit. I'm stumped," Crusher said, turning to Riker, and she didn't know if that was fear she saw in his face.

15

"I must say I'm impressed." Ambassador Sulel swiped through the *Enterprise*'s scans, peering down at them with a discerning eye. "We certainly are fortunate that we had the *Enterprise* at hand."

"And her crew," Picard added, and he saw the hint of pride flash across Worf's features.

"Of course. That goes without saying." Sulel handed the padd back to Worf. She glanced up at Commander Rusina, who stood off to the side, hands folded behind his back. "Which is why Commander Rusina and I have a proposal for you, Captain Picard. Time is of the essence in this situation. I think the *Enterprise* should search this sector for Aviana Virox."

Picard felt a feeling of joy swell up inside him—he could be off Betazed within the hour. Surely as important as it may be to calm the guests, ensuring the safe return of the treasures was a better use of his talents.

"We still don't know it was Aviana!" Lwaxana protested. "Oh, we can't let the other Keepers get word of this—or the House leaders, for that matter. They're already asking so many questions since we sequestered Aviana's attendants." The ambassador had produced a feathered fan from somewhere on her person and was flapping it wildly. For dramatic effect, Picard suspected, as the room was fairly chilly.

"Ambassador Troi, Aviana Virox is our primary suspect," Worf said.

"That's simply not *possible*!" Lwaxana squawked.

"Mother, please, you are here as a courtesy." Troi's tone was even, but Picard was able to detect the edge of frustration in her words.

Lwaxana looked over at Sulel, aghast. "Don't tell me you think she's responsible!"

What Picard could only describe as the faintest *hint* of a Vulcan smile played on Sulel's lips. He had no experience working with her, but something about the ambassador's manner suggested she found Lwaxana—amusing.

"Lwaxana . . ." Sulel started.

"Hopeless. Hopeless!" Lwaxana flung her fan on the table. "How am I supposed to handle the House leaders now?"

"Patience," Sulel said. "Captain Picard, as the Federation ambassador to Betazed, I would like to formally request that the *Enterprise* pursue Aviana Virox's ship."

Picard's hopes flared.

"Of course, Commander Rusina, you will continue the investigation here on Betazed, as we discussed," Sulel continued. "Finish your interviews with anyone who was backstage. Be thorough with Aviana Virox's House and attendants. Perhaps"—she held up a hand to stop Lwaxana—"the *Enterprise* will find Aviana Virox, and discover if she had a hand in this unfortunate incident."

Sulel turned to Picard. "Captain?"

"The *Enterprise* would be honored to assist the people of Betazed in the recovery of Xiomara's treasures."

"Wait," Lwaxana said, rising up from the table. "Jean-Luc, you must stay."

Sheer terror lanced through Picard.

Sulel looked up at her. "Could you explain why, Lwaxana?"

"Yes, please do," Picard said carefully.

"We are facing a potential worldwide diplomatic *crisis*." Lwaxana strode dramatically to the head of the table, sweeping her heavy gown past Commander Rusina. "The stolen treasures are objects of *significant* cultural importance. This could be the opening shot from an antagonistic force."

"Go on," Sulel said.

Was Sulel on Lwaxana's *side*? Picard felt like a specimen pinned to a board.

"Jean-Luc's skills are unparalleled." Lwaxana retrieved her folded-up fan from the table and pointed it in Picard's direction, a plume of trembling feathers. "Why, only a few years ago, he saved me from the clutches of a Ferengi using *Shakespeare*."

Heat rushed to Picard's cheeks.

"As ambassador of Betazed, it's my duty to ensure that no one acts against the interest of my people." Lwaxana stopped a few paces away from Sulel. "If this turns out to be more serious than we thought, then we'll need Jean-Luc here, not aboard the *Enterprise*."

To Picard's horror, Sulel seemed to be giving this proposal serious consideration. "Well, I don't—"

"I am going to need all the help I can get with the House leaders," Lwaxana said to Sulel, punctuating her words with the fan. "They're asking questions, and they are not going to be terribly happy that we handed the pursuit to outsiders." Lwaxana looked over at Worf. "No offense."

"None taken," Worf said.

Picard felt his escape slipping away. *Damn Lwaxana.* They were facing a diplomatic crisis here on Betazed. He had experience. He wished, desperately, that he was a lowly green lieutenant.

Sulel did that small, quick Vulcan smile again. "Captain Picard's assistance here would be invaluable."

Was Sulel making fun of him? Did Vulcans do that?

Picard felt as if the room was filling quickly with water and he was straining to keep his head above the surface.

"Captain," Worf said, "if I may—"

The water was rising. Picard managed a nod.

"I would be honored to command the *Enterprise* on this mission." The Klingon waited for his response.

Deanna Troi was watching him with that clear, implacable counselor's expression. *What is she thinking? That it will be good for me.* Picard didn't need to be a telepath to know that.

"I believe Mister Worf has proven himself more than capable," Lwaxana said. "And quite frankly, the longer we sit around debating this, the harder it'll become to recover the treasures."

Picard couldn't argue.

"Captain?" Sulel lifted an eyebrow in his direction. "Is this agreeable to you?"

He could tell, by the tone of her question, that there was only one answer.

"It is, Ambassadors."

And the water overtopped him and swallowed him whole.

Deanna Troi sat in her chair beside the captain's seat. Worf took the center seat. He glanced at her and she gave him her brightest, most encouraging smile. She could sense his anxiety, his desire to succeed. All around them the bridge crew waited at their stations.

"Lieutenant Besta," he said. "Do you have a lock on the ship's warp signature?"

"Whoever's flying that thing is trying to hide their tracks," Besta reported from the security station.

Troi knew that the Betazoids, by necessity, were not private people. They saw no purpose in lying, or in hiding themselves. What Aviana had managed with her attendants—the private telepathic conversations—was decidedly *un*-Betazoid. But not as un-Betazoid as stealing away the three treasures of Xiomara. *Have I really been gone for so long that I no longer understand my mother's people?*

"Got it," Lieutenant Besta reported. "The ship is heading in the direction of the colony on Uesta. Warp four."

"Match course, warp five," Worf said. "Engage."

The deck plates thrummed as the ship slipped into warp speed, stars streaking into white lines on the main viewscreen. Troi leaned back in her seat, taut with anticipation.

"Sir, we should overtake the ship in forty-five minutes," Besta said.

"Very good." Worf sat ramrod straight in the captain's chair, his eyes fixed forward. He was tightly wound, ready for action.

"What's your plan once we catch the ship?" Troi asked.

He considered her question. "It will depend on what we find. Do you think Aviana Virox is the thief?" Worf paused. "I would appreciate your insight on the matter."

Troi smiled, flush with a surge of affection. "Honestly? I don't know. This situation is an unusual one, certainly."

Worf nodded in acknowledgment. "We will be prepared for anything."

He fell into a meditative silence, the ship maintaining the course. The soft sounds of the bridge always soothed Troi, and she was finally able to really *relax*. *Enterprise*'s midnight had been Betazed's noon. She hadn't slept for hours. Her eyes fluttered, wanting desperately to close, and her chair was so comfortable—

"Sir, we have a problem."

Troi straightened up, feeling the tension rippling through the bridge.

"Go ahead." Worf was already on his feet, moving toward the forward stations. He stopped abruptly, turned around.

"The ship . . ." Besta's hands flew across the security station. "I've lost the trail. Impossible."

Worf asked, "How close were we to the last known location?"

"We would have intercepted in nine minutes. Now—" Besta

studied the readouts. "I've got it again! The ship is looping back around."

"Stay on it." Worf squeezed his hands into fists.

"Lieutenant, the target keeps dropping out of warp," Lieutenant Mosweu said from flight control. "I suspect it's on purpose."

"Keep a sensor lock on that ship," Worf said.

He stalked back to the captain's chair. Troi whispered, "You have this."

"Dropping out of warp," Lieutenant Mosweu announced.

"Match speed," Worf ordered. "Get ready on the ship's flight trajectory."

On the main viewscreen the stars collapsed back into points. Both Mosweu and Besta studied their screens. Troi leaned forward, waiting.

"Got it!" Mosweu said. "Still headed toward Uesta. Taking a roundabout route."

Worf looked over at Troi. "Are there any ties between Uesta and Betazed?"

Troi shook her head. "No."

"Mister Besta, report on Uesta," Worf ordered.

"Uesta is a Class-M planet located in the Kaelon system," Besta said. "Population of 250,000."

Troi said, "It's a Federation colony."

"Yes, Commander. Uesta was settled by Federation and non-Federation citizens."

"Unusual," Worf murmured.

"Why go to a Federation colony? It seems risky," Troi said.

"Federation Security reports an increase of criminal activity clustered in the western hemisphere."

Troi considered this. Uesta seemed like the sort of place a Betazoid would think the best planet to offload stolen goods. Virox could have heard about Uesta's criminal elements.

But how was a Betazoid house leader so skilled at evasion?

"Sir, the ship is still heading toward Uesta," Mosweu said. "Back at warp four. I have a lock on its warp signature."

"Match speed. Let us see where she is going. Keep a lock on that ship. If she moves even a degree off course—"

"Aye, aye, sir."

16

—◆—

The House leaders were far more inconsolable than Picard could have imagined. He was going to need a lot more than Sh'yan and a dusty old replicator to help him now.

He was backstage, standing side by side with Ambassador Sulel, and feeling profoundly absurd in the white pantaloons of his guest costume. Replicating a Starfleet uniform for him was an extremely low priority for Betazed Security.

Spread out before Picard and Sulel were a dozen furious Betazoids, most in elaborate formal wear. The women seemed particularly fond of towering headdresses made out of materials Picard would never have imagined going into clothing items: flowers, greenery, bits of glass, some kind of shimmery floating light fixtures. Their outrage and worry was understandable, but to see it festooned in finery gave everything a sharp, surrealist edge.

"Have you found the treasures?" demanded one of the leaders, the others immediately chiming in with their own similar demands.

"Where's Lwaxana?" someone called out.

"Ambassador Troi is aiding the search for the treasures," Sulel said, unfazed by the emotion welling up in front of her. "She will be joining us shortly."

Mumbles of discontent followed. Lwaxana was at the command station, on standby as Worf led the search for the missing Aviana Virox. Sulel had requested that Picard accompany her as she updated the leaders on the status of the investigation.

Why am I still here? Picard thought. *I could be on the* Enterprise, *tracking down Virox and whoever else might be behind this crime.*

"We are in pursuit of a potential culprit," Sulel said, and the leaders immediately devolved into shouted questions, drowning one another out.

Sulel raised her hands. "Please," she said. "Remain calm."

"Who is this culprit?" someone asked. "Everyone involved has been keeping their thoughts shut *tight*."

"I'm not at liberty to share that information," Sulel said.

"Then why did you round us up?" demanded a man wearing a long, silver tunic. Picard tried very hard not to stare at him. "We don't keep secrets. It is highly *unusual* how little information has been transmitted so far." He narrowed his eyes. "We ask that our High Guests—any guests on the planet, for that matter—adhere to our custom out of politeness."

"Sir, we are not here to keep secrets from you," Picard said. He knew it ran counter to Betazoid mores, but the decision to lock out the identity of their top subject had been Commander Rusina's. *The last thing we want is panic from the House Leaders,* he'd said, frowning.

"We're here to prepare you," Picard finished. He glanced sideways at Sulel. She gave him a small nod of encouragement. "We understand the importance of retrieving the treasures as quickly as possible."

The House leaders went silent. If they were communicating telepathically, Picard couldn't tell. He didn't think they were. Dozens of dark eyes stared at him fervently, waiting for him to speak.

"We want to prepare you," Picard said, "for the possibility that you may need to serve in a diplomatic capacity."

A gasp rippled through the leaders, and they turned to each other, their voices in hushed whispers. That had their attention.

"Why?" one of them asked. "Where are the treasures?"

"We don't have those answers," Sulel said. "We are working to procure them."

"We promise to bring you everything we can as soon as it's possible," Picard added. "But in the meantime—"

Picard cut himself off as Sulel peered at him.

"I want to personally assure you both Starfleet and Betazed Security are working together on this matter," he said. "The *Enterprise* is currently tracking down the potential culprit."

At first, the reaction was only a stunned silence. Picard let out a low breath.

Then the yelling started.

Questions lobbed out like phaser fire. Picard resisted the urge to turn heel and leave, holding himself still.

"There is no need for panic at this juncture," Sulel said, raising her voice slightly to counteract the din. "We are simply looking to honor Betazed custom and asking you to be prepared in the event that you will need to sit in on a diplomatic session."

"With whom?" someone asked.

Sulel said smoothly, "Ambassador Troi and myself will be doing all of the communication. But I know custom dictates the House leaders have the right to be present for any negotiations."

The protestations quieted down into soft murmurs.

"It's our hope that we will have this matter settled quickly." Sulel turned toward Picard. "Captain, if you could share with the House leaders what your starship is capable of."

Picard felt his shoulders loosen. He immediately launched into a perhaps too-technical description of the *Enterprise*'s scanners as well as the skills of Lieutenant Worf, who was leading the chase. As he spoke, he was aware of the Betazoids listening intently, nodding their approval.

"I assure you, we have everything under control," Picard fin-ished.

Sulel said, "Now, we ask that you remain on standby in the event that we do need to open diplomatic negotiations. But remember"—she held up one finger when the Betazoids began to bubble up with questions again—"we are still in the early stages of our investigations."

She and Picard stepped out into the hallway, leaving the Betazoids to their own devices. The captain was anxious to get back to the command center; he was as ready for answers as the House leaders were.

"Thank you again," Sulel said as they strode down the hallway. "Your presence was reassuring."

"I suppose," Picard said softly.

"It was." Sulel paused. "You do not feel comfortable among Betazoids, do you?"

Picard set his mouth into a straight line. "They are marvelous people."

"Of course. But many find their love of pomp and circum-stance . . . overwhelming."

Picard didn't answer.

"I felt the same, during my first year on Betazed." A faint grin curved at the edge of Sulel's lips. "Vulcans have our share of cere-mony, but nothing can compare with the ceremonies of Betazed. They are so imbued with emotion. I believe it is where they get their power from."

Picard looked over at her. "Forgive me, but it's surprising to hear a Vulcan say so."

"My people could learn from the Betazoids," she said. "Their telepathy makes their emotions a strength, not a weakness. The art and music of this world—it's unlike any else. Don't you agree?"

Picard thought back to the pageant, before the treasures had been revealed to be gone. He'd had a limited view from his place backstage, but he had heard the music and narration, the drama of the story of Xiomara. As much as he hated his ridiculous costume and the endless parading around he'd been forced to do, he had to admit that there had been something stirring about it all.

"Betazed is my preferred posting," Sulel continued. "It's important to me that this matter is handled swiftly."

A Vulcan enamored with Betazed. It wasn't something Picard expected to ever encounter. But then, nothing about this had gone the way he had expected.

17

Doctor Beverly Crusher shot awake. The sleeping quarters were dark and cool and quiet, and each of the beds held a sleeping inhabitant.

What had woken her?

She listened, then heard a soft, mechanical *whump* coming from somewhere in the walls, or possibly outside the station. Crusher sat up and listened, holding her breath.

There it was again. *Whump.*

She slid out of bed, wrapped herself up in a blanket, and padded softly out of the sleeping quarters. A single light glowed in the smaller laboratory, but when she peered in through the doorway, it was empty, a dissembled tricorder scattered across a workstation. Data must have heard the noise and was investigating.

Crusher told herself she was overreacting. Data was more than capable of handling any emergency. But her doctor's instincts had her too wired to fall back asleep.

She activated her combadge. "Crusher to Data," she whispered as she shuffled down the hallway. "Where are you?"

"Outside," Data responded. *"There is an issue with the station's power."*

"What kind of issue?" Crusher's thoughts went back to the replicator and the piles of spilled food.

"I am not sure."

"I'll lend a hand."

"Come ahead."

Crusher slipped out through the front entrance. The wind rolling across the grasses swept her hair into her face and she pulled it away with one hand, tucked it behind her ear. Stars sprayed across the sky, the night a deep, rich shade of purple. She followed the trail of safety lights glowing in the biomass of the station structure until she found Data. He had peeled back the outer layer of the structure's organic covering, revealing the delicate network of fine optical data network cables that served as the structure's data system.

"I heard something," Crusher said. "I guess it was the generator." The wind gusted around them. "It woke me up."

"The backup generator failed. Twice, in quick succession," Data said.

A chill crept over Crusher's skin. "Failed completely?"

"Yes, and then immediately rebooted itself."

The doctor crossed her arms over her chest, hugging herself tight. She had woken up because of the whumping noise, but what if it had been the *lack* of noise? All the unusual background hums suddenly silenced.

"The power shouldn't fail," Crusher whispered. "Not on a station like this." Because this type of station was designed to work in all environments. Crusher had been on missions where a failure like this would have been disastrous—at least they could breathe the air on Kota. But the tech itself was the same, regardless of the planetary condition. Which meant it was very troubling, and very unusual, that both the EPS and the backup commands from the station's computer had failed.

Data paused, his hands still buried in ODN cables. "No," he said, "it should not."

Uneasiness crawled up Crusher's spine. "Do you think this is related to the dinner attack?"

"I am trying to determine that the cause of this failure is not related to other issues."

Crusher watched as Data pulled up a fingernail and put a particularly delicate ODN into his fingertip. Instantly, everything lit up. A harsh, arctic glow threw strange, jagged shadows across the grass. Data gazed into the far distance as information raced through the ODN and into him.

To Crusher, the ODN cables inside the biostructure looked like a life-form's nervous system, millions of complicated pathways giving form and meaning to the biomatter that grew up around it. But something as simple as an injury to the wrong part of the body could make the entire system collapse. An infection in the brain and the body would shut down in unexpected ways. A whole litany of effects from one spot of disease.

The lights blinked out. Data had tucked the ODN back into place. "There appears to be no fault in the system."

"There has to be *something*."

"Strange," Data said as he put the biomass back into place, pinching it with his fingers until it melded together. "We are seeing similarities between the technological failures and the medical ones."

An infection in the brain, she thought.

"This'll only sting a little," Crusher promised.

Malisson made a face. "Doctors always say that."

Crusher pressed the extractor against Malisson's arm and collected a vial of her blood. She was cautious about using any equipment, after what had happened last night. But she tested the instrument on herself, and it was functional.

"All done," Crusher said, adding Malisson's sample to the others she'd collected: seven the more common red, and one bright cerulean blue, courtesy of the Bolian.

"Hope you find something useful," Malisson said. "I had those dreams again last night."

Crusher smiled thinly. "I hope so too."

Malisson wasn't the only one who'd had the dreams. The others had complained as well. Images of drowning, of strange drawings scrawled across cave walls, of the stars swirling into patterns. Making notes of the imagery, she then took everyone's temperature. Normal. No surprise.

Crusher carried the blood samples into the laboratory she was sharing with Data. He was studying last night's malfunctioning equipment, currently staring intently at the cylindrical core of the replicator.

"Anything?" she asked him.

"No." He set the core down. "All that remains is to examine the station's computer. But given the lack of issues in the structure's ODN, I suspect I will also turn up nothing."

"Well, let's hope I find something." She shook the tray a bit, making the vials clank together.

"You are excited about the prospects?"

"I wouldn't go that far, Data." She slid in front of the centrifuge.

She fed the vials into the centrifuge and told it to start. A whir rose up from the machine, soft and whispery. The vials whipped around in the machine, humming softly.

Instead of test results, it was displaying nonsense. Strings of words in Standard, Bajoran, Vulcan, binary code, and dozens of other languages. The words rippled down the screen like a waterfall. *Landslide—I left the—inordinate—cloudcraft songs above the sky—*

"Data," she said uncertainly, looking at him, "I think I got something."

The centrifuge let out a screeching, grinding groan. Just as Crusher turned toward it, she saw seven red streaks and one blue jettison toward the ceiling. A heartbeat later came the crystalline shatter and the wet spray of blood.

The two of them peered up at the blood-spattered ceiling. "Jackson Pollock," Data said. "*Convergence*."

"What?" Crusher felt dazed. The centrifuge was still running. Words flowed down the control pad. A few drops of blood dripped onto the floor.

"Data, are you all right?"

"Peachy keen, Billy Jean."

"*What?*" Crusher rubbed her temples. "Data, could you please deactivate your slang program. Now's really not the—"

"I do not have my slang program activated, Doctor."

Crusher studied Data. He was watching her with a quizzical tilt of the head, his confused expression one that she hadn't seen in six years.

"'*Peachy keen*'?"

His brow furrowed. "I did not say that. I merely stated that I am perfectly fine. I—" He stopped. "I did." He looked at her. "Doctor, this is disturbing."

"I'll say." Crusher peered up at the blood splatter on the ceiling. "Computer, biowaste protocol."

There was a long pause, longer than normal. For a moment Crusher was certain that the computer had failed. But then it answered, "*Affirmative. Biowaste detected. Initiating cleanup protocol.*"

Biowaste. Crusher had been so stunned by the centrifuge's failure that she hadn't been thinking properly. The computer should have detected the blood splatter immediately.

It did appear to be cleaning it up now. The blood slowly seeped into the biomass, where it would be broken down and used to reinforce the strength of the structure. That was what it should be doing.

"Something is going very wrong," Crusher whispered.

A knock sounded on the door. "Can I come in?" Riker asked.

"Yes, of course." Crusher went back to the station, where the centrifuge was still running. "Stop," she ordered, and to her surprise, it did.

"Sorry to interrupt," Riker said. "But I need Data's help. We're having issues in the other lab."

Of course they were.

"Everything all right?" Riker stepped into the room, peering around. Crusher leaned against the table.

"Peachy keen, Billy Jean," said Data.

Riker gave him a confused look.

"Again?" Data said to Crusher. She nodded.

"What's going on in here?"

"Something's affecting the technology in the station," Crusher said, "and unfortunately, that includes Data."

"It is true," Data said. "Which is why I feel it is necessary to ask you to deactivate me until we can determine what is happening."

"I don't think that's necessary," Riker said.

"Without realizing it, there is the potential for me to do something I would regret."

"I would tell you to run diagnostics," Crusher said. "But like everything else, I doubt you'll find anything wrong." She looked to Riker. "Are the others okay?"

Riker replied, "Yes. It was just the microviewer. It keeps showing false readings."

"What kind of false readings?"

"Well, that's probably not the best way to describe it. Come see for yourself." He nodded at Data, grinning a little. "You come along too. I'll make sure you don't do anything you'll regret."

Crusher fell into step beside Data as they left the laboratory. "We'll figure out what's going on," she told him. "I may not be an engineer, but I'm still your doctor."

"I appreciate that," Data said.

Crusher smiled, but she wished La Forge were here.

The second laboratory was cramped, and none of the team were working. When Riker walked in, Malisson threw her head back and groaned. "Everything's doing it now."

"Really?" Riker let out a frustrated sigh.

Crusher wove her way up to the microviewer. The screen flashed with light and color, swirls of lavender and green pooling together and spreading apart, puddling into strange, delicate shapes that almost—*almost*—seemed familiar. They were like the faces of a person she had only seen once, or a song she hadn't heard in decades.

What it should have been showing was the magnification of whatever sample had been loaded into it.

"What were you looking at?" she asked, watching the screen. The colors shifted into shades of blue, black lines growing up like jagged, broken trees. Or Lichtenstein patterns. Every time Crusher thought she saw something in the images, it evaporated away.

"Groundwater." Solanko crossed his arms over his chest and scowled down at the machine. "Running a check on potential microorganisms. We shouldn't be able to see anything; even if there were some critters in the water, it wouldn't look like *this*." He flung his hand toward the screen. "Then it started up on the other equipment, even Ensign Rikkilä's tricorder."

"And the padds," Rikkilä called out, "all of them."

"It's either the weird images or words." Talma handed over his padd. Crusher was not surprised to see the waterfall of languages cascading down the screen.

"This same thing happened to me," Crusher offered. "And Data, tell them—"

The room was plunged into darkness.

There was a flurry of confusion. "Where are the emergency lights?" someone called out. Crusher felt around for a light but only succeeded in jamming her finger against something hard, metallic, and cold.

"Everyone, file out to the common room," Riker said. "There are windows in there, so at least we'll be able to see."

"The lights should be on by now," Talma said, his voice floating from somewhere across the lab.

Data said, "Please, allow me to lead you out of the room. I am not hindered by darkness."

Crusher followed Data out into the corridor and into the common room. Thin sunshine filtered through the skylights built into the ceiling.

"The power failed twice last night," Data said, "but immediately rebooted."

"As it's meant to do," Malisson said, fear carving edges into her words.

"I was unable to determine the cause of the failures."

Riker strode across the room and flung open the door, letting in a swell of wind. "Malisson, with me. We're taking a look at it. Solanko, stay here, let me know if anything changes."

"Yes, sir." Solanko tapped on his padd. He muttered, "Worthless."

Riker and Malisson vanished out the door, letting it swing shut behind them. Crusher sat down on a sofa beside Rikkilä. "How do you feel?" she murmured. "Any symptoms?"

The ensign shook her head. She pulled out her padd, still flowing with words. "It's a bunch of different languages," she said, "including Finnish, not standard."

"Finnish?"

Rikkilä nodded. "I learned some of it when I was little. I installed it on my padd when I joined the *Enterprise*."

Crusher frowned. "I suppose that makes sense—it's using the languages included on the padd."

"But I've never seen a padd malfunction in this way." Talma joined them, looking at his own padd. "It's almost like the padd is just throwing words at us. I mean—" He held up his padd. Words flashed by. "Mine is set to Standard. Now it's all Bolian. A number of Bolian words, plus some nonsense."

"Data," Crusher asked, "what do you think?"

"It is far out, Doc."

"Again," Crusher said.

Rikkilä was clearly trying to smother a smile. The Bolian looked confused.

"What I am trying to explain is . . ." Data paused. "These slang expressions are involuntary. The words on the padd are also involuntary. There is no program on a Starfleet padd that does this. I suspect the power failures are an involuntary expression."

Crusher thought of last night, standing in the cold wind, thinking about blood veins and strokes.

"Are you saying the technology is sick?" she asked.

"Isn't that a doctor's way of saying it's malfunctioning?" Talma asked.

"I think that is accurate. There is something foreign in the system. And the technology is trying to expel it," Data said.

Crusher leaned back. That was how she had seen the initial attack on the beach—an infection, one she hadn't been able to identify. Maybe it was an infection, but not a virus or a bacteria. Something else. Something that could affect organic life-forms and technology.

"That's not good," Rikkilä said. "Look at us, sitting in the dark—" She gestured at the room, the thin, murky light. "We can breathe the air, but we don't have a replicator. Our tricorders are not reliable enough to tell us what vegetation is safe to eat." She turned to Crusher. "Sometimes it isn't the *disease* that kills, but the attempts of the body to get rid of it."

Crusher wondered if she was onto something.

"Whatever it was, it's no longer affecting *us*," Rikkilä said.

"We probably shouldn't assume that," Crusher said softly.

"Maybe we expelled it, no problem. But what if it kills the technology?" The ensign's voice had raised an octave higher. "What if the tech is trying so hard to get rid of whatever all this weirdness is, in an attempt to *kill* it?"

The room had gone very quiet. Rikkilä seemed to notice for the first time, and withdrew a little into herself. "Just something I'm thinking about," she said in a rush.

"An astute observation, Ensign. Data, I think we need—"

"Riker to Crusher." His voice cut through the room, louder than the doctor expected.

"Go ahead," Crusher said. "We still don't have power."

"That doesn't surprise me." Silence. *"We have a problem."*

18

⸺◆⸺

Picard and Sulel were back on the floor of the temple. The crowd had settled; attendees and guests looked listless and bored rather than panicked and desperate.

"Captain, I appreciate your help these last few hours," Sulel said. "I know you would much rather have been aboard the *Enterprise*."

Picard didn't want to answer, only in that he had no desire to say something sharp to the ambassador. It was late, he was exhausted, and his dealings with the House leaders had tested the limits of his patience. Still, he appreciated the acknowledgment.

Finally, he said, "It's certainly been an interesting experience."

Sulel studied him. "It is the interesting experiences that shape us, do you agree?"

Picard tugged at the ridiculous costume he was still wearing. "I can't say I disagree."

Sulel regarded him for a moment. "I was uncomfortable with all this . . . ceremony." She gestured out toward the temple, and Picard looked out at the attendees in their elaborate finery, the guests in their extravagant historical costumes, still sitting in their assigned places. Security had paused the questioning when the *Enterprise* left to capture Aviana Virox.

"What changed your mind?" Picard asked.

Sulel tilted her head thoughtfully. "I participated in a ceremony with a similar structure to this one. The five guest groups, the endless pageantry. It was much *smaller*—a local celebration."

"Did Ambassador Troi rope you into it?" Picard said before he could stop himself.

To his relief, Sulel smirked. "Yes. She said it would be good for me."

"She says that a lot," Picard muttered.

"It was good for me," Sulel continued. "I was asked to stand in for a Music Guest. Lwaxana had heard me play the Vulcan lute. As a child, I used to play constantly, to soothe my emotions."

Picard raised an eyebrow and Sulel let his observation go. "I had to dress up in an Lestai-era costume. Are you familiar with that one?"

"No."

"It involves corsetry and quite a lot of capes. I found it all absurd. Why all that *work* to clothe your body? It was illogical."

Picard smiled a little.

"But as the Federation ambassador," she continued, "it was my job to ensure I understood Betazed. I did as I was asked. I wore the costume, I participated in the dances"—she looked sideways at him—"which were *much* more highly choreographed than yours."

Picard felt himself blush.

"I also had to perform in public," she continued. "Something I had never done before."

"I'm sure you played beautifully," Picard said.

"Thank you, Captain." Her eyes sparkled. "It was an unparalleled experience. It showed me that I can learn from the Betazoid people. How much I can learn from Lwaxana. She is a friend."

Picard turned his gaze back out to the crowd. Sulel and Lwaxana had been working together to convince him to stay. He knew it.

So why wasn't he angry about it?

A figure in a white-and-gray uniform strode through the crowd—Commander Rusina. He lifted his hand in greeting as he approached the captain and the ambassador.

"Commander," Sulel said. "Have you received word from the *Enterprise?*"

"They are still in pursuit," the commander said. "I have spoken with my officers, and we have decided to lift the temple lockdown. We know that the culprit, whether it is Virox or someone else, is no longer here. There's no point in keeping people here while we wait for answers."

"A logical decision," Sulel said. "Captain, what are your thoughts?"

Picard managed to keep the glee out of his voice. "I agree. I'm sure the attendees"—he paused meaningfully—"and the *guests* would appreciate a chance to rest."

"Certainly," Rusina said. "It's been an exhausting night." He tapped his combadge, turning away from Sulel and Picard, murmuring instructions softly. A few seconds later, the force fields dropped, and cries of surprise went up from the crowd as they stirred in their seats.

"Can the *Enterprise* contact you in your quarters?" Sulel asked Picard.

"Of course," Picard said.

Picard felt a long, deep surge of relief at the thought that he would no longer have to wear these white pantaloons. "Thank you, Ambassador."

"You were very helpful today," Sulel told him, "and I hope you found this experience helpful as well."

Picard found himself grinning at her. "Ambassador," he said, "I believe I did."

19

"Approaching Uesta," announced Lieutenant Mosweu.

"On-screen," Worf said, and the main viewscreen showed a small and pearl-colored world with massive ice caps. A fragile band of blue and brown wrapped around the equator: the only livable portion of the planet.

Ensign Naysmith reported from the security station. "The ship has landed in the center of the western ice field. No outposts have been established there."

Troi stared at the icy pearl on the viewscreen. "I don't think it's out of the range of possibility a criminal element on Uesta has taken refuge out there."

"Agreed." Worf stood up. "Ensign Naysmith, you and Commander Troi will join me on the away team. Mister La Forge, you have the conn."

Troi frowned. "Worf, you are currently in command of the ship. Surely Lieutenant La Forge—"

"Noted," Worf said. "But I would feel more comfortable leading this mission myself, given my role as security officer."

Troi expected him to say as much. She stood up, heart beating quickly, and followed Worf and Naysmith down to the transporter room. Worf was speaking into his combadge, requesting cold-weather gear be replicated immediately. Two days ago, Troi had been planning to spend three days on Betazed: a warm, lush, and temperate world. Beaming down to a frozen planet had not been in her plans.

The life of a Starfleet officer, she thought wryly.

They arrived at the transporter room and suited up. Cold-weather gear was waiting for them. The pants were bibbed, adding extra warmth to the core. The coats fit snugly around their forms and fell to their knees. Troi pulled up the hood, tucking her hair inside, and then slipped on the heat mask: a shield that would protect her lungs from the icy air planetside.

"Ready?" Worf asked the team. They stepped onto the transporter platform.

The commander didn't want to think about the ramifications; if Aviana Virox was in the ship, it would reverberate across Betazed.

"Energize," Worf ordered.

"The ship is this way!" Ensign Naysmith's voice came in through the heat mask, by way of their combadges. Snow swirled around them and was evaporated into mist when it hit their masks. Worf and Naysmith were two dark smudges on the white backdrop, and Troi pushed forward across the hard-packed snow, her gear struggling to beat back the cold.

Fortunately, it didn't take long before she saw a structure rising out of the smear of snow. It was some kind of thick, dark metal, with a jagged, uneven roof, like black ice jutting up out of the tundra. Naysmith held up his tricorder.

"Inside that building!" he said.

Worf stalked forward, phaser drawn. Troi followed, pushing through her own discomfort to determine if she could sense someone inside. At first, there was nothing, just a dark, cavernous emptiness. Then—

A thread of terror. Despair.

"Someone's inside," she said. "And I don't think it's our thief."

"Are you sure?" Worf looked over at her.

"I can sense fear. Not just fear—" She plunged forward, calling out over her shoulder, "Hopelessness!"

"Understood. Ensign, how do we get in that building?"

"Working on it." Naysmith trudged up to the structure, holding his tricorder. Troi was still reaching out. The emotions she had registered were growing stronger, pulsing out in frantic, panicked waves. She pressed one gloved hand against the building, ice melting away from the heat of her glove and dripping down to the building's side only to freeze in a series of teardrops.

"I found something," Naysmith reported. "It looks like the door is iced over. We need to melt it."

Worf checked the setting on his phaser and then directed it at the door. Steam billowed out as the ice evaporated, landing on the hood of his coat in dark spots of condensation. Naysmith joined in. When the ice was clear, Troi was able to see that the door was made of the same material as the building. Ferengi was etched across the top of the door, and Naysmith's tricorder provided the translation: *Property of the Kotor Brothers.*

Kotor. Ferengi gangsters—they'd been active over a century ago. Now they were a popular subject for holodeck programs where one could either play the Kotor brothers or the Starfleet officers who took them down.

Naysmith pressed his hands up against the door. "This door is reading as unlocked."

Abruptly, the door jerked sideways, letting out a loud, metallic groan, then shuddered to a stop when it was only halfway open. The terror Troi had felt poured out—along with a wave of heat.

"Whoever is in there is terrified," she said to Worf.

The Klingon's features were blurred by melted snow smearing across his heat shield. "We need to be cautious."

Troi said, "Let me go first."

"No."

"Worf." She put her hands on his upper arms and looked straight at him. "Trust me. I'm not sensing any threat."

Worf nodded in agreement, and Troi knew that was the best she was going to get. She squeezed through the half-open door, stepping into a massive, empty space. It was a warehouse of some sort, with old ship parts and packing crates sitting in haphazard piles. She deactivated her heat mask and pushed back the hood of her coat. The climate control was welcome after being outside.

"Hello!" she called out. "We're here to help you!"

The panic shifted, turned to a kind of hysterical giddiness. *Can you hear me?* The voice rang in Troi's head. *You're Betazoid. Please, I need help!*

"Aviana Virox?" Troi whispered, then sent it out with her thoughts.

Yes! I am Aviana Virox, daughter of the Third House of Betazed and Keeper of the Enshrined Disk of Xiomara. I have been kidnapped!

Footsteps sounded behind Troi, filling the space up with echoes. She knew it was Worf and Naysmith, both with their phasers drawn.

"Put those away," she said. "It's Aviana Virox. She says she's been kidnapped."

Naysmith put his phaser away and activated his tricorder. "No life signs," he said. "Just the ship."

"She's here," Troi said. "I can hear her."

Help me! I'm trapped in my ship! That dreadful Romulan commandeered it. She has the treasures! She used my likeness to take the treasures!

"What's wrong?" Worf moved closer, alert.

"We need to find her," Troi said. "She's telling me that a Romulan is behind the robbery. We need to get to the ship."

"Follow me."

The Klingon lieutenant took off across the echoing warehouse.

Naysmith and Troi followed. Starship parts towered around them like sleeping giants, and the air had a musty quality, as if the space had not been touched in decades.

"There." Worf pointed. An old-fashioned Betazoid ship sat out in the open, the floor around it wet with melted snow. The hatchway was open, the stairs extending from it.

Troi started toward the ship, but Worf put his hand on her shoulder. "I will go first," he said.

Troi understood his concern. She shouldn't be scrambling aboard a ship that had likely been used for the heist of the century. "Yes, sir."

I can hear noises outside! Is that you? Who are you?

Commander Deanna Troi of the Starship Enterprise, Troi thought. *Lieutenant Worf is coming aboard now.*

"Madame Virox!" Worf called out from inside the ship. "I'm a Starfleet officer. We are here to help you."

Starfleet!

Troi stepped into the ship. As with most traditional Betazoid ships, it was exquisitely decorated. Filigreed details along the bulkheads, brocaded flight seats, and tapestried carpet covered the decks.

Aviana? We are aboard your ship. Where—

That Romulan locked me up in the storage facility.

Banging echoed through the ship.

Can you hear that?

Troi sent along a wave of affirmation as she and Worf ducked deeper into the ship, following the banging. In the rear, the curtains had been ripped down, and a bar was jammed into the handle of a storage door. Virox banged against it, making the bar rattle.

"We're here." Worf yanked out the bar and dropped it to the deck with a clatter. The door immediately sprang open and Aviana Virox spilled out, landing in Worf's arms. She gazed up at him, blush pinkening her cheeks.

"Are you injured?" Worf said.

"No." Aviana spoke barely above a whisper. She pulled away, shaking out her dress, a simple traveling frock. Troi vaguely recalled seeing a holo of her Betazoid grandmother in one. "Thank you," she added to Worf, and gave him a curtsy. She looked exactly as she had in the memories Loriana had shared with Troi: older, with curly silver hair and a handsome, aristocratic face.

"Aviana," Troi said. "We would like to beam you aboard the *Enterprise*. Is that acceptable to you?"

Yes, please get me out of this awful place.

Twenty minutes later, Troi and Worf sat with Aviana Virox in the *Enterprise*'s briefing room. She had replicated a new dress. *It's not proper to be seen in a traveling frock in mixed company,* she informed Troi. She sipped hot chocolate, her long fingers squeezing the mug as if she were afraid to let it go.

"Aviana," Troi said. "We need to speak audibly." She gestured at Worf.

"Yes," Virox whispered. "Please forgive my voice. I don't use it much."

"That is perfectly fine." Worf folded his hands in front of him and nodded at Troi to get started.

"Tell us what happened," Troi said. "Tell us about the Romulan."

"She tricked me," Virox whispered hoarsely. "She has a device— it allows her to look like anyone she wants. She came to my estate as Sildar Syn." *I've known Sildar for years! I would know his face anywhere. And yet—*

"Out loud, please," Troi said, patting Virox's hand.

"Oh, of course, forgive me." Virox set down her chocolate and pressed her hands into the table. "Posing as Syn, she told me to send my attendants along earlier, that he needed them for . . . I can't even remember what." Virox shook her head. "She wanted me in my ship alone, and I fell for it! I absolutely fell—"

"Aviana," Troi said, "this is not your fault. But we need your help so that we can recover the stolen treasures. Where is the Romulan now?"

"I don't know. She locked me in my ship and left me on that terrible planet. She took Xiomara's treasures with her." Virox's eyes gleamed. "To see them in the hands of a Romulan—"

Worf tapped his combadge. "Worf to La Forge. Scan Uesta for any Romulan presence."

"Oh, she's not on the planet." Virox scowled. "She was taking the treasures elsewhere. We must find her before she does something horrible to them."

"We will," Troi said. "Do you have any sense of where she might be going?"

Aviana closed her eyes and breathed in deeply. "I do remember her grumbling about having to pass through a checkpoint near Creis. Does that help?"

Creis. It was a small moon in the Tasch system, which wasn't far.

"It helps immensely. What else can you tell us?"

"She left me in that warehouse while she was on Betazed. She took the Enshrined Disk. I thought that was horrible enough, but when she came back, she had all *three*."

Her eyes glimmered gently with tears, but the despair and anguish welling out of her was overpowering. Unlike her attendants, she made no attempt to block her emotions.

"We will need to inform Captain Picard and the Betazed authorities about the Romulan." Worf headed for the bridge.

Troi drew Virox into an embrace. "Worf, I'm going to see if I can help her relax."

You have to find them. As she sent words, Virox also sent images:

the Romulan wrenching the Enshrined Disk out of its carrying case while Virox watched, hands bound by an energy cord. The Romulan was telling her "It's nothing personal." She loaded the other two treasures into new carrying cases, and secured all three.

A Romulan. Virox's telepathic skills were refined enough, practiced enough, that Troi could see the Romulan's face clearly. She was older than Virox, and she wore her long, sleek hair pulled back in a ropy braid.

"We're going to find her," Troi said, helping the House leader to her feet. "We're going to find all of the treasures."

20

———

"The *Romulans* are involved?" Picard said with disbelief.

On his viewscreen, Worf gave an apologetic shrug. The captain was back in his guest quarters. Betazed Security had lifted the lockdown.

The Betazoids had been correct: Aviana Virox wasn't the culprit.

"We don't know if it's the Romulan government or an independent agent," Worf said. *"Madame Virox knows that it was a female Romulan who kidnapped her. She was equipped with a device that allows her to change her appearance."*

Picard rubbed his face. He was exhausted, and it looked like he wouldn't be getting sleep anytime soon. He had promised Ambassador Sulel, and Commander Rusina, that he would alert them as soon as he heard from the *Enterprise*. It was the only way he could convince them to let him go back to his quarters.

"Do you know where this Romulan is now?"

"No, sir. After scanning the area, I can confirm that no Romulan warbirds were ever in the vicinity. Or any non-Federation ship."

Picard considered this. He was familiar with Uesta. As a boy, he had explored the panoply of holo-adventures centered around the old Ferengi syndicates. It was a small, cold Class-M planet and underpopulated.

"Any sign of a cloaked vessel?"

"Commander La Forge is setting up a tachyon sweep. We think the vessel is heading toward Creis. I will keep you informed. Enterprise out."

Worf disappeared from the screen and Picard leaned back into his narrow and stylish, but uncomfortable, chair. *Romulans? What would the Romulans want with a few pieces of Betazoid cultural history?* The treasures weren't valuable monetarily, but stealing them seemed like a very convoluted way to start a war.

He was going to recall the *Enterprise* to Betazed and join them on the hunt for this mysterious Romulan. And *that* was something he wasn't keen on telling Lwaxana and the House leaders. They had proven to be quite a handful as he had listened to their grievances along with Ambassador Sulel.

Picard requested to speak to Sulel. She responded promptly, looking put together and well rested. How was she not exhausted?

"Captain Picard."

"Aviana Virox claims she was kidnapped by a Romulan," Picard said, and launched into what Worf had reported to him. When he finished, Sulel nodded.

"Captain, meet me at the balcony conference room immediately."

Picard dreaded that she would say that.

He made his way to Isszon Temple. It was still dark out, and the grounds in front of the temple had been abandoned abruptly, giving the lawn an eerie, apocalyptic feel. Floating lights still drifted between the brightly colored tents, their fabric flapping in the cool wind. The food stands were shuttered, the performance stages empty. The temple was illuminated in a rich, gray light that was the Betazoid color of mourning, and the colorful banners had been replaced by gray ones. The sight made Picard feel empty.

He was supposed to be at some after-party right now, begging off invitations to other, smaller after-parties. Instead, he was walking up to a crime scene that may or may not instigate the next galactic conflict.

Ambassadors Sulel and Troi were both waiting on the balcony.

Lwaxana had changed clothes again—this time to something less extravagant: a plain gray silk dress.

"I knew Mister Worf would get to the bottom of this," she said with one of her usual dazzling smiles. Also not exhausted. Apparently ambassadors didn't need sleep.

"Not quite," Sulel said. "Captain Picard, thank you for joining us so quickly. I have asked Commander Rusina if he wants to cede the investigation to Starfleet. He has consented."

Not a wholly unexpected development. Picard waited.

"Unfortunately, Ambassador Sbrana is currently in negotiations and can't reach out to the Romulan Star Empire on our behalf. With her permission, I have contacted the Romulan ambassador to the Federation, Hakruth, myself."

The conference room door swung open. A tall, well-dressed Betazoid man swept in. Picard recognized him instantly: Jarkko Sentis, one of the Keepers of the treasures.

"Keeper," Sulel said.

"Where is he?" Sentis demanded. "This Romulan ambassador?"

"Jarkko," said Lwaxana, swishing out of her chair like a flower petal caught on the wind. "I am so grateful to have you here." She fell silent, and Sentis's expression softened.

"Telepaths," sighed Sulel. "Still"—she spoke to Picard, her voice soft—"the Federation will honor local customs. This is such a delicate situation."

The rest of the House leaders filed into the room, and Sulel watched Lwaxana, arranging them in a row of chairs behind the left side of the table and clearly communicating with them telepathically, given the hand gestures and facial expressions that were accompanying their silence.

The Betazed House leaders finally settled down. Picard recognized Onora Opeila but none of the others.

Lwaxana bustled back over to Sulel and Picard. "They promise to keep silent," she said. "Traditional modes of communication only."

"Very good." Sulel nodded. "Captain, are you ready?"

"I am." Picard had to admit he was fairly impressed that Lwaxana had managed to corral the House leaders. It occurred to him he'd never paid attention to her skills as an ambassador.

She was very good.

Sulel tapped the combadge she wore. "We're ready. Please forward the transmission to the balcony conference room viewscreen."

"Ambassador Sulel." An older Romulan, his eyes still heavy with sleep, filled the screen. *"Why did you wake me up so early in the morning?"*

"My apologies," Sulel said. "It is very early here as well."

Ambassador Hakruth squinted down, and from their perspective it appeared as if he was squinting down in judgment of them. *"It says here you're on Betazed?"* He looked up. *"I suppose that explains the presence of Ambassador Troi as well. A pity Ambassador Sbrana couldn't join us."*

Lwaxana smiled at him, cocking her head to the side. "It is always a pleasure to see you, Hakruth." Somehow she made the word *pleasure* sound like poison.

Hakruth sniffed. *"The Romulan Star Empire has no interest in Betazed. Stop wasting my time."*

"I would not deign to waste your time," Sulel said smoothly. "I've asked to speak to you because of the kidnapping of one of the Betazed House leaders, Aviana Virox."

"Never heard of her," Hakruth said.

Sulel raised an eyebrow. "Of course not. Why would an ambassador be appraised of a kidnapping?"

"What are you saying?" Hakruth shot back. *"That the Romulan Empire has kidnapped a Betazoid House leader?"*

Lwaxana stiffened, and Picard strongly suspected she was

reminding the other Betazoids of the need for silent communication.

"I would sincerely hope that is not the case," Sulel said. "But Aviana Virox has been recovered. And she has claimed that her kidnapper was a Romulan woman."

Hakruth rolled his eyes. *"Do you think we control every Romulan in the galaxy?"*

"You certainly try," Lwaxana said sweetly.

Hakruth smiled. *"As much as the Tal Shiar would like to believe it, that simply isn't the case. If Aviana Virox has been recovered, I don't understand why you're contacting."*

Sulel kept her expression neutral. "Aviana Virox was not kidnapped for a ransom. Her kidnapping was to aid in the theft of three significant Betazed cultural artifacts."

Hakruth snorted with laughter. *"So the Betazoid fell victim to a treasure hunter."*

"Are you certain?" Lwaxana's voice strained at the edges.

"The Romulan Empire has no interest in Betazed cultural items. Surely, Ambassador Sulel, you can see that there's nothing logical about the insinuation you are making."

Sulel said, "I am looking to rule out possibilities."

"You can rule out official Romulan involvement," Hakruth snapped. *"Now, if that's all, I would very much like to go back to bed."*

"Thank you, Mister Ambassador." Sulel settled back in her chair. When the viewscreen switched off, all hell broke loose.

"It's the Romulans!" cried Jarkko Sentis. "No interest in Betazed cultural items? Nonsense."

"I agree," said one of the other leaders. "He was trying to get rid of us!"

Shouts of approval from the remaining leaders. Picard waited.

"Captain Picard," Sulel said, turning to him, "what are your thoughts?"

Picard tugged his uniform tunic down and tuned out the House leaders clamoring beside him. "Aviana Virox and her ship were found in an abandoned warehouse, once controlled by a Ferengi crime syndicate."

"Ferengi!" moaned one of the leaders. Picard couldn't actually tell which one; their voices were blending together into a symphony of righteous rage. "Are the Ferengi involved?"

"That's not what I—" Picard began.

"The Ferengi and the Romulans are conspiring against Betazed!"

"This matter *must* be—"

"Quiet, all of you!" Lwaxana snapped. "Let Jean-Luc speak." She turned her smile on him. "Go ahead, Jean-Luc."

The captain blinked, the angry faces of the House leaders staring at him. "As I was saying," he continued, "I understand the urge to assign blame for this robbery to the Romulans. But it is much more likely that it was a petty criminal, a Romulan acting independently."

"Boo!" called out one of the House leaders.

An actual boo, Picard thought.

"Calm down, Onora," Lwaxana said. "I agree with him."

Picard glanced over at her. "You do?"

"Of course." Lwaxana waved her hand dismissively toward the viewscreen. "Ambassador Hakruth is dreadfully rude, but for a Romulan, he's honest." She patted the side of her hair. "If the Romulan government *was* involved, he would have been far more polite. Accommodating, even. They think unexpected politeness will throw us. It usually does." Lwaxana dropped her hand to the table. "But I've dealt with him before. He was telling the truth."

"My reason for waking him up was to put him on the wrong foot," Sulel said. "Hakruth's willingness to offer that the items were stolen by a treasure hunter was not, based on my previous interactions with him, an insult. He was effectively washing his government's hands of this crime. I suspect he might know who the perpetrator is and hopes the Federation will handle the problem."

"Exactly," Lwaxana said.

Lwaxana smiled knowingly at the Vulcan. Picard realized they made quite a formidable team.

"If you think Hakruth knows her identity," one of the House leaders said, "why don't you make him tell you?"

"He's a Romulan," Picard said. "They don't give up information easily. And the ambassadors have clearly learned to read this particular Romulan. They are doing their jobs quite effectively."

Lwaxana beamed at him. "Why, Jean-Luc, what a lovely compliment!"

Picard sat very still, his spine stiffening. The House leaders were grumbling among themselves, but the captain suspected there were even more fervent conversations happening between them telepathically.

"Ambassadors, with your permission." Picard stood up, tugging on his uniform. "I will recall the *Enterprise* and find Aviana Virox's kidnapper. By now my crew should have found traces of her ship."

"Excellent," Sulel said. "The *Enterprise* will take up the search."

Picard felt a flood of relief. He realized that he had been waiting the entire meeting for just that. He looked over at the House leaders, their faces red and their eyes wild as they muttered telepathically among themselves. He understood, even if this wasn't a Romulan plot to sow discord on Betazed. Their cultural identity was tied up in those objects. The House leaders would do anything to get them back.

"If you will excuse me, I'll be rejoining my ship."

"No, Captain, you will not." Sulel's tone was low. "You will remain here on Betazed and assist in my efforts to uncover the Romulan's identity."

"Madam Ambassador, I . . ."

"Starfleet Command has already agreed to my request that you remain on Betazed."

21

———

The door to the common room flew open, letting in the wind and a triangle of light. Malisson stomped inside.

"What's the problem?" Solanko asked.

Malisson's shoulders slumped as she raked a hand through her hair. Commander Riker stepped in through the still-open door and pushed it shut.

"The generator is stating the mission is complete," Riker said.

"How's that even possible?" Solanko frowned. "You, as commanding officer, would have to enter those commands into the computer."

"That's how it's *supposed* to work." Malisson leaned up against the wall. "I can't find anything *actually* wrong in the structure, so it has to be in the comp—"

A loud, shuddering *whump* rolled through the room, and the overhead lights started blinking. Crusher watched the lights. *A clotted artery.* If and when the system shuddered back to life, it wouldn't mean they were in the clear.

Riker asked, "Computer, what just happened?"

"Kota is an uninhabited Class-M planet located in the Nilko system," the computer said. *"Kota is an uninhabited—uninhabited—uninhabited Class-M planet located in the Nilko system. Circumference is—"*

"That's not what I asked you," Riker told the computer.

"Repeat, repeat your request?" said the computer.

"Why did power cut out?"

"The power system has a total of ten backup systems in the event of damage or other unforeseen catastrophe." The computer's voice rippled through the room. *"All systems are currently functioning normally."*

"Data, can you do a level-3 diagnostic of the computer?"

"Yepperoni," Data said.

Every absurd piece of slang Data used reminded Crusher that she still had not found out what was affecting the beach team.

"Are you well enough to work?" Riker said.

"Of course, Commander. I do not—" He stopped. "I did it again."

"Yes," Riker said. "Doctor?"

What could she say? She had no answers. She *hated* this feeling, this hopelessness.

"The slang is—*odd*. But I don't think it will affect his work."

"I feel fine."

I feel fine.

An odd thing for Data to say. He was continually reminding her whenever she treated him like another patient that he had no feelings.

"That's it," Riker said. "We can't push our luck. I'm calling for extraction. We're getting out of here."

"No, sir. You . . ." Rikkilä jumped up—then immediately grew bright red, realizing what she had done.

Riker offered her a faint smile. "Go ahead, Ensign, you have my permission to speak freely."

"Thank you, sir. We still don't know what caused the attacks. What's causing our dreams. We shouldn't risk infecting anyone."

"We don't even know if it's a virus!" said Muñoz. "Or if it's an infection, or something endemic to the planet. And why Doctor Crusher and you aren't affected."

Crusher stepped forward. "I appreciate your concerns, but we can be quarantined. I'd like to have access to sickbay; with my equipment, I know I could get to the bottom of this."

"Agreed," Riker said. "If we stay here and the power fails along with the computer, it will only be a matter of hours before the station disintegrates. We'll no longer have access to shelter. We need to request an extraction." Riker glanced at Crusher. "The ceremony will still be going on, but the *Enterprise* won't be gone for long."

The *Enterprise* senior officers made their way to the sleeping quarters, where the comm station was located. Crusher sank down on her bed, watching as Riker hailed the ship.

"Commander Riker." Ensign Rivera's face materialized on the screen. *"How can I help you?"*

"Could you connect me to Captain Picard?" Riker said.

"Stand by, Commander Riker. I'm connecting you now." The screen flickered. A few seconds later, Ensign Rivera reappeared.

"Apologies, Commander Riker. Captain Picard is currently with the Federation ambassador. Stand by."

"Will, is something wrong?" Crusher stood up from the bed and walked over to Riker's side. His expression was serious.

"If the captain is with Sural," he said, "it's not good."

Crusher let out a laugh of disbelief. "Looks like none of us had the shore leave we were hoping for."

"No. But the captain . . ." he muttered.

"Will, don't be unkind."

"I didn't say anything unkind!" Riker looked at her with innocent eyes. "Lwaxana Troi is a remarkable woman. But she and the captain—"

A Betazoid aide answered the transmission. *"Is this* Enterprise? *Have you captured the Romulan yet?"*

What is going on over there? Crusher thought. The poor aide seemed frazzled.

"Romulan?" Riker said. But before he could ask anything, the

United Federation of Planets seal appeared on the screen. Riker looked over at Crusher. "Romulans?"

"Picard here." The captain looked like he hadn't gotten any sleep. His usual crisp uniform was slightly rumpled. He smiled. *"I can't deny it's good to see some familiar faces."*

"Captain, what's happening on Betazed?" Crusher asked.

"The treasures were stolen. Enterprise *has discovered that a Romulan—"*

Picard's voice garbled, and his image distorted, overlaid with other faces of all different species, most in Starfleet uniforms. Their mouths moved but Picard's voice came out: *"—denies involvement. But we have a situation on our hands."*

Crusher put her arm on Riker's shoulder. "We need to do this fast. Before the comm station cuts out completely."

"Captain, we didn't get that," Riker said. "Can you repeat?"

For a moment Picard's face flashed on the screen, looking concerned. Then it was replaced by an Andorian officer, his lips moving silently. Picard's voice crackled out of the speakers. *"What's—tell me what—something wrong?"*

"Captain, I hope you hear this," Riker said. "We need immediate extraction from Kota. We have been exposed to an unknown infection. It affects life-forms and technology, including Data."

"Extractiooooooon?" The word was drawn out in a lilting, melodic wail.

"He can't hear us," Riker said softly.

"Yes, I can hear you." Picard's face came back on-screen, but now the background was a beach, waves crashing high against tall, jagged rocks. His voice was lost in the constant, roaring susurration of the waves, the howl of wind.

The sky was lavender, the water a dark purple. Kota? Was it the beach where the team got infected?

Riker tried to bring the captain up to speed on their situation. "Even the comm station is threatening to stop working as we speak." He gestured at it. "It shows you on a beach."

"*The* Enterprise *is in pursuit. How long can you last in the event of system failure?*" Picard asked.

Riker shook his head. "I'm not sure. A couple of days. But we would be without any equipment—"

Picard was speaking to someone outside the pickup. "*There are no other ships . . .*"

The waves erupting behind Picard suddenly washed over him, filling the screen with an image of murky, violet-tinged water. It sloshed back and forth, a rhythmic, haunting sound.

"Captain?" Riker said. "Can you hear me?"

The water sloshed back and forth, back and forth. The captain was gone.

"Damn," Crusher said.

Voices babbled out of the comm station, bleeding together into what could only be described as *music*. The words became images crowding each other out in a pattern that superseded any individual words. The voices became a hum that turned into a melody and then grew louder, straining the systems.

"Computer, end transmission!" Riker ordered.

The sound increased.

"Manual deactivation!" Crusher said.

"On it." Riker programed in the command. "That should . . . It's not working!"

"I'll get a tool kit." Crusher headed for the lab and ran into Data.

"Data," she breathed. "Thank goodness you're here. We can't get the comm station to shut off."

He opened his mouth to speak—

The song from the comm station, a riotous layer of noise, came out of his mouth.

His brows went up in an expression of confusion. His mouth moved, and the noise rippled in time. Stopped. Tilted his head. Did it again.

"Data," Crusher whispered. "You're—"

Data looked past her, at the comm station. He pushed Riker aside, who let out a shout of surprise. Data bent down in front of the comm station.

Crusher asked calmly, "Data, do you know what you are doing? Do you think you can fix it?"

He plugged his index finger into the port, and his eyes brightened. Immediately, the comm went silent.

Crusher waited.

Opening his mouth to speak, Data unleashed a torrent of binary code. He spoke so quickly that the ones and zeros bled together into a loud, whining hum.

"Data," Riker said, "can you hear me?"

Data kept unspooling binary, unmoving, his gaze boring into them.

"Computer," Crusher asked, "can you translate?"

"Kota is an uninhabited Class-M planet located in the Nilko system," the computer offered. *"Circumference is 160,000 kilometers, with a distance of—"*

"Computer, stop," Crusher said with disgust.

The doctor sat down beside her friend. "Data, can you hear me?" No reaction.

"I'm going to get Malisson," Riker said. "She's the closest thing to an engineer we have here."

Crusher nodded, still focused on Data. There was something she could do, but she had promised him that she would only do it in an emergency.

"Data," Crusher murmured. "I'm going to deactivate you. Please, give me some sign if you don't want me to proceed."

Data kept reciting binary code. There was something so *flat* about his aspect. As if Data weren't there.

Crusher took a deep breath. "I'm going to do it."

He made no move to stop her. No attempt to protest.

"I'm sorry," she whispered. She felt for the deactivation switch on his back, then pressed it.

Immediately Data's head fell forward. The silence was deep and reverberating.

"Is everything all right?"

Riker came in with Malisson. Both looked at Data in horror.

"I promised to only use it as his doctor. It was the one thing I could do." Crusher took Data's head and lowered his body, then gently set his arms by his sides.

Malisson knelt beside Crusher and studied Data closely. "I'm not sure I could have done anything," she said. "Artificial intelligence was never my strong suit." She twisted around toward the communication station. "How are we receiving a transmission from Bluster Beach?"

They had been so focused on Data, Crusher hadn't paid attention to the comm.

The screen showed a beach dotted with tide pools, the waves calm and steady. Lavender water, a rich purple sky.

"Bluster Beach?" Crusher asked. "Where the initial attack took place?"

"Yes," Malisson said flatly.

"That's what I was trying to explain," Riker said. "Data reacted to whatever the comm was doing."

Malisson stared at the screen, reached over, and turned it off. "I'll see if I can make sense of this."

Crusher found Data's off switch again and pressed down hard. Immediately she had the sense of life coursing through him. His fingers twitched. His eyes opened.

"Doctor Crusher," he said. "What happened?"

Crusher took one long, thankful breath. "I don't know, Data. I just don't know."

22

———◆———

"Shields up. Red alert," Worf ordered.

The lighting shifted as the red-alert lights turned on. Standing up, Worf ordered, "Open a channel. This is Lieutenant Worf commanding the Federation *Starship Enterprise*. Deactivate your cloak, drop out of warp, and prepare to be boarded."

"Ship is decloaking," Officer Szczepinski said from the tactical station. Then, a second later: "The ship is responding."

"On-screen."

A Romulan woman filled the main viewscreen. Troi saw the same Romulan woman that she had seen in Vlrox's memories. High cheekbones, angled eyebrows, and long, sleek dark hair wound up in a thick braid tossed across her shoulder.

Troi caught Worf's eye and nodded.

"What the hell do you want?" she snapped. *"I have permission to be in this sector. Just sent it over."*

Worf wasn't as suited to diplomacy as the captain. Troi could feel the tension, his annoyance with the Romulan surging up inside him.

"Confirmed, sir," said Szczepinski. "Her name is Thuvetha. She's a merchant delivering medical supplies."

Thuvetha offered them a cold smile. *"I'm sure the Romulan government will be very interested in hearing that Starfleet is stopping an* authorized *merchant."*

"You were cloaked, a suspicious action for an 'authorized merchant,'" Worf said. "We're investigating a kidnapping. The victim states that her kidnapper was a Romulan woman."

Thuvetha's expression gave nothing away. But Troi could sense her caution, her—not fear, not exactly, but something . . . the need to protect a secret.

"I'm only guilty of being a Romulan," she said.

"Why would an authorized merchant carrying medical supplies need to be cloaked?"

"Orions." She smirked.

"Really?" Worf was getting agitated, but he was doing a good job of hiding it. Troi could feel his frustration bubbling underneath the surface.

"Really." Thuvetha narrowed her eyes.

Troi knew of Worf's disdain for every Romulan.

"*Do you have any evidence to detain me?"* Thuvetha asked coolly.

Worf glanced at Troi. The commander stood up, her heart hammering inside her chest. "Yes," she said.

For half a second, Thuvetha's face flashed with a wild, unbridled panic, intense enough that Troi felt it reverberate down her spine. The Romulan recovered quickly, but not quickly enough.

"Aviana Virox showed me the face of her kidnapper," Troi said. "It was you."

The viewscreen showed only stars.

"What happened?" Worf asked.

"She cut the transmission. Warp nine, sir." Szczepinski shook his head. "I don't know how that's possible. It's an old merchant vessel. They aren't capable of that speed."

"We'll worry about the how later," Worf said. "Follow her. Lock onto her warp engines. Be prepared to fire if necessary."

The *Enterprise* jumped to warp, matching the Romulan's speed.

Thuvetha's ship had not raised its cloak, and it looked like a green smear. Sitting back down, Worf glared at the viewscreen. Thuvetha's ship was getting smaller.

"A decades-old merchant vessel," Troi observed.

"With an advanced warp engine." Worf stared at the viewscreen. "How long?"

"She's pulling ahead," announced Szczepinski.

Worf ground his teeth together.

"She's cloaked." Szczepinski studied his readouts. "Initiating tachyon sweep. I don't . . . I've got her."

Worf said, "Get a lock on her, and plot possible destinations."

"Yes, sir."

How was the *Enterprise* was falling behind?

"Lieutenant," Worf demanded.

"I've lost her again," Szczepinski said. "Wait." He swiped through his controls. Troi held her breath. "Got her, sir. There's only one place she could be headed." He looked straight at Worf. "Issaw II."

"I demand to speak to that Romulan ambassador. Get him *now*."

Picard let the door swing shut behind him and found himself staring into the angry face of yet another Betazoid. He didn't recognize him. Somehow the House leaders, who had been listening to the communications with Ambassador Hakruth, had multiplied.

"Sir, that isn't possible right now," Picard said with as much benevolence as he could muster.

"Isn't possible?" The Betazoid threw up his hands, nearly hitting Picard in the face with a fluttering flag of purple sleeves. "Isn't *possible*? Who were you speaking to just now?"

"Lord Oreste!" Lwaxana's voice sailed over the din. How had this conference room gotten so crowded? Picard inched back toward a door. It led into a closet that had been converted into a communications station, and it was small, hot, and airless. A welcome refuge right now.

"Lwaxana." Oreste tossed the draping sleeves of his dress coat back behind himself with a flourish as he turned to greet her. "This . . . *person* is refusing to allow me to speak to the Romulan ambassador!"

"As well he should." Lwaxana swept up and slipped her arm into Picard's, pulling him back into the room. "We've already determined this is not a matter to discuss with the Romulan government officials."

"How could that be?" cried Oreste. "Jarkko and Enni and the entire Third House are already talking about preparing for war!"

"Jarkko and Enni are terrible gossips," Lwaxana said. "Literally. They are terrible gossips; none of their information is up to date." She smiled. "Let's speak to Auni Kazmera. She can tell you everything."

And with that, she flung open the door to the communications room and pushed Oreste in.

"I never liked him," Lwaxana said when the door swung shut. "Far too ostentatious for his own good."

Picard looked at her sideways, trying to keep his thoughts to himself.

Lwaxana dragged the captain out of the conference room and onto the balcony overlooking the temple floor. "My apologies for intruding uninvited." She looked at him, her dark eyes deep and intense. "You can talk to me, Jean-Luc."

Picard sighed. The communication with his away team had ended so abruptly: freezing and fragmenting until it cut off. Picard didn't have a full picture of what they were facing. A threat of total system failure, he'd gotten that much. Then, the request for immediate extraction. They couldn't be under attack; Will had said they could survive for a few more days.

"Jean-Luc?" Lwaxana said gently.

Picard pulled himself out of his thoughts. "I have an away team helping out a Starfleet science team," he said. "And they seem to be in some sort of danger. The transmitter cut out before they could give me the details." He paused. "They requested an extraction."

Lwaxana nodded along to his words. "You're worried about them." She smiled. "No, I'm not reading you. I can see it on your face."

"They're experiencing some kind of equipment malfunction. I'm concerned for their safety."

"Who's commanding the mission?" Lwaxana said.

Picard softened a little. "Will Riker."

"Oh, Will!" Lwaxana clapped her hands together. "I always liked him." She beamed. "They'll be fine."

"Captain's burden. I'm worried about how much worse it might get."

Lwaxana stepped closer to him. For a moment, Picard was sure she was about to say one of her usual outlandish things. But instead she asked, "Did my daughter ever tell you the story of Xiomara?"

"Excuse me?" It took him a moment to place the name: Xiomara. The reason for all this madness. "No, she didn't."

Lwaxana tsked softly. "Well, she *should* have. Once you accepted the position of High Guest—but I digress."

"I felt I got the gist of it from the performance before the—" Picard wasn't sure what to call it. "Incident."

"Oh, no." Lwaxana waved her hand. "Sildar took quite a few artistic licenses in the choreography." She drew herself up, straightening her shoulders. "The performance was all about the founding of the Houses. He had to do that, to keep the House leaders happy."

Picard snorted a little.

"Yes, exactly. You see how they are." Lwaxana tossed the loose curls of her hair over her shoulder. "But the real story is in the treasures. Xiomara was a Betazed leader over a thousand years ago. Before we made it into space." Lwaxana flicked her wrist with a flourish. "Her rule was under threat from a rival leader, and she was preparing for war. And then the unthinkable happened."

"She lost her telepathic ability," Picard said, thinking back to the flashes of the performance he had seen backstage: swirling dancers, the constant fluttering curtains. A backdrop to a robbery that threw the celebration to a halt.

"Yes. How could Xiomara lead her armies into battle if she could not communicate with them?" Lwaxana shook her head. "Was she supposed to use *words*? In those days, it was unthinkable that a woman of her standing should speak. Her armies would never have obeyed her commands."

"I'm glad you no longer hew to that custom," Picard told her.

"Well, of course not!" Lwaxana said. "We are part of the Federation. But this was long ago."

Picard nodded.

"However, Xiomara was a clever woman. Like all Betazoid women." Lwaxana winked and Picard felt his face pink in spite of himself. "She knew she couldn't march on her rival. Instead, she sent an emissary to challenge the rival to a contest of wits."

"A contest of wits when she's at a clear disadvantage?"

"It seems so, doesn't it?" Lwaxana's dark eyes glittered. "No one who had lost their telepathic powers would do such a thing. Which is exactly why she did it: to stave off the rumors that would follow if she refused to fight her rival." She looked up at Picard. "A traditional Betazoid battle of wits is fought by pitting one's mind against another's." Lwaxana shook her head in disgust. "A brutal, disturbing affair. It usually ends with the loser going mad."

"I've read about it," Picard said.

Lwaxana laughed. "Do you think we would celebrate anyone who drove her opposition mad? No, Xiomara saw the battle as an opportunity to flex her wits in another way: by *faking* her telepathy."

Picard was amused in spite of himself.

Lwaxana continued. "The day arrived. Her rival traveled into Xiomara's land with a great deal of pomp and circumstance. Giant feathered callowbirds draped with jewels, dresses with fifteen-foot trains, and so on. Xiomara came out to greet her rival in a simple white serving dress, carrying a platter of butter cakes that she had prepared herself."

Butter cakes. Sh'yan had been eating one before the performance, a thick golden disk dripping with honey. "I've had one," he said.

"Oh, yes, every vendor was competing to be named the best," Lwaxana said. "But it's not the butter cakes that are the important part of this story. Xiomara was dressed as an attendant because, in those days, attendants and leaders would not interact directly."

"Ah," Picard said. "I see. So the rival would be thrown off."

"Exactly!" Lwaxana's smile deepened. "Xiomara had one of her most trusted attendants dress in her clothing and communicate with her rival. That attendant went on to become the founder of the Third House, and was given the platter on which Xiomara served the cakes."

"The Enshrined Disk," Picard gasped. "It's a serving platter?"

"It was hand carved by artisans," Lwaxana said, rather defensively.

"Anyway, the rival demanded to know how they could possibly have a battle of wits when Xiomara wouldn't communicate with her directly. The attendant, acting on Xiomara's coaching, deflected the challenge back at the rival. *What are you so afraid of? Don't think you're strong enough to get through me?* And so on. Taunting."

"And?" Picard asked.

"Now, there was a great deal of ceremony whenever someone requested a battle of wits—"

"To be expected," Picard said.

"—Xiomara used that to her advantage. She found an old urn that had been gathering dust. During the ceremony, she swapped out her old urn with the beautiful, delicate urn that her rival had brought to make her offerings to the old gods of Betazed. With the help of her attendant, they convinced her rival that her beautiful urn had been transformed into an old, rusted one by the gods themselves."

"It was my understanding," Picard said slowly, "that Betazoids don't see the point of lying."

"Well, why should we?" Lwaxana gave him a stern look and then started to laugh. "But Xiomara had no choice! This was a battle of wits. There were no draws. Someone had to win." She wrinkled her nose. "The past can be distasteful."

"I agree."

"Now," Lwaxana said, "that urn came to be known as the—"

"The Hallowed Urn of Rus'xi," Picard finished. "Because she gave it to Rus'xi as a dowry. I remember that from the ceremony."

"So that leaves us with one last item." Lwaxana grinned devilishly. "The most important of them all. The Sacred Silver of Xiomara. It is, in reality, a spoon. It's a fragile, flimsy spoon," Lwaxana explained. "Practically worthless for eating with, but it had a curious property."

Picard raised an eyebrow.

"It *glows*," said Lwaxana. "If that dreadful Romulan hadn't stolen it, you would have seen it glowing during the unveiling. We understand now that the reason for the glowing is because the metal it had been forged with was tainted with iclonide—"

"So it glows when heat is applied to it," Picard said.

Lwaxana nodded. "But at the time, the Betazoids hadn't yet discovered the properties of iclonide. Things simply didn't *glow*. During the ceremonial dinner, Xiomara swapped out her spoon, so that when she began to eat her soup, it looked as if she were holding starlight in her hand."

"Let me guess," Picard said wryly. "Her attendant claimed she had been chosen by the gods?"

"Of course. And at that point, the rival decided that she simply could not engage Xiomara in a battle of wits. Xiomara was too powerful—so powerful, in fact, that she lived as an attendant rather than risk harming her subjects with the power behind her thoughts. The gods were warning the rival off, and she signed a treaty right then and there. Eventually that led to the formation of the Fifth House." Lwaxana touched her chest humbly. "Of which I am a descendant. But that is a different story."

Picard laughed. It was the easiest he'd ever felt in Lwaxana's presence. He realized with a start that he had been so involved in learning what happened that he had, just for the few moments it took her to tell the story, allowed himself to forget about Kota, the *Enterprise,* and the Romulan, and simply *relax.*

"Thank you for sharing that with me," he said. "I can— Well, I can see where Troi gets her talent for counseling now."

"Oh, Jean-Luc! What an odd compliment. And thank you." She stood up, smoothing down the lines of her dress. "You should share it with your team on Kota, when you get through to them. We all need a reminder sometimes that we can exist without those things we take for granted." She tapped her temple. "Like telepathy. Or Starfleet's technology."

"An important thing to remember," Picard said softly.

"Your people will be fine until the extraction," Lwaxana said. "They are *yours,* after all." She held out her hand, her nails painted a shimmery gold. "Now, let's go back out into the conference room and convince the House leaders we have everything under control."

23

———•———

It looks so much like Betazed, doesn't it? Aviana Virox turned away from the port. When Troi had come to update her on their progress, she found the House leader watching the planet as they entered orbit.

Most Class-M planets do. Troi sat down beside the House leader and looked out at Issaw II. The surface was a swirl of green and blue, brown and white. More blue than green.

Are they down there? Virox asked, and an image of the three treasures flashed in Troi's mind.

We don't know, Troi thought. *But that's our working theory.*

Virox stood up. She had changed out of her traveling dress and into a pair of rather un-Betazoid-like coveralls.

I thought we were being attacked earlier, she said.

Troi felt the start of a headache throbbing behind her eyes.

"Do you mind if we speak aloud?" the commander asked. "I'm not used to communicating this way."

I don't mind. She felt Virox's warm pulse of reassurance.

"Thank you." Troi smiled. "The red alert is why I came to talk to you."

"You found her. The Romulan." Virox's face darkened and she turned back to the port.

"Yes," Troi said. "We believe she's here." She nodded toward Issaw II. "We're preparing an away team."

"I'll come with you."

Virox's insistence made the headache bloom inside Troi's skull. She jerked her head back as the House leader went toward the door. "Aviana, wait. You will not be . . ."

Why not? Virox whirled around. *I was kidnapped and impersonated. Three of our most revered treasures were stolen.* Images flashed through Troi's head: of the Romulan, of Aviana Virox in her ship, of the Enshrined Disk sitting in a place of honor. Each image made the pain in Troi's head pulse.

"It isn't safe," Troi said. "We don't know what's down there."

Virox drew herself up, her expression stern and haughty. Troi could already sense that there wasn't anything she could say that would make Virox change her mind; the firmness of her decision radiated off her.

"I demand satisfaction," she said in her raspy, disused voice. She stared at Troi, daring her to protest.

"You can't be serious," Troi said.

Oh, I am.

"You can't *do* anything to the Romulan," Troi said. "You'll be in violation of—"

Virox laughed, audibly, and telepathically Troi could feel the mocking edge to it. *I don't mean literal satisfaction! This isn't one of our old myths!* Virox strode forward and stopped a few paces away from Troi. *But I will be there when she's captured by Starfleet.*

Virox was twice the age of her mother. Every Betazoid woman was a matriarch, and Virox was the head of a House. And when they had lived as long as Virox had, they weren't used to hearing no.

"Very well," Troi said. "But you'll have to convince Lieutenant Worf."

• • •

"You would like to accompany the away team?" Worf looked down at Virox in bafflement.

Virox nodded, her expression fierce.

Worf turned to Troi, who was standing behind the House head. "Commander, do you think this is a good idea?"

"No," Troi said.

Worf made a rattling, irritated noise in the back of his throat.

"Please, Lieutenant," Virox rasped. "The Enshrined Disk has been kept by my family for generations. I have *dishonored* them."

Worf's expression flickered, and Troi felt something in him shift. "It was not your fault that the treasures were stolen," he said.

"But it was!" A quaver worked its way into Virox's voice. For someone who supposedly only communicated nonverbally, she certainly was adept at it. "Please, Worf—"

"Lieutenant," Worf interrupted.

Virox pressed out a smile. Was that impatience Troi detected? Worf was clearly impatient; the bridge crew was awaiting his orders and he was in the ready room with a Betazoid House leader making demands. *This* impatience could only belong to Aviana Virox. It was subtle, quiet, but there.

Troi wondered if Virox was trying to repress it, and failing. *Why* was it so important to her that she come along? To put herself in danger? Honor wasn't a driving force for Betazoids.

"Lieutenant Worf," Virox said. "Please. I would like—" Her voice cracked. "Forgive me," she whispered. "I'm so unused to speaking—"

Worf's expression softened.

"But I have dishonored my family—"

Worf held up one hand. "You can come with us."

Troi realized that Virox was more savvy than she let on.

"You will stay close to Commander Troi," Worf said sternly. "And we will beam you up at the first sign of trouble."

Virox's annoyance rippled through her. She thought to Troi, *He doesn't mean that.*

"He does."

"Bridge to Lieutenant Worf," Szczepinski said. *"The ship is in orbit, but there's no sign of her on board."*

"Understood." Worf nodded at Virox. "Madam," he said. "You will stay with Commander Troi when we are on the surface." Then he swept out of the ready room. Troi moved to follow him, but Virox's voice snagged in her.

Why isn't she on board? Virox asked sharply—back to the role of Betazoid matriarch. *Did you follow the wrong ship to the wrong planet?*

"Of course not," Troi said. "Come. We'll be beaming down soon."

They left the ready room. Troi took her seat on the bridge. Virox followed, keeping her thoughts to herself, much to Troi's relief.

The emotions on the bridge were running high. Worf studied the main viewscreen, which showed Thuvetha's ship in orbit of Issaw II.

"Is she the only Romulan on the planet?" Worf asked.

"No, sir, she's not the only Romulan on the surface," Ensign Lara reported from the security station.

"How many?" Worf asked.

"One hundred and sixty-eight," Lara said.

She's not here! insisted Virox.

"What about the treasures?" Troi asked. "We know their signatures. They're all unique."

Worf gave Troi a hint of a smile. They worked well together.

"Ensign," Worf ordered Lara.

"I've got them. They're all together, but are behind some sort of transport dampener. We won't be able to beam them up."

"As expected," Worf said. "At least they're all together. Let's go."

Troi looked over at Virox, who wore an expression of fierce determination, her eyes blazing. Her concern about the treasures was genuine.

They followed Worf down to the transporter room. The rest of the away team—Bombardo, Divan, and Sral—was waiting.

Troi reached out to Virox, but she couldn't get through. Virox was locked up tight. It was a strange reaction from a Betazoid.

"Energize," Worf said.

They were standing in the middle of a thick, damp forest, trees zooming up to dizzying heights. Thick, woody vines draped over the leafy underbrush.

There's no path, Virox said.

There usually isn't, Troi said.

Ensign Sral held up his tricorder. "This way."

"Phasers on stun." Worf flicked his gaze around the greenery. "This forest provides the perfect cover for an ambush."

Troi took a deep breath and pulled out her phaser, which Virox eyed with envy. *Shouldn't I have one?*

"No," Troi said calmly, and then she stepped in front of Virox. Sral and Bombardo were on point. Worf was one step behind them. Troi and Virox were followed by Divan, who was bringing up the rear. Troi kept her guard up, reaching out for any emotions.

The forest pressed in around them, stickers clinging to their uniforms as they wove through the thick underbrush. The air was cool and damp, and a clammy sweat beaded up on Troi's brow. She squeezed her phaser in her slick palm.

Sral stopped, lifting one fist. Troi grabbed Virox's arm as she tried to push past and got a blast of annoyance.

"We're close," Sral murmured. "I'm picking up life-forms. Forty-seven."

Worf peered down at his tricorder. "Inside a structure," he muttered.

"We're near the Essar ruins," Divan said. "Whoever it is probably adopted them as a base of operations."

I knew it was some kind of Romulan plot! Virox said.

We don't know that, Troi thought back.

The away team moved forward. Worf pushed back the underbrush by hand, taking point. Troi kept her eyes on her charge.

They crept along, keeping quiet. Their footsteps were drowned out by the constant rustling of the trees, but a single broken branch could echo for klicks.

Troi felt a surge of emotion from Worf—surprise, concern.

He caught Sral's eye and nodded.

They all pushed through the final tangle of underbrush. Distant movement of something flashed through the trees, along with patches of blue sky. Worf was crouched behind a particularly wide tree; the root system, jutting out of the earth, was almost as tall as he was.

He glanced back and made a quick *come here* gesture. Troi turned to Virox. *Stay here!*

She's here. Virox's eyes flashed. *The Romulan. I can feel her.*

Troi grabbed Virox's arm and tugged downward; Virox's annoyance washed over her. But she did crouch down behind the tree's roots. The House leader moved slowly with practiced ease.

She's done this before, Troi realized with a jolt as Virox squatted silently alongside Worf. She hid it in her thoughts, but there was no denying how comfortable she was creeping through the woods.

Virox threw an unreadable look back at Troi as she joined her. Troi forced herself to concentrate on the matter at hand. Virox could keep her secrets.

At first, all she saw were the Essar ruins: massive stone structures that had been built by the beings who inhabited this system millennia ago. They once reached higher than the trees, but now all that was left of them were one- and two-story structures of polished boulders thick with moss.

But then a slick hoverbike zipped by.

It's her, said Virox.

Troi looked over at her. "How did you—"

I told you, I can sense her.

"Scans show the rider is a Romulan female," whispered Sral.

The hoverbike turned sharply, kicking up a cloud of dust. Shouts of protest came from a trio of Ferengi who were perched along a bench carved out of the ruins. The rider slammed to a stop, hopped off, and jeered back at them from underneath her helmet.

The rider threw something at the others and then stomped off through the grass.

She stopped in front of another piece of the ruin. Troi leaned closer, trying to read the Ferengi writing across the top half of the stone.

"Can you see what they're doing?" Worf whispered to her.

"No," she whispered back.

With a hiss, a door slid open, revealing a pair of Ferengi with loops of blue electric whips hanging from their belts. They patted down the rider and all three disappeared into the stone.

"Pull back," Worf whispered, stepping away from the roots.

What! cried Virox. *What is he doing? That was her, and they're just Ferengi. Surely we can—*

Troi gave her a sharp look. "No," she snapped.

Virox's eyes narrowed, but she withdrew with the others. They walked for a few moments, ensuring distance between them and the Ferengi at the ruins.

Worf turned to his team. "Are there any records of a Ferengi settlement on Issaw II?"

Divan was checking his tricorder. "No, sir. But we are in unclaimed space, so it's possible."

"Why didn't we pick up this place on our scanners?" Worf asked Sral.

"It read as natural ruins. Low-power sensors blockers," Sral said. "Best guess."

"In all likelihood, it's some kind of criminal enterprise," Bombardo said.

Virox sent out a surge of agreement. "Yes," she said hoarsely.

The others looked at her with surprise.

She cleared her throat. "The writing above the door." She thought to Troi, *How do you do this all day?* "It says, 'Property of Bryt the Baron. Trespassers shot.'"

"You can read Ferengi?" Worf asked.

"I wasn't always a House leader," Virox said sweetly.

"What were you?" Troi asked.

Virox ignored the question. *Tell the others I can't speak aloud much more. It hurts my throat.*

"I'm running Bryt the Baron," Divan said.

Virox smiled knowingly. Troi felt the smugness roll over her.

"He's wanted on Ferenginar," Divan said, "although it doesn't say for what."

"Probably for repaying a debt," Worf muttered.

"Worf!" Troi suppressed a laugh.

"Regardless," Worf said, "this Bryt the Baron isn't in the ruins alone. And that rider, whoever she is, didn't get inside easily. We need to develop a plan before acting."

Virox sent over a surge of wordless protest as Worf put in the request for extraction.

You didn't answer my question, Troi said. *And you clearly know what you're doing out here. More than you're letting on.*

The transporter beam shimmered around them, and Troi had the sense of Virox laughing.

24

"We're just going to have to ride it out," Riker said. "The captain knows our situation. I'm sure we can manage for a few days."

Crusher, Riker, and Data were sitting in the second lab, away from the others, considering their options.

"It appears we have no other choice," Data said. "However—"

The lights flickered.

"Not again," Crusher said.

The windowless room was plunged into darkness. All she could see was the vague outline of Will and Data. She pushed herself up and felt her way toward the door, brushing her hands along the surface of the lab equipment. The path was narrow, and she knocked her knee up against something that let out a loud metallic clang upon impact.

"Data," she asked, "can you pry the door open?"

"Of course."

She squeezed herself up against the table so he could step past her. If the pattern held, another technological malfunction was next.

With a harsh, metallic grinding, the door opened and thin light spilled into the lab. Even though it had only been a minute, the air from the corridor seemed fresher, cleaner. Crusher knew it was her imagination.

"How are you?" she said softly to Data.

"I am fine." They walked side by side down the corridor, Riker behind them. "However, before we see the others—" He stopped, a few paces from the entrance into the common room. Crusher could hear Rikkilä and Talma through the wall. Rikkilä moaned, "We are never going to finish this."

"What's even the point?" grumbled Talma.

"I *know*—"

Crusher agreed with the Bolian, although she also understood why Riker had told them to get back to the lab when the power came back up. Maybe there was something they'd missed.

"Data?" Riker asked.

"Commander, it is likely I will experience another failure," Data said. "As they seem to follow with the failures of the technology in the station."

"You're not just technology, Data," Crusher said.

"I appreciate that, Doctor," Data told her. "However, I may begin to experience a disruption. And when I do, I would like you to examine me in any way you see fit."

Crusher took a deep breath, not sure how to respond.

"Examine you? What do you mean, exactly?" Riker pressed him.

"I am offering myself," he said, "as a test subject. Unlike the other pieces of technology, I have a more robust communication system. It is my hope—"

His words garbled and turned to a hissing, rhythmic static.

"Will, it's starting—"

"—source of the problem." He paused, looked at the others. "Oh. I see. It—"

More static.

"Data," Crusher asked, "can you understand *me*? Nod your head yes or no."

He nodded.

Well, that was something.

"Data, I'm not an engineer. I'm not the best choice."

He opened his mouth and a burst of static spilled out, then sharpened into words: "—my best interests. I trust you."

Crusher smiled in spite of herself.

More static. "Assistance?"

Crusher put her hand on Data's shoulder. "Data"—she glanced back at Riker—"I know Malisson doesn't have a lot of experience with cybernetics, but I'll need all the help I can get."

He nodded.

"As for the rest of the team," Riker said, "we need to focus on preserving power. If this keeps happening—" He gestured up at the darkened lights. "We need a plan."

"Doctor, what do you need?"

"I'll need light." Crusher looked at Data, who stood quietly, listening. The previous attacks had been the same. He could understand what was happening; it was just communication that was difficult. Crusher filed that observation away. "I think the sleeping quarters is our best option for now." Other than the common room, the sleeping quarters was the only space with windows.

Crusher watched as Riker turned the corner into the common room. She turned back to Data. "Are you ready?"

He nodded.

Together, they walked to the other end of the corridor, past the common room where Riker was handing out orders. Malisson darted out. "Doctor, you need me?"

Data turned and tried to speak. This time the static sounded more like wind, low and keening.

"Whoa." Malisson jerked back. "Okay. I don't know how much help I'll be, but—"

"Anything we can learn," Crusher said, "I'll consider a success."

The sleeping quarters were dim without any power. And silent. There was a stillness to the station when the power was off. She

192 CASSANDRA ROSE CLARKE

wondered if the station computer believed the assignment was complete, and it was time to dissolve the structure.

Crusher shoved the thought aside. The power failures had never lasted long.

Data and Malisson were both staring at her expectantly.

Crusher took a deep breath. She was a doctor, and she had a patient.

"Data, if you could have a seat on one of the unused beds."

He nodded and perched on the edge of a bed that was shoved up against a wall. For a moment Crusher studied him, frowning.

"Let's start with the basics."

Data tried to speak again, but there was more of that howling wind noise, rising and falling the way the static had. She shook her head at him, and he stopped, peering up at her.

"That sound he's making," she said to Malisson. "What does it sound like to you?"

Malisson frowned. "White noise?" She shook her head. "No. It's—honestly, it reminds me of Bluster Beach."

"The beach where all this started?"

"Yeah." Malisson pushed her hands through her hair. "Crazy, I know. But the wind down there—" She asked Data, "Commander, can you say anything?"

Data tried, but the sound of the wind swirled through the dim room, dancing over the rows of empty beds. Crusher's skin prickled.

"Keep talking," Crusher said to Data. She closed her eyes, listening. Earlier his words had dissolved into static, into true white noise, chaotic and harsh. But there had been a rhythm to it, a rising and falling like Crusher was hearing now.

"Thank you, Data."

The howling wind didn't stop. Crusher's eyes flew open. Data's mouth was still open, his expression slack.

The howling grew louder.

"What's wrong?" Malisson dropped down beside Data. "Commander? Can you hear us?"

No response.

Crusher stepped over to the bed. "Data," she said. "Data, I don't want to shut you—"

The sound rose up around them, louder and sharper. Her fingers tightened around Data's arm.

"I hear waves," Crusher whispered. "Do you?"

Malisson listened. "I do," she whispered.

"The comm station showed Bluster Beach." Crusher's pulse quickened. It wasn't an answer. But it was a *connection*. Whatever was happening, it wasn't random.

"Data." Crusher tilted his face toward her. "We're going to look inside your brain. See what might be causing this."

He didn't react; he didn't seem to hear her. It was like *Data* wasn't there, that he was just playing back a recording. The endless howling moan of wind on an alien beach.

"Okay," Crusher said. "I need my tricorder."

Malisson jumped to her feet. "It's back in the lab. I'll go grab it."

Crusher sat back on her heels, watching Data, waiting— hoping—for a change in behavior. But he just kept up that strange, haunting wail.

Abruptly, Data's mouth shut. The room fell into silence.

"Data?" she said hesitantly.

He turned his head toward her, the movement stiff. Crusher tensed. It wasn't *him*.

Suddenly the power flared back on, flooding the room with light. The computer's voice spilled out: *"Kota is an uninhabited Class-M planet—"*

Somewhere else in the station, someone shouted.

"Data," Crusher said. "Data, can you hear me?"

"Kota is an uninhabited Class-M planet," he said. Crusher took his hand and squeezed, but he didn't react.

He wasn't *there*.

Where was Malisson? Distracted by the generator coming back on? Had she been the one to shout?

"—located in the Nilko system," he said. "Circumference is 160,000 kilometers."

"I'll be right back," Crusher said, jumping to her feet. "I promise."

"—Oxygen, 21 percent. Nitrogen—"

Crusher rushed out of the room and slammed hard into Rikkilä.

"Doctor Crusher!" Rikkilä cried. "Lieutenant Solanko is injured." She held up her hands, streaked red with blood. "I tried to use the combadge, but it didn't work—nothing's working—"

The doctor could still hear Data and the computer reciting the database's entry on Kota. "Where is Solanko?" Crusher asked.

"The common room." Rikkilä took off down the hall at a jog and Crusher followed. "When the power came back on, a phaser fired."

"*What?*" Crusher careened through the common room door and skittered to a stop. The room was in chaos. The computer was reciting the Kota database in here, too, and Solanko leaned against the wall, clutching his arm to his chest. Sand was piled up beside the replicator.

Sand—

"Your medical tricorder's not working," Rikkilä said briskly as she handed it to Crusher. Rikkilä had wrapped what looked like a scrap of uniform around the wound. "Nor the replicator."

Phaser fire blasted through the door, scorching the far wall.

"Lieutenant Talma!" Riker shouted. "I told you to get that thing away from the station, not set it to kill!"

"I *did*." Talma was already yanking open the door. "And it must have changed the setting on its own somehow."

Another phaser blast zipped through, this one leaving no scorch marks. Talma ducked out through the door.

Concentrating on Solanko, Crusher knelt down beside him and examined the dressing. Rikkilä had done a good job.

"Cecil," she said, "what happened?"

"The damn thing just fired." Solanko groaned. "I've been hit with phaser fire before, but never when I didn't expect it."

"I'm going to check the wound," Crusher said, unwrapping the dressing. Solanko grunted.

Talma flew back into the room and slammed the door shut. "I threw it out the door, but it's burning the grass out there. I tried taking out the power cell, but it was jammed."

"Kota is an uninhabited Class-M planet in the Nilko system—"

"Good enough. Doctor?" Riker asked.

Crusher peeled away the fabric from Solanko's arm. The wound underneath was clean, the skin charred shut. The phaser had been on a low heat setting.

"You're lucky," she said. "It barely grazed you."

"Shouldn't have fired at all," Solanko replied. "It was locked away in the supply closet. Suddenly, zap."

Rikkilä nodded in agreement.

"It's clean but painful," Crusher said.

Solanko leaned back. "Hurts like hell."

"I should have something for that." Crusher looked up at Josefina. "My medkit is in the lab."

Rikkilä was already moving. "On it."

"You'll be fine," Crusher said. Right now she wondered if it was a comforting lie she was telling herself.

The computer was still chattering out the database's information about Kota. Riker and Talma were no longer in the room. She hadn't been paying attention while she treated Solanko. Where were they?

Rikkilä jogged into the room, clutching the medkit. "Got it," she said, heaving it up triumphantly.

"Was Malisson in the lab?"

Rikkilä shook her head and knelt down beside Solanko. She checked the dosage and administered the painkiller.

"I'm going to check on Data." Crusher slipped into the hallway. It was slightly quieter; there were no comm speakers here. But she could hear the computer's voice coming from all of the other rooms.

"Doctor Crusher?" Malisson's head popped out of the doorway leading into the sleeping quarters. "Thank goodness you're here. I just— I don't know what to do."

I wish I did, Crusher thought.

"Have you seen Commander Riker—" Crusher stopped. The computer was still reciting from the database. Data was not. He lay on his back, and the top of his head opened up to reveal its inner workings.

A loud, shuddering *whump*, and all the power failed again.

For a moment, Crusher reveled in the silence. Distantly, she heard shouting coming from outside.

Then the room erupted with loud, piercing shrieks, high pitched and squealing.

"Now what!" asked Malisson.

Crusher clamped her hands over her ears and whipped around, trying to find the source. All the power was still out. Data was unmoving, lights rippling across his circuitry.

Her combadge.

All of them.

"The combadges!" she yelled, and yanked hers off. The shrieking rose in pitch—

Then silence.

Crusher flung it on an empty bed in frustration. "It's like Data said—you were infected on the beach, and now the technology is infected. How? And with *what*?"

The same question, over and over.

"I don't know," Malisson said. "And why did it start when the *Enterprise* away team arrived?"

Data jerked up to sitting, so abruptly that Crusher jolted in surprise. For a moment he didn't move, only sat in that perfect right angle. He turned his head.

"Doctor," he said, "you must go outside immediately."

And then he slumped over.

"Data!" He was motionless, his head lolling against his chest.

"Did he shut himself off?" Malisson said uncertainly. "Can he do that—"

"No." She was struck with that familiar, sick feeling that came when she was on the verge of losing a patient. She tamped it down through her own determination.

Not Data.

"Why did he tell you to go outside?" Malisson said.

Crusher eased Data onto his back. He was dead weight. She would give anything for her sickbay.

She pressed the pattern on his skull to pull the top of his head back into place.

"Doctor?" Malisson said softly.

"I don't know." Crusher looked down at him. "I'm not sure opening Data up will give us the answers. All the other technology has been going haywire, and we never found anything wrong with it."

More shouting was filtering through the walls from outside.

Malisson moved to the window. "Do you think they are trying to get in contact with us?" She tried her combadge. Nothing.

"Possibly," Crusher said. "Rikkilä tried her combadge, but that was when the power was still on."

Malisson had to stand on her toes to peer out the window. "I don't see— There's Commander Riker. Everyone else is outside." She pulled away from the window. "They're all around something."

The only thing outside was the phaser. Talma had thrown it out when it kept firing—

"We should go out there," Crusher said.

"Will Data be okay?"

Crusher frowned. "He told us to go outside." She took a deep breath. "And that was the first comprehensible thing he said since the attack started."

Malisson nodded. "Okay."

They made their way out through the common room. "Look at the replicator," Crusher said.

"Sand," Malisson said. "That damn beach keeps coming back up."

"Almost like—" Crusher shook her head. "Almost like something doesn't want us to forget about it."

Malisson's frown deepened.

The door was open, letting in a cool, damp breeze. The wind was singing—unlike the wail she'd heard from Data or the comm station, but close enough. They walked around the side of the station.

Malisson put her hand on the outside wall of the station.

"It's not—" Crusher started.

"No," Malisson answered before she could finish the question. "Not yet."

Not yet.

"How soon?"

"I don't know." Malisson picked her way back through the grass. "Under normal circumstances, the structure shutdown wouldn't begin until both the commanding officer and their second give the command to initialize." They walked together, grass brushing against their uniforms. The voices of the team were drifting on the wind to them. "But there's a fail-safe in place. If the power has been inactive for twelve hours, shutdown will commence. The system assumes emergency evacuation."

Twelve hours. They would have to be here for at least another two days.

"Doctor, you've been on lots of away teams," Malisson said quickly. "Have any of them been as bizarre as this one?"

"No, it's one for the books."

Riker spotted them and shouted, "There you are. We've been trying to get in contact."

"Combadge. Another malfunction," Crusher answered. The grass was burned in some places, sliced off cleanly in others. The malfunctioning phaser. Crusher looked up at Riker. "Is it safe to be here? That phaser—"

"We destroyed it," Riker answered. "But not before it did this."

Crusher's pulse quickened. She strode quickly through the grass, swatting it away with her hands, and stepped up next to Riker.

The phaser had burned a pattern into a patch of grass. A series of circles linked together by lines radiating out in jagged, uneven paths.

"How," Crusher whispered, "is this even possible?"

Riker pointed silently back toward the structure. Malisson gasped.

The biomass had expanded along the ground, seeping through the grass in a narrow, dark line, then lifting itself up like a snake. Crusher could see the form it had taken to hold the phaser.

"That can't be," Malisson said. "The biomass can't expand like this. Not without explicit commands—"

"The phaser was covered in biomass," Riker said matter-of-factly. "Somehow—we don't know how—the station did this."

Malisson shook her head. "I don't— There's some pulses in the biomass, but it shouldn't be enough to form . . . I mean, not unless someone *programmed* it."

Crusher studied the patterns in the grass, her mind racing. It all started with the team collapsing on Bluster Beach.

The beach, appearing on the screens. How? Data's howling. The replicator, making sand.

Dreams. The affected crew members all talked about dreams. With water. A beach. *The* beach.

Could all the people, all the technology, even Data, be reacting to the sensory input it received? Impossible. Crusher dismissed the thought. However, Malisson had said the same thing about the biomass expanding.

Is something programming the station? Crusher thought. *Is something spilling strange, watery thoughts into the team's dreams? Into Data?*

25

———

"Aviana Virox knows more than she's letting on," Troi said.

Worf looked over at her. They were in the ready room; Troi had joined him to share Virox's reactions while they were down on Issaw II.

"She insisted that rider was Thuvetha," Troi said. "Which could just be the result of her being such a skilled telepath, but—" She shook her head. "I get the sense there's something more. She's hiding it from me, of course. But she let part of it slip while we were on the planet."

"In what way?" Worf asked.

Troi told him about Virox's insistence on pursuing the Ferengi. "She was ready to run in there herself."

"That does not exactly fit with the frightened Betazoid woman we found on Uesta, does it?" He frowned. "I'll admit this information cements some of the doubts I had about her. The insistence on coming with us on the away mission. The detailed image of Thuvetha she was able to give you—"

"Exactly," Troi said. "Something's going on here."

Worf nodded and hit his combadge. "Worf to Bridge. Please send Aviana Virox into the ready room." He looked over at Troi. "We'll get to the bottom of this."

He walked around behind the desk and sat down. Troi slipped into the guest seat just as the door whisked open and Virox stepped into the ready room.

We shouldn't be having meetings, she said. *We should be storming into—*

"Aviana," Troi said, "could you please speak out loud, for the lieutenant's sake?"

Aviana gazed evenly across the room at Worf. "Of course," she said in her raspy voice. "Lieutenant Worf, we know the location of Thuvetha. We shouldn't be *here.* We should be down *there.*"

"I'm not convinced it's our best course of action," Worf said.

Troi concentrated on Virox, trying to get a sense of her emotions. She was working to keep them blocked, but a few impressions slipped through. Virox was frustrated and impatient.

"And why not?" Virox demanded. Was that Troi's imagination, or did her voice seem stronger, more clear? "If we're dealing with a criminal element, I'm sure the Ferengi Alliance will be pleased that we can bring them this Bryt the Baron. I'm not requesting a declaration of war here."

Worf studied her. "You are a much more—*forceful* woman than I originally thought, Madam Virox."

Something flickered in Virox.

Virox smiled sweetly. "All Betazoid women are forceful."

"Yes," Troi said, "but not all Betazoid women are as traditional as you."

Virox eyed her coolly. Whatever mask she had up was slipping, and Troi caught a whiff of desperation. A sense that all of this was *personal.*

"Aviana," Troi said, "what aren't you telling us?"

Virox looked between the *Enterprise* officers.

"Madam," Worf said, "if you have been withholding information from us, I need to know immediately. We are *trying* to get these artifacts back as smoothly as we can."

Virox took a deep breath. Her eyes burned. "I haven't always been a House leader," she finally said.

"Yes, you mentioned that," Troi said wryly.

"What did you do before you were a House leader?" Worf said. "It's uncommon to find someone who can read Ferengi."

Virox sat for a long moment. When she finally spoke, her voice rang out clear and steady, without any hint of the disuse that had plagued it before. "I used to be Betazed Intelligence."

Troi gaped at Virox in shock. She'd heard stories about the branch of Betazoid military that operated in the shadows. It had always seemed vaguely outlandish.

"You were a spy?" Troi spat out.

Virox crossed her arms over her chest and lifted her chin slightly.

"Betazed Intelligence?" Worf's frown deepened. "Why didn't you tell us from the beginning?"

"I've been retired for ten years," Virox said darkly. "It's customary for those retired to return to an everyday existence."

"With all due respect," Worf said, "it is not normal for a Betazoid civilian to accompany an *Enterprise* away team."

"I was desperate to have this matter handled," Virox said.

"And so you lied," Worf said.

"I most certainly did. The Enshrined Disk is my responsibility. My old skills could be useful. *If* I was allowed to use them instead of sitting in this ready room discussing my past."

Troi studied her. She still couldn't get over the sound of her voice. It was the rasp that had made her seem so frail. All an affectation.

It was all just so—un-Betazoid.

And suspicious. Why keep it a secret? And how did a Betazed Intelligence operative, even a retired one, get bested by a Romulan mercenary?

Troi could sense that Worf had similar thoughts. Suspicion and doubt rolled off him.

"Madam, if we are to successfully retrieve the three treasures," Worf said, "I need to know any information that could potentially be useful. Surely, as a former intelligence operative, you understand that."

Virox hesitated.

"Commander Troi told me that the image you sent her of Thuvetha was startlingly accurate," he continued. "Which is, as I understand, rather unusual for a situation in which you would have only briefly seen her face."

He had caught her. Virox's eyes glittered darkly. "Fine," she said, throwing up her hands. "Thuvetha and I have a—past."

An overwhelming relief poured off her. "She's telling the truth," Troi said.

"Good." Worf narrowed his eyes. "Now, I would like more of it."

Virox sighed. "Thuvetha's from an old Romulan family that had"—Troi sensed a burst of discomfort and guilt—"a high standing in Romulan society. I say *had* . . ."

"Go on," Worf urged.

"They were involved in smuggling weapons," Virox continued. "I intercepted one of their ships. Thuvetha's father had been in charge of that ship, and while he escaped from me, he didn't escape from the Tal Shiar."

Virox took on a distant expression, her face soft. "Thuvetha was trying to frame me," she said. "As revenge for what happened to her father, and to her family afterward. They fell out of favor. Left Romulus. I believe she grew up on an Orion colony."

"That's why you wanted to charge into the compound," Troi said softly. "If you can get the treasures back yourself—"

"Then there could be no doubt of my innocence," Virox finished. "You know how the Betazoid House leaders are. Even if I was officially cleared, the gossip would have been unbearable."

Worf frowned. "Commander," he said, "are you sensing deception from her?"

"She's telling the truth," Troi said.

"Of course I am," Virox snapped. "Now that you know my reasoning, could we develop a plan?"

"I have every intention of retrieving those artifacts," Worf said.

"Then why not attack?" Virox said. "The *Enterprise* should be able to attack Bryt's holdings with minimal risk. Ferengi are not fighters by nature. When they see how easily we can overpower them, they'll surrender."

"Or flee," Worf said. "Taking the treasures with them."

"The *Enterprise* couldn't catch them?" Virox arched an eyebrow. Worf stated, "This must be taken care of quietly."

"This would be quick!" Virox said. "There is no reason that a team of Starfleet officers could not successfully infiltrate a Ferengi gangster's place, with minimal planning and minimal loss of life."

"You mean Starfleet lives," Worf said. "These Ferengi do not deserve to be killed, criminals or not." Worf shifted in his seat. "Frankly, madam, I'm unclear why you are so keen on attacking. You were a spy, not a warrior—" He stopped himself. "Warriors," he murmured.

"Worf?" Troi leaned forward.

"The Ferengi aren't warriors either," he said. "They're businessmen. They're *negotiators*."

He looked at Troi. "There was something you shared with me once. You said your mother told it to you, when she first became ambassador."

Troi nodded, remembering. "Yes," she said. "About how Betazoids don't find lying necessary." She glanced over at Virox. "But she had learned to lie when she took up her position as an ambassador."

"An ambassador is just a spy who works out of the shadows," Virox said.

"Exactly," Troi said. "And what my mother said—"

"When the situation calls for it," Worf said, "sometimes the only way to negotiate is to lie."

Troi felt a prickle on her neck: Virox was agreeing.

"I know how we'll do this," Worf said.

"Let's hear it." Virox seemed relieved.

"If a Ferengi gangster has the three treasures," Worf said, "what do you think he's going to do with them?"

Virox blinked. Then she laughed.

"He's going to sell them," she said.

"Exactly." Troi smiled. "I doubt he cares who he sells them to, as long as the seller has the latinum he wants."

"Are you suggesting we *buy back* the artifacts?" Virox asked.

Worf gave a sly grin. "Or at least pretend to."

Virox's approval was immediate.

"You want to scam a Ferengi," Troi said dryly.

"We need to retrieve the treasures without the Ferengi knowing Starfleet is involved," Worf said. "And Virox has the experience we need for this sort of operation." He paused. "Obviously, Commander Troi and I will accompany you," he said to Virox, "to assure your safety."

"Yes," Virox said. "I like that. Two Betazed criminals with a Klingon bodyguard."

Worf frowned. "I suppose that will make as good a cover as any."

"This is a good plan," Virox said.

Troi took a deep breath. She looked over at Worf. It *was* a good plan, one that would avoid any unnecessary violence. Still, she could sense he was nervous. None of this was how he did things. She knew she wouldn't want to carry out this ridiculous plan with anyone else.

When he caught her gaze, she gave him a smile.

Which he returned.

26

—◆—

"I need to go to Bluster Beach," Crusher said.

Riker stared at her.

"Beverly." Will peeled himself off the wall he'd been leaning against. "You're our only doctor. Why do you want to go down to the beach?"

Crusher walked over to the bed where Data was still stretched out, unmoving. The rest of the team was prepping outside: setting up a makeshift camp in the grasses, determining what technology wasn't affected by the outage. Ensign Muñoz and Lieutenant Solanko were trekking out to a small spring in the nearby caves to secure potable water. Then they would scour the fields for the wild tubers Solanko said were safe to eat.

But Crusher couldn't get the images of the beach out of her head. "Everything that's happening here started on the beach. Or, most of it." She looked at Data. "The science team was here for six months," she said. "Everything they did confirmed all of the scans. No threat."

"Until we got here."

"Exactly," Crusher said.

Sitting down in the chair she had pulled up alongside Data, Crusher was concerned that she didn't know how long he had been under completely. With the power out, and all their devices malfunctioning, precise timekeeping was impossible. She knew it had not been twelve hours.

"Will," Crusher said, "whatever is on the beach is trying to communicate. We need to listen."

Riker blinked. "Are you certain?"

"No," Crusher said. "That's why I have to go to the beach. If there's a chance that there is a life-form trying to speak with us—we can't simply ignore it."

"The station is in danger of collapsing. We don't have time—"

"I understand that." Crusher walked up closer to him. "Which is why I'll be going alone. The rest of the team can continue their work on setting up camp outside. If I haven't returned within two hours or so, send someone for me."

Riker squeezed the bridge of his nose. "I don't like this, Beverly." He looked over at her. "Tell me. What makes you think this is a life-form? That it's trying to speak to us?"

"This infection, for lack of a better word, has affected both our crew and our technology. I saw it as an infection in the crew, because that was how their bodies reacted to it. But the dreams." She nodded. "The dreams all suggested Bluster Beach too."

Crusher glanced over at Riker.

"Dreams in most life-forms are a way for the mind to process the day's events," Crusher continued. "I thought the dreams were related to a possible infection. I think whatever this is, it was shaping the crew's dreams. *That's* how it's trying to communicate."

"And the equipment?" Riker said. "Data?"

"It's the same thing," she said. "I don't—don't know how, or what it even *is*, but I think it's essentially reprogramming the station's technology. The way it *reprogrammed* the crew's dreams." She strode over to the window and peered out, standing on her tiptoes. The pattern was still scorched into the grass, and beyond it, she could see that the team had managed to get a shelter tent set up. "The biomass walls directed the phaser to create that," she said. "But the whole station is controlled by the station computer. And what controls the station computer?"

She turned away from the window, back to Riker.

"We do," she said. "We program the computer to do what we need it to do. Data was also programmed, by Noonian Soong. To think and act as a human does."

Riker frowned.

"This life-form—it's treating the crew and the technology the same," Crusher said. "It's planting the message it wants to send directly into the crew's subconscious, *and* it's altering the equipment programming somehow." She paused. "That's why Data is affected. It made the crew sick, it made Data sick." She gestured up at the walls, the darkened lights. "It made the whole station *sick.*"

For a moment, Riker was silent. Crusher dropped her hands to her sides, feeling out of breath and desperate.

"All of these messages," Riker said slowly, "are of the beach."

"Exactly," Crusher said. "It's showing us the beach over and over again. That symbol out there"—she pointed at the window—"that's the one piece that doesn't fit the pattern. But I think if I can go to the beach, to the same place where the crew originally fell ill—"

Riker held up one hand. "Is there any chance what you learn might bring the station back online?"

"I don't know. My hope is I can find the root cause," Crusher said. "And once we have that, we *might* be able to fix the station."

Riker nodded. "The generator has been off for about six hours at this point."

"That gives us six more," Crusher said. "The beach is a twenty-minute walk from here." She smiled thinly. "Please, Will. It's worth a shot."

"How dangerous do you think this is going to be?"

That was the question Crusher had been dreading. Mostly because she didn't have an answer.

"With the exception of Data, the infection didn't cause harm to the team," she finally said. "I believe that there's an acceptable level of risk."

Riker considered this. "Very well," he said. "But you're not going alone."

"The team needs to work on our shelter . . ."

"And they will," Riker said. "I'm coming along."

"Will, that's not necessary."

"I don't want you going out there alone," Riker said. "And I can't in good conscience send someone who's already been infected. So it looks like it's going to be the two of us or neither of us."

Crusher and Riker waded through the tall grass. They each carried bags filled with containers of water that Malisson had managed to get from the replicator before it started pouring out sand. Their combadges had stopped squealing and appeared to be working normally, as did the tricorders, so they took both with them. However, the larger equipment was still malfunctioning. More mysteries.

Crusher gripped her medical tricorder. She pushed forward through the grass. The wind blustered across the team, damp and laced with the strange, sweet scent of this place. She peered up at the sky, a pale lavender at this time of day. The small, white sun was hidden behind layers of cotton-candy clouds. Kota would be a wonderful place to live if they could solve this one problem, she thought. The refugees deserved a beautiful home after what they had been through.

Crusher had seen so little of the planet since their arrival, but now, as she trudged through the silvery grasses, she realized how much it reminded her of Caldos, where she had grown up. The endless sweeping fields, battered by the wind. She could imagine colonists building stone manors out here, laying paths through the grass down to the beach. Would they keep the name, Bluster Beach? Or would the colonists give it a name of their own?

It was easy to daydream, thinking about Kota as a world filled with people and *life*, as she walked through the grass and the wind. But then her thoughts wandered further, and she saw the refugees dealing with Kota as it was now. Plagued by power failures. Replicators pouring sand out like it was a broken hourglass. Children opening padds to find waterfalls of languages. Crops tilled into strange symbols by their plows. Everyone on the planet dreaming simultaneously of the sea.

"We're getting close!" Riker called out over his shoulder. Crusher took a deep breath. She couldn't smell the salt yet, just the sweet scent of the grasses.

He stopped while she caught up with him. "I have a strange feeling," he said in a low voice. "Like something's watching us."

Crusher turned her head, looking around. "What do you mean?" She lifted her tricorder. The grass rippled around them. Uninhabited. Hundreds of scans had confirmed it.

"Just—you know that prickly feeling you get, when someone's watching you?" Riker rubbed the back of his neck. "It might be nerves. You don't feel it?"

"I don't—" Now that Riker had mentioned it to her, she felt the hairs on the back of her own neck, and the strange feeling of some being's eyes on her. The power of suggestion, she told herself. She was on edge; she hadn't slept much. *Focus.*

"I know what you mean," she finally said.

Crusher flicked her gaze around the field. The grass seemed dense and endless, and suddenly she could imagine millions of glowing eyes watching them as they trekked to the beach.

They fell into step together, not speaking. The ground was tilting up a little, the grass thinning out. White sand kicked up onto the black of Crusher's uniform.

Then she heard it. The ocean.

"I wish we could have used the transporter," Riker said wryly.

Crusher gave a tight, nervous laugh.

And then, abruptly, she was there, at the crest. She stepped up beside Riker and saw the Kotan ocean for the first time, stretching out to the horizon. It was high tide, the water lapping at the base of the dunes.

The sky was turning a sickly bruised color. The horizon was nearly dark, and she thought she smelled the faint tang of metal.

A storm was rolling in.

Crusher stepped forward.

"Let's go down," she said. "And see what we can find."

27

———•———

Deanna Troi adjusted her jacket one last time, ensuring that her combadge was well secured in a pocket. Worf had created their identities—black-market treasure hunters, with ready latinum.

"It's been a while," Virox said, smoothing her hair back into a severe bun. She smiled at her reflection and Troi felt a radiance of contentedness spilling out of her.

"You're looking forward to this," Troi said.

Virox smiled slyly. "You have no idea how dull my life has been. Dinner parties, high teas, and ceremony after ceremony, sitting in the garden waiting for something to happen." She turned back to her reflection and gave it one last appraising glance.

"Is that why you used doubles?" Troi said. "So you could—" She couldn't actually think of how Virox's doubles would have alleviated her boredom.

Virox laughed. "Training them to hide their thoughts was one of the only ways I kept myself sane."

It was still strange to hear Virox speak. Her audible laughter was at odds with the old grand madam image she had cultivated on Betazed.

Of course, Virox said. *No one suspects an ultratraditional daughter of the Third House to have been a spy.*

Virox whirled away from the mirror. She was wearing a shabby outfit, a bland brown skirt with work boots, and a canvas vest. "Your grandmother pulled me out of any number of sticky situations when I was younger."

"What?"

Virox winked and strolled across the room. "Is Mister Worf ready?"

Troi shook her head. She dug into her pocket and tapped her combadge. "Troi to Worf," she said. "We're ready."

"I'm ready."

"I hope you didn't put him in anything too absurd," Troi said as they stepped into the corridor.

"Absurd?" Virox's eyes twinkled. "Of course not. He looks like a proper Klingon."

Troi resisted the urge to roll her eyes.

They stepped into the transporter room. Troi let out an audible gasp.

She had seen him in Klingon dress before, but usually a Klingon uniform, with the imposing shoulder pads and the House sashes and the various decorations. Virox had dressed Worf in dark leather trousers and heavy black boots, a fur-lined cape tossed over one shoulder.

"You look—" Troi started.

"Ridiculous," Worf grumbled. "No Klingon warrior would wear this."

"I was going to say impressive." She smiled up at him, feeling a rush of affection from him.

"You are not a warrior," Virox said. "You are a criminal."

Worf glowered at her. Still, he had been on undercover missions before, so he knew how important it was to blend in.

The commander also felt the barest *hint* of vanity. She suspected that Worf liked how he looked, and the fact that he liked it embarrassed him. Troi could feel that just beneath the surface.

It was unexpected and quite charming.

"Weapons?" Worf said as they stepped up onto the transporter pad.

Troi pulled out her type-1 phaser from a pocket. Worf gave it an approving nod. As fitting his role as their Klingon bodyguard, his *mek'leth* was strapped to his back, and a Klingon disruptor hung from his hip.

Worf had refused to arm Virox. "You have a bodyguard," he pointed out. "I will protect you." He smiled. "Energize."

They were back on Issaw II, in the thick of the forest. "Ready?" Worf asked.

Troi nodded. Virox just smiled, looking—and feeling—excited. "Very well."

It was about a five-minute walk to the edge of the forest. Troi felt her heart flutter as they got closer, the Essar ruins towering over them.

Their appearance was immediately noted by a Ferengi standing near the entrance. He leaped to his feet and hurried over to greet them, energy whip in one hand, a disruptor in the other.

"Who are you?" he demanded.

Worf sneered at him. "You speak to the great collectors of antiquity, Dorota Cusk and Amica Cossio!"

"Who?" The Ferengi stepped closer and Worf pulled his disruptor. The Ferengi stood his ground.

He's enjoying this, Virox said.

Yes.

"Forgive our bodyguard," Troi said, moving up alongside Worf and putting her hand softly on his arm. "As he said, I am Dorota Cusk, dealer of ancient curiosities, and this is my associate, Amica Cossio."

"Never heard of you," the Ferengi snapped. Immediately his eyes flashed up to Worf, then back to Troi.

Troi smiled. She stepped closer to the guard. He swallowed

nervously. "Your knowledge gaps are not my concern," she said haughtily. "I'm not here to see *you*."

You would have made a good intelligence operative, Virox thought.

"Bryt's never heard of you either," the Ferengi said, pointing to Worf's disruptor. "Could you please lower that thing?"

"No," Worf said.

"I heard from an acquaintance that your employer has recently acquired items of immense interest to my associate."

The Ferengi's eyes settled on Virox. "I don't know what you're talking about."

Worf growled.

"We both know that's not true," Troi said. They had rescanned the planet. Now the ship sensors only recorded a dead spot in the middle of the Essar ruins. Worf was certain that Xiomara's treasures were there.

Virox's voice in Troi's head was warm and oddly disconcerting. *This is all about the big lie to get what we want.*

Troi had to resist the urge to share her disgust with Virox. But she had to admit that the House leader was right.

"Look," the Ferengi said. "Bryt's not seeing anyone. Situation's hot."

Troi raised an eyebrow. "Hot? Is it because Bryt recently acquired *three* items of cultural significance?"

The Ferengi's eyes went wide, and Troi knew she had him. Suddenly, Worf yanked the energy whip out of his hand and tossed it away, out of reach.

"Hey!" the Ferengi protested. "That's not your property!"

"But *this* is yours." Worf slipped a half slip of latinum into his pocket.

The guard looked insulted.

Virox lifted an eyebrow. Worf pulled out a whole slip.

Before he could grab it, Troi stepped in front of the guard, aware of Virox following behind her. "Take us to see Bryt the Baron."

The Ferengi gazed up at her, something like panic in his eyes. "You don't know much about Bryt, do you?"

You don't have to lie about everything *when you're under cover,* Virox offered.

"No," Troi said finally. "I am bound and determined to obtain those artifacts."

Virox stepped forward. "Profit enough for everyone."

"That's well and good," the Ferengi said. "Bryt doesn't *see* anyone."

Troi frowned. "He is not interested in our latinum?"

Good, said Virox.

"He's very interested," the Ferengi said, and Worf stepped back. "*Finally.* Thank you." He smoothed out his shirt. "Bryt doesn't let anyone see him face-to-face. Not me, not his contractors, and not even clothed fe-males."

Troi narrowed her eyes at him. "Can we *speak* to him?"

The Ferengi hesitated. Worf slipped the latinum into his pocket. "Uh, that I can probably manage. No promises."

Troi felt her shoulders soften. She hadn't realized how tense she was.

"Bryt will be very interested in hearing from us when he finds out what we can offer," Virox said, sweeping her arm about grandly. "Unless the Ferengi are no longer interested in profit." She leaned down and traced her finger along the Ferengi's ear, making him tremble.

Worf watched Virox's display stone-faced. Troi stepped over to him while Virox whispered something into the Ferengi's ear.

"Is that really necessary?" Worf murmured.

"*Hija*," Troi answered.

"You've been practicing."

Troi winked at him.

The Ferengi let out a shivery little noise of delight while Virox grinned wickedly and Troi schooled her expression.

"Fine, fine!" he yelped. "You can wait inside. I'll see what I can do about getting you in contact with Bryt."

Virox peeled away from the guard, looking pleased with herself. "Thank you, darling," she purred. "I know Bryt won't be disappointed." She smiled slyly. "Nor will you."

Worf made a sound like a strangled cough.

Aviana Virox looped her arm into the guard's as he led them over to the entrance. He slapped his hand on the identity pad while he gazed dreamily up at her. The door slid open, releasing a sweet, heady scent. Some kind of incense. It smelled expensive.

"I have potential buyers," the Ferengi announced to an Orion woman lounging behind an ornately carved desk, positioned at the entrance to the structure. She looked up at the group appraisingly as they stepped inside. The space was small and dark.

"Bryt's busy," she cooed, picking up a slim silver nail tipper and then fitting it over her index finger. It buzzed and when she slid it off, her nail had been transformed into a sharp, curling black talon. She held her hand out and admired her work.

"I know that," the Ferengi said, scuttling up to the desk. "They can wait until he's ready."

The Orion dropped her hand in her lap. "Fine," she said. "But the Klingon has to give up his disruptor." She frowned. "And run them through the weapons scanner."

"You heard the lady." The Ferengi turned to Worf with a grin, although it quickly vanished once Worf met his eye.

"I'm keeping my *mek'leth*," he snarled.

The Ferengi looked nervously at the Orion woman, but she just waved one hand dismissively. "Fine," she said, returning to her nails.

Worf glowered. He dropped the disruptor on the Orion's desk.

"Right this way," the Ferengi said solicitously.

"Weapons scanner," the Orion called out without looking up.

The Ferengi scowled at her, but he did pull out a scanner and waved it apologetically over Troi and Virox. It beeped at Troi's hip, and she sighed and gave him her phaser. Then he scanned Worf.

"All clear," he said. "Now—" He held out his hand toward a darkened staircase.

"Absolutely not!" Worf barked out. He put his hand on Troi's shoulder. "I am not allowing them to go down in the dark."

The Orion woman was now watching them with bemused interest.

"What do you care?" the Ferengi said. "You'll be with them."

Worf growled. The Ferengi skittered backward, bumping up against Virox.

"Oh, don't mind my Klingon associate." Virox drew the Ferengi closer to her and brushed her fingers over his ears. "I'm sure it's perfectly safe."

To Troi, she sent a thought: *Tell Worf not to be so overprotective.*

Troi touched Worf's arm. "It's fine," she said in Klingon.

She felt Worf's worry and his frustrated distrust of the Ferengi, of Bryt the Baron, and the inky darkness waiting at the bottom of the stairs.

"Yeah, nothing to worry about, big guy." The Ferengi eyed the *mek'leth* as he squeezed past them and started down the stairs. Worf stepped right behind him. Troi followed, with Virox right behind her.

This Bryt is apparently reclusive, Virox thought, *although our Ferengi friend there won't tell me much more than that. No one knows much about him, only that he's terribly rich and feared in the criminal underworld.*

Troi glanced back at Virox. *You got all that?*

Virox smiled, her thoughts sparkling.

She was having *fun*, Troi realized.

What do you think I was talking to him about? If this Bryt the Baron is as reclusive as our friend says, we're going to have our work cut out for us.

They reached the bottom of the stairs. The air was cooler down here, lit by pale lights that traced a path through the stony walls. A cave deep underground was exactly what Troi pictured when she imagined the lair of a wealthy Ferengi criminal.

"The VIP lounge is *right* this way," the Ferengi called out, stepping sideways to avoid Worf.

"If this is a trap—" Worf started.

"It's not!" The Ferengi looked over his shoulder. "The baron just prefers his spaces *dark*."

Eventually, they came to a door set into the rock of the wall. "Here we are," the Ferengi said. "The VIP lounge, for VIPs." He grinned at Virox for half a second before whirling around and pressing his hand against the ID pad.

The door whisked open, and Troi was grateful to see that it was well lit with warm golden lights. Soft, tinkling music spilled out into the hallway.

The Ferengi gestured for them to go in, still beaming at Virox. Worf stepped inside. Troi tried to check out the room.

Recognition shot through Worf.

Troi reached into her pocket, ready to call the *Enterprise* for an extraction.

There was another person in the lounge. She sat in an elaborate brocaded chair in the corner, her legs kicked up on what looked like a rather expensive and very old Bajoran-style table.

She looked up, a smile curved across her lips.

Thuvetha.

She'd spotted them, and it was clear from her expression and from the sense of giddy delight pouring out of her that she recognized them.

28

———•———

"First order of business," Cecil Solanko said. "Get Commander Data to the camp."

The crew was standing outside the station, which was still without power. Solanko had estimated that they had another seven or eight hours before the autoshutdown would start, and tensions were high. Josefina Rikkilä felt as if she were racing against the clock. Earlier, no tech was working; now the combadges had reconnected. It should have been a relief, but it wasn't— it just meant another unknown variable.

"Transporters are still down," Malisson said. "And I wouldn't recommend using them."

"Agreed," Solanko said.

Rikkilä raised her hand. "Permission to speak freely, sir?"

"Go ahead."

"I went through the full round of field-medic training at the Academy. I can put together a simple gurney to transport the lieutenant out of the station." She gestured over at the table. "I can dismantle some of this furniture."

"Perfect," Solanko said. "Talma, you help her. Malisson, keep working on that replicator. Get as many rations as you can out of it."

Malisson turned back to the replicator, below which sand still littered the floor. She was running the replicator off a battery she'd retrieved from dismantling some of the laboratory scanners. It gave the replicator power, but that didn't mean it was functioning normally.

"Muñoz, you and I will focus on moving equipment over to the camp." He nodded once. "Let's go."

Rikkilä joined Talma over by the table. "We can use this as the frame," she said. "Although we're going to need to break it in half." She frowned. "It's too big. And the phasers—"

"No phasers," Talma said glumly. That had been one of Riker's orders before he set out for the beach with Doctor Crusher.

"Much harder without our equipment," Rikkilä muttered. Her field-medic training had covered some of these kinds of contingencies—what to do if you didn't have access to a replicator or a padd—but it hadn't covered a full-on power failure. Still, she had learned how to create a gurney using standard equipment.

Like phasers.

"The table's not one piece," Talma said, flipping it on its side. "We can separate the top from the legs easily enough."

"Good point," Rikkilä said. The table had clearly been replicated in pieces and then assembled afterward. They quickly removed the legs and set them aside. "If we can brace the tabletop," Talma said, "I bet we can snap it in half."

Rikkilä's eyes were itching—smoke. It was coming from the common room.

"Sorry!" shouted Malisson from over by the replicator. "I'm trying to get some protein packs from this stupid thing—"

The smoke belched out, thick and black, and hung around the rafters of the common room.

"Is that the battery?" Rikkilä asked.

"No, it's the replicator itself!" Malisson sounded exasperated. The smoke grew thicker, forming into dark clouds. "There's no fire," she added.

"That's something, at least," Rikkilä said.

The smoke hung heavy, like an encroaching storm. Rikkilä

hoisted up the table and leaned it against a clear spot on the wall and nodded at Talma.

"Let's see if my Bolian martial-arts training comes in handy," he said with a grin, and then he hoisted up his left leg, hooking it at an angle. Rikkilä held her breath as he slammed his foot into the table.

There was a loud, sharp *crack*. A line arced through the material of the table.

"It's working," Josefina said.

Talma brought his foot down on the table a second time. Splinters of material scattered up into the air. The table cracked in the center.

"Third time's the charm," Talma said, and kicked again.

The table snapped in half, the bottom piece skittering out across the floor. But the top piece didn't clatter down like Rikkilä expected. It had jammed into the wall.

"Oh no," she breathed. She ran up to inspect the wall. "The biomass," she said. "It's getting soft!"

"That's not possible," Talma said. "We have eight more hours, and Commander Riker hasn't given the execution code."

"I know. But look!" Rikkilä grabbed the piece of the table and tugged. It came away easily, bringing with it a few flecks of biomass. She pressed her fingers against the indentation. It still felt solid, but there was a faint sponginess that sent a chill down her spine.

She tapped her combadge. "Rikkilä to Solanko."

"Go ahead."

"We have a problem here."

Josefina Rikkilä knotted the last bedsheet around the makeshift gurney, securing the final handle. She was in the sleeping quarters, working quickly. It was hard to stop herself from looking up at the walls, trying to see if they had gotten softer in the time it had taken her and Talma to assemble the gurney.

"Malisson can't find out what's happening with the station." Solanko strode into the sleeping quarters. "But the biomass is definitely starting to decay."

"It shouldn't be starting so soon," Talma said.

Solanko's face was dark. "I know. Which is why we need to work fast. I hope you have some good news for me." He gestured at the gurney.

"We do," Rikkilä said. "Just finished."

"Perfect." Solanko walked over to where the gurney was set up on a bed. Rikkilä had wrapped the table in sheets stripped from the beds, knotting them the way she'd learned in training to create the handles. Now all they had to do was transfer Lieutenant Data onto it.

"As soon as the lieutenant is secured at camp," Solanko said, "I want the two of you gathering as many supplies as you can from the station. With the biomass softening, we don't know how long we've got."

"Understood," Talma said, and Rikkilä nodded in agreement.

"Now, Ensign," Solanko said, "how do we do this without an antigrav device?"

"Push the beds together," Rikkilä said. "Minimize the space."

Talma was already on it, shoving the bed with the gurney up against Data's own bed.

"One of you at his head, the other at his feet," Rikkilä said. "I'll help lift from his center." She had learned how to transfer patients in training—antigrav devices and transporters weren't always available in the field—but she hadn't expected to have to do it on her first away mission.

Talma and Solanko arranged themselves. Rikkilä slipped her

hands under Data's hips. He was unmoving, his face blank. She only hoped they would be able to bring him back once they were on the *Enterprise* again.

"Count of three," she murmured. "One. Two. Three."

With a burst of breath, all three of them lifted Data off the bed. Josefina's grip was light, but she could see the strain in Solanko's and Talma's arms as they moved Data sideways, setting him on the gurney.

She allowed herself a sigh of relief. "We did it."

Solanko was already twining the handle around his arm. "Let's get him to camp."

As they lifted up the gurney, Rikkilä's chest was tight: she had visions of the sheets unwrapping, of Data crashing onto the floor. But her work held, and Solanko and Talma headed toward the exit, the gurney holding fast between them. Josefina grabbed ahold of the third handle, which she had affixed to the front of the gurney, and guided them into the hallway, toward the front exit.

Malisson was back at the replicator, muttering under her breath as more sand piled up.

"I got some water," she called out as they moved Data past her. "But it's salt water. At least the battery is holding up."

"Keep trying," Solanko said. "I can send Muñoz foraging for food. Water's going to be more precious."

The smoke was still hanging in black clouds near the ceiling, and Rikkilä thought she caught a dark, earthy scent. A whiff of mulch.

Biomass.

They spilled out into the sunlight. The sun was at a high angle in the sky, bright and golden. Doctor Crusher and Commander Riker said to come find them if they weren't back by sunset. Which seemed like too long.

The team had started building the camp about five hundred

meters away from the station, to give themselves plenty of space in the event that it collapsed unexpectedly. It didn't seem far when they'd been hiking out here with the initial supplies. But carrying the lieutenant made the walk feel like a hundred kilometers. The sun was sweltering; sweat dripped down Rikkilä's spine. She could see the flash of red from the emergency tarp, a stunning contrast against the endless sweep of pale grass.

"Almost there," Solanko grunted.

Rikkilä's arms strained. The tent loomed up ahead, the material flapping in the breeze.

"Place him out of the sun," Solanko said as they approached, and Rikkilä directed them into the tent proper. With a sigh, all three set the gurney down in the grass. Rikkilä stumbled away, her arms shaking.

Data's eyes flew open.

"Lieutenant?" Solanko's eyes were wide beneath his sweat-soaked forehead.

Data lifted his gaze. "Lieutenant Solanko. Lieutenant Talma." He turned his head. "Ensign Rikkilä. Where am I?"

Rikkilä pulled out her tricorder and knelt down beside him. The tricorder appeared to be reporting that everything was normal with the android.

"We brought you outside to the camp," Talma said.

"The camp?" Data sat up abruptly.

"A lot has happened since you've been out," Solanko said. "But the most pressing thing is that the station is going to collapse."

Rikkilä kept scrolling through her tricorder readings. Why had he woken up? Taking him out of the station seemed to be the differentiating factor. Isolating him from the rest of the tech in the station—

A loud, distant *thump* rang out across the field. Rikkilä scrambled to her feet, her gaze turning toward the station.

A dark plume rose up against the violet sky.

"The station," Rikkilä gasped.

Commander Solanko's combadge chirped, and Malisson's voice chimed out.

"Commander—it's starting."

29

―――

At first, neither of them moved from the top of the dune. Crusher took it upon herself to make the first step, sand avalanching down around her as she slid sideways toward the shore.

Immediately, she heard the rustling of Riker following her. A few paces away the water broke against an outcropping of stone in little firecracker bursts, sending sea spray soaring across her face. She pulled out her tricorder. The expected readings: oxygen levels, moisture levels, trace gases in the air. Everything was normal.

"So?" Riker stood beside her, and they stepped into wet sand at the dune's base.

"Still working," she said, "so far."

"Mine's working too." Riker looked up from the screen. "I'm reading a number of those fossils the team told us about."

The fossils. She looked down at her tricorder. She scrolled through the readouts. *Fossilized matter: 398 individual pieces.*

Something flashed on the edge of Crusher's vision.

She looked out over the waves rolling gently in. The storm seemed like it was closer, the clouds thick and black.

"How dangerous are the storms here?" she asked.

"One did kill Commander N'yss. But this one is a ways off. We have time. It helps that the tech seems to be working."

Crusher was studying her tricorder, the readings shifting slightly as the wind lifted or a wave crested and sent sprays of water pluming over the beach.

Another flash of movement. Will? She was farther out than she expected—the water was nearly to her ankles. How had she not noticed?

Another flash of movement. This time Crusher turned, following it. She saw a dark blur skimming across the top of the water. The doctor tapped her combadge. Dead.

"Will!" she shouted.

The dark blur stopped. What was it? She lifted her tricorder. No change. Nothing.

Then, as Crusher watched, it blinked out, like a flare of sunlight.

Crusher moved forward. She was vaguely aware of a tricorder alert; she glanced down at it. No change.

A particularly big wave slammed into her knees. She hit the water and sank, her eyes wide open. All she saw was the dark, murky water. Where was the bottom? It wasn't that deep here. Why was she drifting downward, a sense of vast enormity stretching out around her?

She brought the tricorder up. Except it wasn't a tricorder. It was a ball of light. No—several balls of light, linked by sharp lines at odd angles.

Crusher gasped and stood straight up.

She was on the beach. On the sand. The waves rolled in around her; the ocean stretched out to those looming black clouds.

But she was soaked, drenched in salt water, and exhausted. She fell back in the wet sand and stared up at the violet sky. The clouds moved fast, dark spots on the sky's endless canvas.

They're communicating, she thought, and hit her chest. No combadge.

"Will?" she cried out hoarsely. She pushed herself up. The tide was going out, the water pulling back, revealing the tide pools among the rocks. "Will?" she called out again, more loudly.

Her head was so heavy. "Will!"

The waves answered, a constant, steady roar.

And then another voice answered, a low, steady howl. The wind. *Data.*

She forced her head up. A dark-gray rain line moved across the water. She could smell the metal in the air.

Someone was walking on the water.

Who?

With a burst of strength, Crusher crashed down onto the beach. Her head spun. The first drops of rain fell on her face. "Will!"

The figure watched her. She turned; it was amorphous and ill-defined, billowing like the clouds.

"We aren't here to hurt you!" Crusher shouted at it, the howling wind swallowing her voice. She imagined it opening its mouth and letting the sound of the wind roar out, as Data had done.

A chill raced down her spine. From the cold air? From something else?

The dark mass on the water dispersed into wisps, and then the rain hit, a torrential curtain that made Crusher feel as if she were drowning. She raced back to the shore, ducking her head, sputtering at the rainwater.

Crusher splashed through the tide pools, their surfaces churning with rainfall, and flung herself at the base of the dunes. She whipped her head up and down the beach—where was Will? He wouldn't have left her here.

The team had passed out on the shore. Data had found them.

"Doctor?"

Crusher craned her head around. Data was there standing on the dune, smiling placidly.

"Data?" It didn't make sense. Even if he had gotten better, why would he come out here? "Why are you here? I need help. I can't find—"

Data's smile widened and widened until his mouth was open wide. Then, he was howling.

Crusher stumbled backward, over her own feet. She landed hard on her backside and her hands sank into the wet sand. Her fingers brushed against something solid. The edge of her tricorder stuck out of the sand.

She scraped the sand away, grains clumping on her fingers. The rain made her grip slick as she pulled the tricorder out of the sand.

She looked back over her shoulder. Data was gone.

"Data?" she called out uncertainly. She looked back at the tricorder. It didn't look right. The case was cracked and decaying, the screen murky. It looked as if it had been buried for—

Years.

Crusher's heart thumped. She whirled around on the empty, rain-swept beach.

Dreams. The others had complained of dreams. It was their primary symptom after the initial attack.

She looked back down at the tricorder. It didn't feel like a dream. It didn't have the hazy, distant quality that her dreams had. She felt soaked through and was shivering. The tricorder felt solid.

Not real. Not exactly.

A burst of thunder erupted from the clouds, so loud Crusher felt it in her chest. A few seconds later, lightning cracked down through the sky, striking the point on the dune where "Data" had stood. A smell like ozone drifted on the air.

That didn't make sense—thunder before lightning?

The lightning struck again, with no thunderous explosion, hitting the side of the dune. Crusher jumped.

Again. Now it was on the beach.

It was moving toward her.

Crusher clutched the tricorder to her chest and ran, her feet sinking into the sand as she heard the explosion of thunder behind a crackle and sizzle of lightning each time it hit the sand. She veered toward the tide pools, the jagged outcropping of rocks where the waves slammed with a shuddering, violent force.

Then she heard something, distantly—a steady, mechanical beeping.

Another lightning bolt struck behind her, close enough that she felt the searing heat of it. She flung herself up against the rocks, whirling around in time to see another lightning strike—this one moving away from her, back up the sandy strip of the beach.

Crusher took a few deep breaths. The tricorder was still beeping. How was it working? It had been destroyed.

Light moved across the tricorder screen, the words blurred by sand and water. Crusher wiped it clean with her hand, scraping the sand away. She thought she'd see binary code or streams of random words, but instead there was an actual reading. The elements in the air, the barometric pressure.

She scrolled through it, watching the lightning as it continued to strike the beach. Then the rainstorm came, and she could see the dark holes where the lightning hit the ground. Oddly, dark fractal lines splayed out across the sand in sharp angles.

Circles and lines, she thought.

The thunder crashed again, loud and violent. This time, the lightning stayed in the sky, frozen in place, illuminating the clouds.

The doctor looked down at the tricorder readings. Everything was *normal.* Except—

Fossilized matter: 98,309 individual pieces.

She gasped, pushed herself up to standing. Could inert, microscopic fossils suddenly exist in such high concentration? It made no sense. She braced herself against the rocks as droplets of water from the rain scattered across the tricorder screen, distorting the words.

Those fossils had always been there, lurking in the background. They were the key.

The storm was calming, the rain falling steadily but less harshly. The thunder rumbled off in the distance. Crusher peeled herself off the rock and moved forward, toward the site of a lightning strike. She held out the tricorder, scanning the dark hole that had been left behind.

Nothing. The tricorder didn't pick up even the charged ions, nor the subtle changes in the sand's composition.

Which meant it wasn't working, she told herself. Even though it *seemed* to be.

She moved on to the next hole, only a few steps from the first. The dark lines tangled together in the sand. They were all like that, she realized as she followed the path of the lightning down the beach. Circles arranged in a loop, connected by angled lines. Crusher scrambled over to the dunes, her feet sinking deep into the wet sand. She grabbed fistfuls of sand and grass as she pushed herself upward. Finally, she was standing on the top of the dune, the soft patter of rain falling around her. From here she had a view of the entire beach, of the pattern etched across it.

The same lines as had burned into the station grass.

Dozens of dark circles connected by a complicated tangle of lines. Even the rain, falling gray and steady, couldn't wash it away.

She drew up the tricorder, but it had turned into the same pattern, made out of light.

Rain dripped into her eyes. She was underwater, everything murky and dark. But then a line of light shot out of her hand— out of the tricorder, fractaling and branching until it hit another point of light.

Will?

Crusher pushed herself forward through the water. The beach was underneath her, the sand covered in the lines. Riker floated, his hair drifting loose around his face.

And then a line of light shot out of him, carving its way through the water until another point of light bloomed.

You need to go outside, Data's voice whispered in her head.

The tricorder offered up streams of words. Communication.

Water filled her lungs.

Then she was sputtering on the beach, coughing up ocean water as she lay on her back in the dry sand. She rolled onto her side, spitting out the water until her lungs felt clear.

"Communication," she murmured. Images drifted through her thoughts. Lines and circles. Light. Riker floating in the water.

She pushed herself up, the left side of her head throbbing. The rain had stopped. No, it hadn't rained at all—the storm clouds were still gathering on the horizon.

Crusher stood up, her legs shaking. There was an ache in her joints usually associated with high fevers. The sunlight, dim and filtered through the clouds, still seemed too bright.

She stumbled sideways, turning in a circle, and nearly tripped over Will, who was sprawled out on the sand.

"Will!" Crusher cried, and she knelt down to check his pulse. It was sure and steady, his breath warm on her hand.

A flash of lightning. Thunder rumbled off in the distance. She froze.

Lightning.

It had chased after her, in her dream.

Communication.

The lightning hadn't chased her.

It had carved a message into the sand, just as the biomass had used a phaser to carve a message in the grass.

Crusher hit her combadge. "Crusher to Kota Station," she shouted. "I need immediate assistance."

The only answer was the crackly, staticky wind sound.

The doctor realized she didn't have her tricorder. Did she

drop it in the water as she stumbled ashore? She'd had it in her dream.

Crusher leaned back on her heels, brushing the sand off Will's face.

"Not a dream," she said.

The wind howled through the rocks jutting out into the water.

The realization came with the storm clouds darkening, the waves rolling in.

Something had used the biomass. Something was using her and the others.

"Damn." She'd been right. Something on this planet really *was* trying to communicate.

30

"Come in, come in," the Ferengi guard said, bustling into the center of the lounge. "Don't mind her. She *bullied*"—he shot Thuvetha an angry glance—"her way in here."

"I did not," the Romulan said coolly. She studied the others. "Do come in," she said. "It will be a while."

The Ferengi ordered her, "Quiet, fe-male."

Troi waited for Thuvetha to announce their true identities.

Nothing. When the commander eased down on a nearby chair, Worf glowered and took his *mek'leth* from his back. When Virox walked in, Thuvetha's expression darkened, but she still kept silent. Virox, for her part, kept her face blank, as if she'd never in her life seen Thuvetha before. Inwardly, though, Virox was seething; Troi could feel it.

"I'll tell Bryt you're here," the Ferengi guard said. "Then we can open negotiations." He glared at Thuvetha. "And get rid of *you*."

"These are the buyers?" The Romulan raised an eyebrow.

The Ferengi sniffed. "Potential buyers, yes."

"I should be paid first." Thuvetha grinned coyly at Virox. "As stated in the contract . . ."

"I told you." The Ferengi bristled. "Bryt will see you *shortly*."

The Ferengi offered Troi and Virox an apologetic smile, then crept nervously past Worf, shutting the door behind him.

The room fell into silence. Troi could feel the Romulan's hostility.

Worf stepped forward, the *mek'leth* balanced in his hand.

"Klingon, what are you doing here?" She tossed her braid over her shoulder. "Madam Virox, I'm glad to see you are fine."

"We both know that's not true," Virox snapped.

Thuvetha rolled her eyes. "Whatever you're trying to do isn't going to work. It was Madam Virox who stole the treasures."

"And the real Madam Virox who returns them," Virox shot back.

"You think I won't try again? Framing you was an afterthought."

"Where are the artifacts?" Worf growled.

Reaching into her jacket, Thuvetha extracted a small disruptor. "I handed them over to Bryt the Baron."

"Please lower your weapon," Troi said, feeling Worf's rage.

"This thing?" Thuvetha laughed. "It barely stuns. But I can get it past Bryt's weapon scanners. I'm surprised they let you bring that in here." She nodded at the *mek'leth.* "What's with the clothes?"

Worf bristled.

"I'm not interested in shooting you." Thuvetha slipped the disruptor back into her coat. "What are you doing here?"

"We are trying to retrieve the items you stole," Troi said calmly.

"They're with the baron."

"Why are you still here?" Worf demanded.

Thuvetha sighed dramatically and flung herself back onto the sofa, kicking her legs up on the nearby table. "I wasn't *just* trying to frame Virox. That was a bonus. But Bryt's trying to rip me off." She smiled. "He doesn't know how patient I can be."

"Rip you off?" Troi frowned.

Thuvetha laughed. "This isn't the Federation. I expect to be compensated for my work."

Troi resisted the urge to roll her eyes. "So you stole the items for the Ferengi? And not just to—" She gestured at Virox.

"For *a* Ferengi. Bryt."

"What did Bryt want with the artifacts?" Virox demanded.

"Profit?" Thuvetha shrugged. "I suppose. I really don't know." She shot an angry look at the three-quarter round Ferengi door in the wall. The commander supposed it led to wherever Bryt the Baron was secreting himself away. "Are you recording me?"

She looked at Worf when she asked the question. Worf drew himself up, straightening his back, and didn't answer.

"You can't be. The scanners would have picked up on any devices. Unless"—her eyes glittered—"new Starfleet technology?"

Worf looked at Troi. "I don't get a sense that she's keeping something from us. At least nothing important."

Thuvetha laughed. "Well, I *was* going to tell you what I know about Bryt."

She's angry at Bryt, Virox said to Troi. *Furious, in fact. She hides it well, but I know how she thinks.*

I would like to know how she kidnapped you, Troi said. *She doesn't seem* that *keen on revenge.*

Virox sent a wave of exasperation. *My fault. I got rusty.*

"Why should we trust what you tell us?" Worf asked.

Thuvetha smiled. "You shouldn't."

Worf let out a loud, frustrated sigh as Thuvetha's grin just widened.

The Klingon looked at Troi.

"She's not lying," Troi said. "She's more aggravated at Bryt the Baron than she is at us."

"True," Thuvetha purred. "I have a children's toy for a weapon and if you were to search my ship, you'd find it full of perfectly legitimate medical supplies."

"We know that you stole the treasures," Worf said.

"If I tell you everything I know about Bryt, you'll just forget about the theft?" She smiled sweetly. "I'm just some simple Romulan off a colony world." She spread her hands out.

A lie, Virox thought.

"How long have you been waiting for Bryt?" Troi asked.

"You mean you don't know exactly when I arrived here?"

"Answer the question," Worf snapped.

"Six hours." Thuvetha settled back on the sofa. "You might wait less. I wonder what they'll do when they figure out you don't actually have any latinum."

"Oh?" Troi said.

"Is Starfleet replicating latinum these days?"

"Enough." Worf's voice was a menacing whisper. "Tell us what you know. If we are able to retrieve the items"—he took a deep breath and spoke the next part slowly, as if it was a threat—"then I will see about getting you a pardon for their theft."

"Bryt's criminal enterprise rose to prominence ten years ago," Thuvetha said. "Ferengi always have the most interesting . . . interests." She grinned. "I kept hearing his name: Bryt the Baron just sold a chest of Gorn gold, Bryt the Baron bought out the Fa'ud gang, Bryt the Baron purchased the Essar ruins." She laughed. "Derak reached out to me about a job on Betazed, I thought why not?" She winked at Virox. "It would be a perfect time to visit an old friend."

"Who is Derak?" Worf asked.

"Oh." Thuvetha waved her hand around. "Bryt's little mouthpiece. He'll be bustling in here eventually to talk to you."

"So it's true," Troi said. "We won't speak with Bryt directly."

Thuvetha looked at Troi for a moment, then burst into laughter, her disdain apparent. "No one sees Bryt. *No one.* Derak doesn't even see Bryt. He talks to him through a combadge."

"How does Derak know who he's speaking to?" Worf asked.

"Who cares?" Thuvetha said. "Maybe Derak's running the whole operation, I don't know. And I don't care. *Someone's* behind it. Someone's stockpiling latinum." She glowered. "And not paying their *contractor.*"

Unusual for a Ferengi, keeping his identity secret, Troi thought. *Maybe Bryt isn't a Ferengi, but someone who wanted to convince everyone he was. Why?*

"The three treasures of Xiomara," Virox asked. "Why would a Ferengi—"

Troi felt that Virox already knew the answer; she was just toying with the Romulan.

Of course I am. Toying with Romulans was my job for over a decade.

Get out! It's rude, Troi said, not even bothering to try to hide her irritation.

"There are buyers who are interested in cultural artifacts." Thuvetha shrugged. "I have to say, your disguises aren't half bad." She looked appraisingly at Worf. "A Klingon is pretty unusual."

"Is there anything else?" Worf said. "Anything *useful?*"

"Bryt's trying to rip me off," Thuvetha said. "Useful enough for you?"

A chime sounded through the room, and the Ferengi-style door slid open. Out stepped an exceedingly well-tailored Ferengi carrying a padd tucked under one arm. Troi assumed this was Derak.

"Ah," he called out. "My buyers. How *lovely* to meet you!"

He glided forward, clearly avoiding Thuvetha.

"Where's my payment?" she asked.

The Ferengi stopped, drew himself up. "I *told* you, Bryt is working on it."

"Fifty bars of latinum," Thuvetha said.

"Madams," he said, bowing slightly to Deanna and Virox. "My name is Derak. I will be working with you today to find an arrangement that meets all of our needs." He turned to Virox. "Are you Amica?"

Virox stood up from her chair. "That is correct," she said softly. "My associate, Dorota, our bodyguard."

Derak checked on his padd. "Oh, marvelous, marvelous." He peered up at Troi. "Your names aren't in our database."

"Yes," Troi said. "We had a—*disagreement* with our previous patron and decided to strike out on our own." She smiled sweetly, aware of Thuvetha's amusement radiating off her.

"Excellent." Derak plastered on an unctuous grin. "Would you like to see the artifacts?"

Troi felt Worf's interest pique behind her, and a surge of hopeful relief.

"Of course," Virox said, and Derak led them back to the small door, which he opened with the press of his palm. Thuvetha glared at him, her arms crossed. He ignored her.

"This way," he said, and Worf stepped up in front of the women, *mek'leth* at the ready. Derak eyed it nervously. "You won't be needing *that*," he said as Worf ducked through the doorway.

They were standing in a large, sleek showroom. Items were displayed behind faint shimmers of force fields: weapons, jewelry, antiques, technology Troi didn't recognize. What she didn't see were the three treasures.

"I don't see them," Virox said sharply.

Derak chuckled apologetically. "Forgive me. We're keeping those particular items in a special storage room. They're quite valuable, as you know."

Troi sighed. So much for grabbing them and beaming out. But that was always a long shot.

"Why," Worf said, "did you bring us in here?"

Derak laughed. "Oh, we have holoscans! The items are safe and sound." He tapped on his padd.

"Lot 489," he said as the holo of the Sacred Silver materialized. A well-worn spoon, with a fine filigreed handle.

"Lot?" Troi looked at him sideways, trying to keep her voice light. "You aren't selling them as a set?"

Derak's smile widened. "Well, no, of course not. But I'm sure we can reach an arrangement—"

"The other two items?" Virox interrupted.

An arrangement, Troi thought.

"Of course. Lot 490." The holo changed and the Enshrined Disk came into view, a flat clay platter, hand painted and fired in a kiln until it shone. "And Lot 491." The Hallowed Urn. A round, fat vase, unadorned and simple.

"How do we know you actually have these items?" Worf said, his voice booming through the hush of the gallery. "A hologram is no guarantee."

Derak deactivated the holo and tucked the padd into his coat. "Sir, how could we earn a profit if we didn't have the items to sell?"

"How much?" Virox demanded. "For all three lots?"

Derak pulled his padd back out and checked it. "We have these lots priced at five thousand bars—"

"*Five thousand* bars?" Troi asked.

"Apiece," Derak finished. "And that's a steal, considering that Lot 489 should really be priced much higher, given its direct lineage back to the Betazoid hero Xiomara—"

"We know who Xiomara is," Troi snapped. She took a deep breath, calming herself. "What about the arrangement you mentioned? Surely we can get a discount for purchasing the set."

"Oh, I don't set the prices," Derak said. "My employer does."

"And how did he reach those numbers?" Virox asked.

"He has *many* interested buyers," Derak said smoothly. He coughed a little. "*Others,*" he added cryptically. "You're lucky you arrived here as soon as you did." He paused, settling his gaze onto Troi. "So soon after they were delivered by our acquirer."

"Things that were separated for five hundred years? News travels fast," Virox said.

"Of course. Now, how will you transfer the bars?" Derak looked up brightly.

"That price," Worf said, "is absurd. No one buyer will have fifteen thousand bars of gold-pressed latinum at hand."

Troi stepped forward. "Agreed. Bryt can't possibly expect anyone to pay that price."

Derak's eyes glittered. "Bryt is always open to negotiation. If you have a counteroffer—"

Troi nodded. "Five thousand for all three."

Derak burst into laughter. "You can't be serious. Five thousand is far too low."

"Fine." Virox stepped forward. "Ten thousand. I think Bryt will find that offer *most* generous."

Again, Derak looked at his padd. "Reasonable," he said. "But what else do you have to offer?" His eyes zeroed in on Worf's *mek'leth*.

"Absolutely not," Worf growled.

"What about the cloak, then?" Derak reached out to touch the thick fabric, but Worf slapped his hand away. "Was it handwoven on Boreth? It certainly has the look."

Troi felt a burst of hopefulness. The Ferengi thought the cloak was genuine. It wouldn't pass muster under any kind of scan, but if they could sell it for the treasures—

"Yes," she said, stepping in front of Worf. "It has been in his family for generations."

"It's why we hired him," Virox said. "We wanted a bodyguard who understands history."

Derak reached out to the cloak again, but this time Worf brought his *mek'leth* up. It was enough. Derak's hand shot back to his side.

"No," Worf said.

Derak's eyes widened. He tapped something into his padd, and his eyes widened even farther.

He said excitedly, "Perhaps we can come to some sort of arrangement after all."

"I certainly hope so," Virox purred.

Worf scowled, smoothing his hand over his cloak protectively.

"Are you sure he'll sell it?" Derak asked.

Worf smiled, showing all his teeth. "I can be convinced, for the right price."

31

———

Ensign Josefina Rikkilä raced through the fields, grass slapping at her uniform. Up ahead, the station looked *wrong*. Lopsided.

"Half the roof has collapsed!" Talma shouted behind her. "How did it happen so fast?"

The tech is sick, she thought. *It's fighting the infection, and failing.* She pumped her legs harder, ducking her head lower. It was too early. The autocollapse shouldn't have started. They'd hardly had a chance to pull out the last of their supplies.

A loud noise cracked across the field, and the right side of the station's roof tilted down, unleashing a cloud of evaporating biomass.

"Grab as much as you can!" Solanko called out, bolting past Rikkilä. Up ahead, Muñoz burst out of the station, bedding fluttering out behind him. The door was gone, sucked back into the walls to prepare for the self-destruct. "If we can use it, grab it!"

The mossy, wet-dirt scent of the biomass as it decomposed was thick and overwhelming. Solanko slowed and turned around to face Rikkilä and Talma. They had agreed that Data should remain back at the camp; the last thing they wanted was for him to risk failure again.

"Move fast," Solanko said, his eyes dark and determined. "We'll be buried if this thing comes down around us."

The ensign nodded, and the three of them stepped through the gaping doorway. The common room was unrecognizable, the remaining furniture half melted into the floor, the walls wet and glossy and dripping. The scent of dirt was so strong that Rikkilä wondered if this was what it smelled like as you were buried alive.

"Talma, you and I will tackle the labs," Solanko said. "Rikkilä, you grab medical supplies. And remember"—the walls shuddered—"if it starts coming down, get out immediately."

He and Talma vanished into the hallway, ducking under a dripping curtain of biomass. Rikkilä picked her way over to the supply closet. The replicator was gone—Malisson must have grabbed it when the collapse started. The alcove where it sat was gleaming and inorganic, startling against the decay. The things that were supposed to be long gone by the time this process was underway.

The supply closet was cramped and shrunken, biomass oozing down the walls in long, thick rivers. It dripped onto the top of the ensign's hand, surprisingly warm. She choked back a gag.

Something crashed in the back of the station.

"Solanko," Rikkilä said into her combadge, "are you all right?"

"We're fine. It was the other lab. Keep working."

She peered into the closet. The shelves had decomposed into a pile of black, rotting strips, like leaves in late autumn, but silver gleamed amid the detritus. Rikkilä swallowed back another gag and plunged her fingers into the wet biomass, digging around for anything inorganic. She pulled out a tricorder and stuck it in her uniform pocket. There had been a medkit in here, full of supplies. Rikkilä scooped up the biomass and flung it backward, scraping out the remains of the closet shelves. She pulled out a padd, another tricorder—and a hypospray.

Rikkilä cursed softly. The medkit was buried too deep to find.

A groan carried through the common room, and the air filled with damp, swirling dust.

"No!" Rikkilä cried, biomass sticking to her tongue. She scraped more fervently through the pile, looking for the rest of the medical supplies, like vials for the hypospray.

Her fingers squelched through the biomass and then closed around something cold and hard. A vial. She let out a long sigh of relief and yanked it up.

Another shudder rippled up from the floor, violently enough that it tossed Rikkilä backward. She landed in a puddle of biomass and immediately scrambled to her feet, gathering up the supplies she'd salvaged. The air was filled with a swirl of mud and decaying matter.

"Ensign!"

Solanko's voice cut through the murk. Rikkilä whirled around, clutching the supplies to her chest, as Talma and Solanko appeared through the dust, gleaming lab equipment in their arms.

"Station's collapsing," he said. "We have to get out now."

"Where's the entrance?" Talma moved forward, his blue skin mottled with the dark biomass. He turned around. "It's collapsed already. We're trapped."

Rikkilä shook her head. "This material is soft," she said. "We can dig our way out."

"Agreed." Solanko plunged forward, Talma and Rikkilä following. At the wall, the ensign dropped the supplies at her feet, took a deep breath, and plunged her hands in. The biomass here was warm and wet, like the inside of a living body. She raked her fingers through it, dropping damp clumps of biomass on the floor. Solanko and Talma were doing the same. They carved through the wall, the ceiling groaning and sinking lower and lower. Rikkilä scraped frantically—how thick *was* this wall?

And then her hand punched through the other side. Sunlight came streaming in, falling in a sharp line across her knees.

"I'm through!" Rikkilä shouted.

A chunk of the ceiling collapsed behind her, making the wall shudder.

"Go, Ensign," Solanko said. "We'll hand the supplies to you."

Rikkilä dove in, squeezing her eyes shut. The biomass showered around her and for a terrifying moment she was sure it was going to envelop her.

But then she burst into the sun, rolling out into the grass. She immediately spun around and thrust her hands into the wall. Something cool and solid was placed in them. The hypospray and the one vial she had found. She yanked them out.

"Got them!" she yelled.

"Talma's coming through."

A spot of blue appeared amid the collapse. Rikkilä grabbed his arm and tugged, pulling him out into the grass, along with a microscanner. Biomass tumbled around them. "The wall's collapsing!" She spat out biomass.

Solanko burst through the wall with tremendous strength and a shower of biomass, rolling clear of the station just as the wall tumbled inward, collapsing into a pile.

"Where's Malisson?" Rikkilä gasped.

"She's clear," Solanko said. "Crawled out through an opening in the sleeping quarters, where the window was. I had to make sure you got out."

Rikkilä nodded. Her entire body was trembling; sweat dripped down her forehead. The air was thick with evaporating biomass. She pushed herself up on one arm just as a great, croaking screech rang out across the field. The roof of the station had bowed inward.

"Solanko!" A familiar voice cut through the groans of the collapsing station. Lieutenant Malisson appeared several paces away, her face covered with biomass, hair matted. "I got the replicator and another scanner," she said. "I think we've got enough scanners that I can cannibalize the batteries."

"We need to get clear of this station," Solanko said. "Now."

The Starfleet officers trudged through the grass, clutching the tech they had rescued. The mulchy scent of biomass was everywhere, like the damp blanket of a forest floor.

A loud *thump* blew through the fields, and a dark cloud rose into the pale sky. Biomass. The station.

Disintegrating.

32

The life-form is here on this beach, Crusher thought.

Why wasn't it detected? It should have been when the planet was scanned.

Crusher pushed herself up to sitting. Wind blew off the water. She had confirmed that there was a life-form. Now she just had to learn how to speak with it.

A piece of driftwood had washed ashore; it jutted up into the air, half buried in the sand, and Crusher dug it out with her fingers. She had so many questions. Why did she remember the hallucinations—the communications—when the others hadn't? What was different?

Crusher stopped digging, sat back on her heels, and wiped her forehead with a sand-streaked hand. How could Starfleet's sensors *miss it?* The dozens of probes that had been in orbit of Kota to record and observe. Nothing.

She yanked out the driftwood, sending an arc of sand glittering on the air. The wood was smooth against her palm, like a stone, and she jabbed the end into a clear patch of sand and drew a circle.

It was a start. She dragged the driftwood through the sand, re-creating the spidery patterns she could picture so easily in her head. Would this work? She had no idea. It was the only thing she could think to try. Communication.

No life signs. She scraped lines and circles all the way down the beach. *How was it missed?*

What if the sensors didn't recognize the life-form *as* one?

Crusher dropped the stick and raced back down the beach, flitting her gaze across the sand, looking for her tricorder. When she'd been under, or dreaming, the number had leaped up to nearly a hundred thousand.

Or was someone trying to *speak* to her?

She slowed to a stop beside Will, who was still stretched out on the sand, fingers twitching, feet scraping furrows in the sand. Alive. There was no sign of her medical tricorder. The number of fossils had been low when the science team discovered them, before the *Enterprise* away team arrived.

It had always been there.

Not fossils.

Something their equipment didn't know. Something—

Again, a flash of movement to the side of Crusher's vision. She whipped her head around, but of course there was nothing there. Crusher could see her handiwork stretching down the beach, the lines wriggling and creating new paths around the circles. She watched as the sand moved on its own. She knelt down on the edge and watched as it moved, working with all the frantic energy of ants.

Distantly, she was aware of her own voice: *You never woke up. They are still speaking to you.*

"Hello?" Crusher called out, her voice uncertain.

The sand didn't stop its motion, rippling and cascading. She thought that it was going to erase her lines, but it was actually adding to it, generating new lines that winged between the circles with an ever-increasing rapidity.

And then one of the lines barreled toward her.

The doctor forced herself to not move. The line stopped so abruptly beside her that it threw up a cloud of sand; then it shot off behind her, heading toward Riker.

"Hello!" she called out. "My name is Beverly Crusher. What's yours?"

Nothing. Likely it didn't understand her. She watched as the line in the sand coiled around Will, forming wide circles connected by lines. Then it took off again, this time running toward the sand dunes. Up the sand dunes. Into the grass.

Scrambling up the dune, Crusher chased after it. The line was cutting through the prairie, the grass rippling upward to mark its path.

She watched the line vanish into the horizon. The doctor felt a strange, hollow emptiness, as if she were watching someone she knew walk away.

The wind blew off the shore, tossing her hair into her face. She stared at the dark imprint left behind in the grass. Was it going toward the station?

Suddenly the dune collapsed. Crusher dropped down into the cool, dry sand, and then she was falling through open air, the wind howling in her ears. After a few moments her fear turned to resignation. This again. She was vaguely aware that she was still on top of the dune, lying on her side, the sun beating down on her. But she was also falling fast, sand glittering around her—

Now she splashed in the ocean, the shore a distant pale streak. Crusher treaded water, kicking her legs above a vast, unimaginable emptiness. Like space, like the vast emptiness she served in.

More howling. The same as before. Lightning flashed behind her. Thunderstorms gathered.

It was repeating. The dream. The message.

Crusher swam toward the shore. "I don't understand you!" she screamed. "I don't know what you want!"

Thunder roared through the sky and the lightning flashed so brightly that for a moment Crusher was blinded. As color came back into the world, she saw that she was closer to the shore, riding on the tops of the waves. The beach was once again empty.

Crusher let the waves pull her to the shore. She sighed, staring out at the black storm clouds, watching the lightning.

Again, she thought. A storm breaking on the ocean. Lightning striking the beach *after* the thunderclaps. The pattern of interconnected circles—

The sand roiling like ants. A million grains moving as one.

The first drops of rain fell across her face.

Howling winds. Lightning burning patterns in the sand. Patterns—

The patterns were here. She could see them. She just didn't know what any of them meant.

"I don't *understand*," she shouted at the air.

The rain fell harder. Crusher stood and ran to the dunes, then up into the grass, toward the station. It was the only thing she could think to do; she had exhausted her options on the beach. She had to let the others know Will was there. Was she still there? Unconscious?

Everything blinked out.

Crusher stumbled to a stop, whirling around. Nothing was here. She was in a dense, shrouded darkness, without any sign of the surrounding fields.

"Hello?" she murmured. Then louder, "Hello?"

She moved in the direction she thought was forward. The darkness made her feel—empty. Abandoned. Like she was the only person on this world.

Something fell.

Crusher thought it looked like a meteor, dropping out of the sky. She moved closer to it through the murk.

Another one fell, leaving a small trail of light.

Another.

Another.

Numbers. She was watching *numbers*, ones and zeros. Binary code. Cascading down like rain.

Something's reprogramming our machines. Something's trying to program us.

"A code," Crusher whispered. The code filled the space around her. She couldn't decipher the code, but she had a strange, certain feeling that she was sharing this dream. That she'd been unconscious.

"We don't know what you're trying to tell us!" she shouted at the storm and the lightning on the beach. "We don't—"

And then she was falling backward into darkness.

Beverly Crusher sat up with a gasp.

"You're awake! That happened faster than I expected." Rikkilä knelt down beside her, running her tricorder over her. "Signs are normal."

Crusher blinked rapidly. She was sitting in the field, surrounded by the tall grasses—although she couldn't see the lumpen shape of the dunes, she could hear the ocean in the distance. She hadn't gone far from the beach.

"How did I get here?" she mumbled. The sunlight felt too bright, blazing into Crusher's eyes. Her throat was dry and scratchy—it didn't look like Rikkilä had any water. She and Riker had brought some. She would need to find it on the beach.

"No idea," Rikkilä said. "But we estimated two hours went by, so I came out here to check up on you, like Commander Riker asked us to." She frowned. "I really wasn't expecting to see you in the grass. I haven't looked for Commander Riker yet—"

"He's probably on the beach." Crusher pushed herself up to standing, wary about her surroundings. The last time she thought she had woken from the trance, she'd actually still been embroiled in it. But she had to admit the air around her did feel—more real, somehow. She didn't have the sense that she was viewing the world through someone else's eyes.

"Bad news, Doctor," Rikkilä said. "No transporter. The station's self-destruct triggered early."

"What?" Crusher said. "I thought we had more time."

Rikkilä shook her head. "So did we. We got as much of our equipment out as we could. One good thing is that Commander Data woke up when we brought him to the camp."

At the mention of Data, Crusher had a flash of memory: the slow-falling code. She looked down at the grass and saw the indentation where she'd been lying. Somehow she had walked over here and then collapsed.

Just like the crew had collapsed on the beach after they were affected.

"Finally," Crusher said. "Some good news. But we need to check on Commander Riker."

Rikkilä nodded and followed Crusher across the grass, toward the dunes.

"If he's passed out, we'll just have to pull him off the beach, won't we?" Rikkilä said. "I can call Data and Malisson to help. Solanko and Muñoz are still out foraging."

"It's not just a beach." Crusher's chest felt tight. The beach was part of the equation. It wasn't the whole thing.

This had never happened until the *Enterprise* away team arrived. Until they had extra hands.

"Doctor? What are you thinking?"

"The equipment isn't dead," Crusher said softly, her walk speeding up into a jog. "It's just passed out."

"What do you mean?"

Crusher took off running, slapping the grass away with her palms.

"Doctor Crusher!" Rikkilä's voice wavered out behind her, caught on the howling wind. "You know you shouldn't be running like that—"

Crusher skittered to a stop on the top of the dune. And let out a long sigh.

Riker was still spread out on the sand, baking in the sun.

"Commander!" Rikkilä cried, and surged forward. Crusher grabbed her by the arm and pulled her back.

"He's safe," Crusher said. "At least until the tide comes back in." She squinted down at the waterline. It was definitely closer to the shore than she remembered. "Do you have your combadge?"

"Of course. They seem to be working fine—"

"Call Data and Malisson," Crusher said. "I'm going to check on Commander Riker."

Rikkilä nodded and handed over her tricorder. Crusher skittered down the dune, half holding her breath. The last thing she wanted was another communication attempt, but she was still inside her own head.

Riker's signs were all normal, his breath steady. She retreated back to the dunes, away from the beach.

"They're on their way," Rikkilä said. She frowned. "Doctor, are you okay? You look pale—"

"I'm fine. I think I know what's going on." Crusher shook her head. "At least some of it."

Rikkilä looked up at her questioningly.

"They're trying to tell us something," Crusher said.

"What?"

"There's a life-form on the beach," Crusher said. "I think it's tied to those fossils you found our first day here." That first day felt like a lifetime ago.

"What?" Rikkilä shook her head. "But the scans—"

"Showed nothing, I know." Crusher stared off at the purple line of the horizon. "It doesn't register as a life-form on our scanners, I think. But it's *talking* to us."

Rikkilä didn't say anything, just listened.

"I thought of it as reprogramming, because the technology was affected, but I think—" Crusher stopped, looked at Rikkilä. "When you passed out on the beach," she said, "do you remember what you saw?"

Rikkilä frowned. "I didn't *see* anything. I just— Everything went dark. I was overwhelmed." She frowned. "It was later. That night. We all had the same dream. Drowning—"

"Yes," Crusher said, her pulse quickening. "You all said that. A shared dream."

Rikkilä tilted her head.

"When I left the beach," Crusher said, "I moved closer to the station—I saw *code*."

"It's trying to tell us something," Rikkilä whispered.

"*They're* trying to tell us something," Crusher corrected. "I think—I think they didn't see us as intelligent until there were more of us. And with the computer—" She shook her head. "They thought our technology was sentient too."

Why did it talk to her on the beach? It had never communicated with just two people before.

It learned about us, Crusher realized.

"Wait here for the others," Crusher told Rikkilä. "I have to go down to the beach—I have to test something."

"What?" Rikkilä cried. "Doctor, are you sure—"

But Crusher had already skittered up to the dunes. It had spoken to her. And she was going to find a way to speak back.

33

———

They were getting nowhere.

Derak had returned with news from Bryt. "He's terribly sorry," Derak said, bowing a little, "but even with the cloak, Bryt feels ten thousand is simply *too* low." Derak's eyes glittered. "But he is very interested in that *mek'leth*."

"You have been told no," Worf growled.

Derak held up his hands apologetically. "Of course, I understand. But unless you have something else to offer . . ."

"This cloak is a masterpiece!" Virox cried, gliding over to Worf. The Romulan was still lounging in the corner, tapping listlessly on a padd. "You won't find anything else like it in the galaxy. Why, there were only three Klingons who could have *produced* this kind of stitching."

Worf stiffened as Virox pulled on the cloak, running her fingers over the rough fabric, forcing Derak to look. Troi could see Worf was close to losing his temper.

Eventually, Derak relented. "Madam, I will take this information back to Bryt. But I can't make any promises."

Derak backed away, vanishing into the depths of the building. Virox unleashed her frustration. *We're losing.*

"Your plan isn't going to work."

Thuvetha dropped her padd into a pocket and kicked her legs back up on the table.

"You could have surrendered the treasures," Worf said. "And saved us the trouble."

"If you'd offered *me* the latinum, I would have taken it." Thuvetha raised an eyebrow. "And I wouldn't have even asked you to throw in that replicated Klingon cloak."

"We don't negotiate with thieves," Worf said.

Thuvetha burst into laughter. "That's what you're doing here."

Worf glowered at her.

"You know how culturally important the items are," Troi said.

The Romulan sprung up and prowled around the edge of the room, kicking at the door sharply when she passed it. "I need to stop working for Ferengi," she muttered. "They have no honor."

"What would a Romulan know about honor?" Worf snapped.

"Enough to know you should honor your contracts. Bryt and I had one," Thuvetha said. "Now he's refusing to abide by it. And I will be sitting here until he does." She circled back around and kicked the door again.

Troi felt a sudden, unexpected burst of hopefulness from Worf.

The Betazoids studied their "bodyguard." Worf looked thoughtful, his brow deeply furrowed.

Thuvetha stared at them from across the room, suspicion rising off of her. "What?"

"Worf," Troi whispered, "I can sense that you've thought of something."

"Ferengi are without honor," he said.

"Glad you agree with me," Thuvetha called out.

Virox glared at her. "This conversation does not involve you."

"Then stop having it in front of me."

Worf moved to the far side of the lounge, gesturing for Virox and Troi to follow. "We can use that against them," he said. "Their lack of honor. Commander, can you sense the emotions of Ferengi?"

"Occasionally, if they're especially heightened. But I've got nothing from Derak."

"But I'm sure he would not know that," Worf said. "As some Betazoids are more adept at it."

"That's one skill I'm afraid I don't have," Virox confessed.

They were interrupted by the door sliding open. Derak stepped back into the lounge.

"I'm dreadfully sorry," he said, ignoring the Romulan's dagger-sharp glares. "But Bryt is simply *not interested* in the cloak. I'll be happy to sell you some Romulan ale, at cost, for your troubles. It appears—"

"No." Worf strode up to him, and Derak shrank back a little, his eyes wide.

"We learned from the Romulan," he barked, "that Bryt has a secret. Something no one else should know."

Derak's eyes darted over to Thuvetha. She shrugged at him.

"I don't see why that's relevant—" Derak started.

"Do you know that secret?"

Derak's mouth dropped open. "I don't—don't see why that's relevant."

Thuvetha barked out a laugh. "He doesn't know."

"Do you want to?" Worf's grin widened.

Is he doing what I think he's doing? Virox thought.

I believe so.

A sense of mirth roiled through Troi's mind. *Good for him.*

"I don't see what any of this—" Derak glanced over at Troi and Virox. "Betazoids can't read Ferengi minds."

"Dorota can," Worf said.

Troi stepped up beside Worf, saying, "I can tell that you're very interested in finding out."

Derak laughed nervously. "No." Although he sounded unsure.

Troi focused on him; years of playing poker had taught her to read tells. "You've been wanting to know a long time."

"No," Derak said too quickly.

"We both know that's a lie," Troi said.

"Fine!" Derak snapped. "I'm still not going to betray—"

"Get her close enough, and it will only cost you five strips of latinum," Worf said.

Troi felt a flash from Thuvetha. She was impressed.

"Wh-what? One slip," Derak said.

"Two," Worf countered.

Derak pulled out two slips and held them up. "Fine," he said. "What is it? The secret?"

"I need to be in much closer proximity," Troi said. "As close as you can get us."

"Just you." He looked at Worf and dropped the slips back into his jacket. "You'll get paid when I know."

Derak gestured wildly at Troi. "Come along then. I'll bring you into the antechamber. Bryt will just be one room over. Will that be close enough?"

"Yes," Troi said, even though she didn't like the idea of going back there alone.

"No funny business."

Troi looked at him, her eyes wide with innocence. "Of course not."

"Good." Derak turned over to Thuvetha. "And if I find out this is some scheme of yours—"

"I don't know these people," Thuvetha snapped. "All I want is the payment I was promised."

Derak puffed up his chest a little. "And you'll get it, when there's a buyer."

"And this buyer isn't good enough?" Thuvetha countered.

"That is none of your concern." Derak glanced over at Troi. "Shall we?"

Troi nodded. She could feel Worf's worry as she followed Derak across the room. He led her through the door, and then through the gallery.

"What's in this for you?"

"Information," she said. "The better we know our seller, the more—attractive an offer we can make."

Derak glanced over at her. "If you are working with the Romulan," he said, "it won't matter."

They had come to the far wall of the gallery: cave stone, dark and jagged and laced with delicate filigree mineral patterns.

"Why would we work with *that* Romulan?" Troi asked coyly.

"I don't know." Derak turned to the wall. "I don't know why you'd care about Bryt's secret. But I could see why the fe-male Romulan would."

"Thuvetha only wants to be fairly compensated," Troi said. It immediately sounded wrong; that wasn't how a criminal talked. But Derak didn't notice; he was busy tracing patterns into the wall with his finger. The patterns began to glow and then, to Troi's surprise, they split, and the wall opened slowly apart in jagged, uneven segments. A false wall.

The wall ground to a stop. "This way," Derak said. "Keep quiet."

Troi stepped through the opening into a narrow, dimly lit corridor. Screens set into the walls showed the outside of the compound as well as the entryway: there was the Ferengi guard who had brought them down to the VIP room, the Orion woman at the front desk, the ruins, and more Ferengi patrolling the grounds.

Derak jerked his head for Troi to follow. The corridor ended abruptly at a sliding door that Derak opened with a retinal scan. Inside was a small, cramped room, a desk with a stack of padds, and a rather large screen filled with Ferengi writing.

"He's just through that door there," Derak whispered. "What can you sense?"

Troi moved over to the door and pressed her forehead against it. She closed her eyes, took a deep breath, and concentrated.

She felt the presence in the room easily enough. She usually couldn't read Ferengi, but she knew there was one in the room—and that there was something different about him. Troi couldn't quite put her finger on it.

"Well?" Derak hissed. "What is it?"

Troi looked over at him. He shifted his weight from side to side, nervous.

"No," she whispered back.

He frowned, and Troi could sense he was weighing his options.

She focused on the presence in the room. It was undeniably Ferengi, but there was something unlike any Ferengi she had ever encountered. Something threaded through the presence. Different.

"This is taking too long," Derak snapped, and grabbed Troi's arm. His own presence flooded into her head, and suddenly the difference was illuminated, clear and sharp. Derak was male.

The Ferengi in the other room, Bryt the Baron, was a female.

Troi pulled away from the door, careful not to react, not to show her hand.

"Do you hav—"

A siren wailed out of the walls, and the room was plunged into red light. And then a voice, deep and distorted, boomed into the room.

"Derak," it snarled. "What have you done? Who is this fe-male?"

Derak moaned, covering his face with his hands. "Noooo!" he cried. "He knows you're here!" He grabbed at Troi, trying to pull her toward the exit, but she shook him off. Worf was not going to be happy with her.

"Bryt the Baron," she said into the air. "I know your secret."

Derak squawked in horror.

"Let's make a deal."

34

———

Crusher crested the dune and curled her hands into fists. The waterline had moved a little farther onto the beach, drowning the tide pools among the rocks. Riker was still stretched out on the sand.

She checked his breathing again. Still steady. Then she walked toward the slowly encroaching water. Was the entity here, in the water? Or was it in the sand? They had found traces of the fossils in both. Maybe it was in both. An organism with a cellular structure that appeared ancient when it was separated from its fellows and invisible when they were together. So unusual it had passed by unnoticed on the Federation's most advanced scanners.

A wave crashed around Crusher's stomach and she jerked her head up, realizing suddenly that she had waded out into waist-high water without realizing it.

"You're reaching out," she said, the sound of her voice reassuring, a reminder of who she was. "I'm ready to talk to you."

Another wave broke around her, knocking her slightly off balance. She steadied herself, resting her hands on the surface of the water, concentrating on the chill of it against her hot skin.

Stay grounded. Focus.

Suddenly, the ground dropped away, and she was falling through the water. Bubbles streamed out of her mouth, spiraling up around her to the water's surface that seemed light-years away. "You are not drowning." The words echoed throughout the water, so that it rippled and shimmered. Crusher pushed herself downward into the darkness below her feet. "You can breathe," she told herself. It was true, and each breath was a reminder that all this was inside her head. A dream.

Communication.

Crusher kept swimming down into the depths, telling herself over and over that she was really on the beach.

Then that's where she was. On the beach while a storm crashed wildly overhead, rain falling in sheets.

Crusher sucked in her breath. "A dream," she said, the words thudding inside her head. She turned to look down the beach and was startled to see not only Riker, but the entire team—Rikkilä, Muñoz, Solanko, Malisson, Talma. And Data. Everyone who had been affected.

They looked around, spinning in place, looking past one another. Each caught in their own versions of the dream.

Lightning arced behind the clouds.

Crusher's breath quickened. *It's working.* She concentrated on the lightning and sent it bolting down at the sand, a meter away from Riker, who jumped and tried to run. "Stay." He was back where he started.

She sent the lightning around him, spinning the sand into a circle with Riker at the center. She imagined black lines cracking across the sand, and they appeared.

And then she lost the lightning. It went off on its own, veering in her direction. Her breath caught and she remembered: *This isn't real.*

She braced her body, digging her heels deep into the sand, as the lightning raced toward her—

And stopped.

It stopped midstrike, a shiny, jagged line connecting the sand to the sky, lines fractaling out against the dark, rain-swept beach.

"Hello," Crusher whispered.

The lightning sucked down into the sand, giving it a silver, vibrant glow. The grains trembled and moved, piling on top of each other, forming legs, then hips, a torso, a head. Crusher smiled a little when she saw the sand-figure was her, the sand sliding over itself in constant motion.

The sand-figure made a barking sound. A laugh?

Crusher touched her chest. "I am Crusher. I am *one*." She pointed behind the sand-figure, to the others. "They are different. We are one, not many. But you had discovered that already, hadn't you?"

The sand-figure nodded. It understood. Crusher knew this the way you discover things in dreams.

It tilted its head, the sand still sliding in a constant flurry of movement. Then it exploded, sand glittering as it fell, coating Crusher with each fine grain. She screamed in surprise, and brushed the sand away. It fell to the ground, inert.

"Yes, we are separate," she said, trying to picture the words, trying to shape the dream so that the life-form would understand. "We are alive. We don't have to be together."

The sand drew itself back up, this time into two forms: one in her shape, one in Data's.

"One," said the sand-Data, in the same way.

"Data?" Crusher whispered. "Do you want to speak with Data—"

The two sand forms dissolved into a whirlwind of glittering light. It wrapped around Crusher, pulling her upward, away from the beach, toward the black storm clouds. She felt herself pulling apart like taffy, blending in with the life-form—life-forms. She could feel their voices inside her head. Images. Impressions. They lived in the sand and the water and the air, billions of them, tiny diatoms swirling in a constant, surging movement. And *dreaming*. This dreamscape was their civilization. She listened, and as she let herself sink into their movement, she saw it: a city glittering with glass and light, thrumming with bright music. A city wasn't what they had experienced. What they experienced, she couldn't understand. They were using her own memories.

Welcome, they were saying. *Welcome. Another One.*

Crusher drifted down, among the tops of buildings, their sides glittering like diamonds. A shared dream. "Was this what you were trying to show us?"

Yes. It wasn't a word so much as an understanding of affirmation. *Welcome. Welcome.*

Crusher lifted her gaze to the sky, which was not violet but the brilliant blue of Caldos. She wondered what they saw.

And then, the sky began to shift and roil until it was an ocean, dark and dotted with millions of tiny lights. Suddenly, the city below was sand and rocks filled with glowing, brilliant swirls. Crusher understood she was seeing a tiny glimpse of their dream.

She drifted downward and landed in the sand, beside a tide pool brimming with multilegged creatures scrabbling over the rocks, tiny flecks of light darting like fish. Then she looked closer and saw the creatures were made of other, smaller creatures, compressed together so that their many legs propelled them through the shallow water. The creatures of light moved in tandem, flickering to some internal rhythm Crusher couldn't hear.

"If I separated any of you from the others," she said, "you'd die. That's what you were showing me earlier?"

Affirmation. One of the knots of multilegged creatures skittered out of the tide pool and balanced on a rock, eye level with Crusher. It said in her voice, "You are one mind, alone. The others? Not here in our place."

"Where are they?" Crusher asked.

"Dead, we thought." The creatures teetered sideways, fell, and scattered across the rocks in a liquid movement, like water. Then they surged back into a knot. "But really—lonely."

"No," Crusher said.

"Even connected minds, lonely." The creatures unwound themselves into a bridge across the tide pool and joined with another knot of creatures, who surged up, twisted around the first knot until they were indistinguishable. They're all indistinguishable, Crusher reminded herself. They only looked like shiny black sea urchins and glittering spots of light because that was how her brain interpreted them.

"Connected minds?" she said, watching as the new knot of creatures splashed into the tide pool and swam furiously around, gathering the light flecks like motes of dust to a feather.

"Yes." Her voice, again, but this time from the light swirling over the sand. It coiled around her shoulders like a scarf. "Strange minds. Stranger than yours. Connected but separate."

The equipment in the station

"You tried to invite our technology here," she said. "The replicator, the station computer—"

"We found your minds, full of images, like ours." The thread of lights settled into the nape of Crusher's neck; there was a warmth to it, like a tiny candle flame. "Too few, at first. Those minds dead. Then more came—but still not connected."

That is why the attacks—the *communications*—hadn't occurred before. There hadn't been enough people.

"We found the connected minds. Bright minds, filled with images. And we found the one mind."

"Data," Crusher breathed.

"Bright mind, but lonely. Not dead. Strange! Tried to speak. To know more."

They *had* been trying to speak with Data. The one mind that didn't fit into their understanding of the world, and they tried to reach out to him.

"Why'd you try to speak to me?" Crusher asked. "Even though I was a one?"

"Curious. One mind not dead? A test."

More light had come swirling around her, and Crusher felt a splatter of rain across her cheek. Odd, that they would imagine rain.

But then she saw raindrops fall into the multilegged creature, and *become* multilegged creatures, and she understood they were showing themselves as rain too.

"Our minds," she said, "are different. Not just because we aren't connected." She took a deep breath. "To see this place, to hear you, we have to sleep."

The light uncoiled itself and soaked up the rain, and Crusher had the sense that the entities did not understand.

"We rest, retreat into our minds. That's how I'm here now," she explained.

"Bodies drift on sand," the entities said. "Like ours."

Crusher pressed her mouth into a flat smile. "They sleep. The connected minds, our technology, it is broken." She hesitated. "Dead."

A surge of panic rose up from the entities, and the world turned dark and stormy. Crusher felt the entity's panic. Regret.

"Stop communication with the connected minds," she said. "We can repair the connected minds."

The entities all swirled together, light and rain shimmering into an indistinguishable mist.

"Bring back the dead?" The question was asked with a surge of fear.

"Only them," she told them. She wondered if they rested. Most biological life-forms they had encountered needed sleep. Perhaps these life-forms, who created entire worlds inside their shared minds, lived in dreams.

"The ones." The chittering arthropods in the tide pool splashed across the sand. "Even the strange one. No communication. You communicate. Why you?"

Crusher took a deep breath. "I learned. I will share. We will communicate. We will speak. That's how my people share their minds."

"Tell them welcome?" the entities said. "Welcome."

"I will tell them." Kota could never be a colony. Even this conversation could be considered a Prime Directive violation, but she had been given no choice.

The entities swirled around her, and she felt a sense of warmth, of comfort. Before there was confusion, sickness, and panic.

"Show them ours," the life-form said. "Can you show?"

"Yes," Crusher said, the words for what she saw floating into her mind: the beach, the tide pool, the constant motion.

"They cannot add," the life-form said. "Show. Be like you. Then can add."

Crusher smiled a little. No one would be adding anything to this place. It was not theirs.

"It is," the life-form said, "sharing our mind."

Crusher's smile deepened. "Thank you."

The life-form seemed satisfied. They lifted up, each tiny creature glittering as it floated toward the blackened sky.

The rocks lifted up, the water left in the ocean. The rain fell up. Everything receded into the black storm clouds. The world became brighter and brighter and—

Beverly Crusher opened her eyes.

Her face was hot from the sun, but her feet were cold. Water splashed up around her legs.

She sat up, pushing against the side of the dune, blinking. The tide had come in, lilac water turning plum as it stirred up the sediment.

She scrambled to her feet, splashing sea foam.

"Finally! We were starting to worry."

Riker's voice was clear, strong, sure. Crusher whirled around and found him sliding down the side of the dune. His face was red, his uniform coated with sand.

"You're okay," she said.

Riker nodded.

A shadow moved across the dune; it was Data. "Are you all right, Doctor?"

"Fine. How are you?" Crusher was reaching for her tricorder, but it wasn't there. Riker laughed.

"I already got checked out by Ensign Rikkilä."

"Did she find anything?" Crusher squinted up at Commander Riker.

Riker shook his head. "No. Although I've got some bad news— the station came down while you were out."

Crusher took a deep breath. "That's fine. We can scavenge the tech we need."

Riker frowned.

Crusher started climbing up the dune. "I know what caused it," she said, and then she told Riker and Data everything she had discovered.

The rest of the team were pacing around in the sandy strip where the grass was sparse. When Rikkilä saw Crusher, she let out a whoop and started racing toward the edge of the dune.

"They were attempting to communicate using me," Data said.

"They were," Crusher said, just as Rikkilä reached the top of the dune.

"I'm so glad you're all right!"

"I'm fine." Crusher smiled. "We're all fine." Then she turned to

Data. "You were their introduction to the concept of the singular. But I think they were interested in communicating with all of us."

"So everything that's been happening . . ." Riker started.

"Communication," Crusher said.

"Who are they?" Rikkilä asked.

"They don't have a name," Crusher said. "They don't have a spoken language. They communicate through dreams."

Rikkilä frowned with confusion.

"Doctor," Riker said, "the illness, the technological breakdowns, that was all caused by these life-forms creating *dreams*?"

"A shared dream. It didn't happen before to the science team because they didn't have enough members. Once our away team beamed down, the numbers were right. They're a hive mind." She tried to find the right words. "They live inside their minds."

"And they're down there"—Rikkilä pointed down at the beach—"or their physical forms are. Right?"

Crusher nodded. "As best as I can figure, they were intrigued by Data during that initial visit to the beach. When we brought back the samples, they used that as an opportunity to attempt to communicate." She thought for a moment. "I'm fairly certain those fossils you found—they weren't fossils at all. They were isolated entities that had gone dormant."

"The scans did not pick up on them," Data said, "because of their unusual structure. We have never encountered anything like it before."

"Exactly," Crusher said.

Data stepped to the edge of the dune and slid down. Crusher joined him.

"Doctor," he said. "I am glad to see that you are well."

"Thank you, Data. I could say the same thing about you." Crusher watched the waves. "Can I ask you a question?"

"Of course."

"What did *you* see, when you were sleeping?"

"I was not sleeping," Data said. "I was merely in a—"

Crusher stopped him. "What did you see?"

"I—" Data paused. "I saw this beach. This ocean. I saw—" He lifted his eyes to the sky. "I saw the *Enterprise*."

"The *Enterprise*?" Nothing from her life had shown up in her "dream." She had only seen the life of the hive mind. Their world, their thoughts, their message.

"Data," Crusher said. She slipped her arm in his and felt him jolt in surprise.

"Doctor, what is the matter?"

"Nothing." Crusher looked up at the sky. Commander Beverly Crusher, Chief Medical Officer of the *Starship Enterprise*, had made first contact with a new life-form.

35

—◆—

Derak offered stammered apologies to the air.

"Derak," Bryt demanded. *"Who is this? What have you done?"*

"The buyer interested in Lots 489 to 491," he cried out. "She tricked me!"

"Bryt," Troi said, "let me speak to you." She looked at Derak. "I don't want him to profit from what I have to say."

"You tricked me," Derak said.

"I'm sure there's a Rule of Acquisition that applies."

"What do you know about the Rules?" Derak hissed.

"Bryt," Troi said, "you can talk to me, or I can talk to him."

The siren stopped, but the room was still stained by bloodred light. "You bargain better than I expected."

Troi said, "Let me speak to you face-to-face. We have—a lot in common."

A burst of feedback erupted out of the speaker; Troi took it as evidence that Bryt had deciphered her meaning.

"Derak," Bryt said, the distorted voice booming through the room. *"Leave us."*

"Baron!" Derak said. "Are you sure?"

"Get out!"

Derak eyed Troi nervously. "You *lied*," he snarled.

Troi smiled sweetly. "Everything's fair in war and business."

"That is not a Rule!"

Bryt's voice was strained, even with the distortion. *"Now!"*

280 CASSANDRA ROSE CLARKE

Derak gave an annoyed little growl and slunk out of the room, glaring backward over his shoulder at Troi. She gave him a satisfied little wave.

As soon as the door slid shut behind him, the red lights dimmed.

"Well?" said Bryt.

"You're fe-male," Troi said calmly.

Then there was a soft *click* followed by the sound of an opening door, not the door that Troi had come in through.

"Let's talk," Bryt said, her voice still distorted. *"Face-to-face."*

Troi moved forward cautiously. The door opened into a sort of foyer, a small round room decorated with items like the ones in the gallery.

Another door opened, leading into a luxurious sitting room. A sweet, dark scent wafted out. *Hallyon flowers.* She'd only had the chance to smell them once. The flowers were notoriously difficult to grow, but she would never forget that scent, like brown sugar and fire.

She stepped quickly through the foyer and then moved into the main sitting room. The lighting inside was dim, the furniture dark and heavy. The walls were lined with shelves, filled with actual books and pots of Hallyon flowers. At the far end of the room was a massive, glittering crystal, lights strung up to catch the angles in it and make the crystal gleam. It took Troi a moment to realize the crystal was actually the wall of the cavern.

In the middle of all this was a massive desk, and sitting at the desk was a slight, unmoving figure.

"Bryt the Baron?" Troi said, moving deeper into the room.

"How'd you know?" Her real voice was soft and mellifluous. She lifted her head and Troi caught the glint of long, gold chains she wore draped from her lobes—much smaller than male Ferengi ears.

"You felt different." Troi stepped closer, and she was able to get a better glimpse of Bryt's face: her brow knitted with determination, her eyes fierce.

"I thought Betazoids couldn't read Ferengi," she said.

"We can't generally, but sometimes we can get vague impressions. I could tell yours was different." Troi stopped a few paces from the desk. There was nowhere to sit, so she stood awkwardly before Bryt, who glared up at her.

"I was so careful. I knew I shouldn't have let you and that other one in." She was clothed, another break with custom. Her purple robes rustled as she walked around the desk. "I suppose you think you can get the lots you were interested in"—Bryt sneered—"for *free*."

Troi looked down at Bryt. When she'd beamed down, the last thing she'd expected to find was a Ferengi woman earning profit.

"What are you doing here?" Troi asked.

Bryt blinked in surprise. "Trying to make a profit. Why are *you* here?" She leaned forward accusingly. "Do you even have the latinum?"

"You're not here *just* to earn profit," Troi observed.

Bryt's eyes widened. "Damn."

"You know you can ask for refugee status in the Federation. You wouldn't be the first Ferengi to do so."

"Ferengi *fe-male*," snapped Bryt. "The Federation?" She shook her head in disgust. "No, it's better here, at the fringes."

"You're doing something else here," Troi said.

Bryt leaned against her desk. "Who are you, really? Tell me the truth."

"Lieutenant Commander Deanna Troi of the Federation *Starship Enterprise*."

Bryt groaned. "Oh, that's the end of it," she cried. "Wrap it up, fe-males, we're done."

"Fe-males?" Troi said. "There are more of you?"

Bryt glared at Troi. "Yes," she said, drawing herself up. "Fe-males make up more than half of the Ferengi population." She slouched back down with a sigh.

Troi found herself liking Bryt. "You're doing all this in secret," she said. "Understandable."

"Not just me." Bryt shook her head. "There are dozens of us. I have fe-male partners scattered all over this sector." Bryt straightened her shoulders and spoke in a stage whisper. "Fe-males tell other fe-males, 'Go to Bryt the Baron. He'll get you started.'"

Troi let out a gasp. "You—you're *giving* profit to other Ferengi females."

"No! Absolutely not!" Bryt looked horrified. "They work *for* me. I set them up, and they do business on my behalf. They become Bryt the Baron. *I'm* all over this sector." She fixed a dark glare on Troi. "I take a percentage of any profit they earn."

Ferengi and profit. Troi really didn't understand it. But she understood wanting to be all you could be.

"Someday there will be a Grand Nagus who will change everything," Bryt said. "I wanted a head start. And if some fe-males have a head start too—" She spread her hands wide.

Troi grinned.

"It's not funny."

"Why did you want Xiomara's treasures?"

"They're *treasures*. I can sell treasures for a profit."

"I see," Troi said. "You know the treasures don't have any intrinsic value."

Bryt narrowed her eyes. "What are you saying?"

"Once you know the history behind them," Troi said, "you'd know that they don't." She shrugged. "An old serving platter? A beat-up urn? A worn spoon?"

"Their history. That's their value," Bryt said. "You wouldn't be here otherwise."

"Exactly." Troi shifted her weight. "Those treasures aren't worth much in latinum, but they are tremendously important to Betazed, which means they're important to the Federation."

"That makes no sense."

"It doesn't matter if it makes sense to you," Troi said. "They're culturally significant, and Betazed is clamoring to get them back." She leaned forward, pressing her hands on the desk. "The Starfleet flagship is currently in orbit of your prime marketplace. If I make one hail, in just five hours I could have five starships checking every vessel that enters or leaves this system."

"You wouldn't," Bryt said.

"No sellers would come close to this place." Troi smiled. "And all the lovely things in your VIP room—"

"What about them?"

"Are any of them stolen?"

From the expression on Bryt's face, the answer was clear.

"*Enterprise* security teams will confiscate all of them and check their provenance," Troi said. "You have what, ten guards? An Orion receptionist? We know about Orion females, and we have enough female security officers to ensure the objects' safety. As for your guards—" Troi shrugged. "We got one to turn on you for just two strips of latinum."

"Enough! I understand!" snapped Bryt. "Why aren't you making that hail right now?" She studied Troi. "Not *very* Starfleet of you to toy with me like this."

"I'm not toying with you," Troi said. "I can appreciate what you're doing here. Earning profit when your society tells you that you can't."

Bryt rolled her eyes.

"Here's the deal: if you give me the treasures, we'll take the Romulan away for the theft. And, if my captain agrees, we will give you a twenty-four-hour head start. The *Enterprise* will be otherwise engaged, returning the items and the thief to Betazed."

Bryt snorted. "And where's your captain?"

"He's here in the compound." Troi stood up straight. "My Klingon 'guard.'"

"You have to be joking," Bryt said.

"I'm not. It'll take five minutes for me to guarantee your head start."

"Very well." Bryt stepped up to Troi, her wrists pressed together, her two hands forming a cup. "Twenty-four hours."

Troi copied the gesture. "It's a deal."

36

A chime sounded on the door to Jean-Luc Picard's quarters at Isszon Temple. He had been taking a much-needed break after spending the bulk of the day reassuring both Betazoids and other High Guests that the *Enterprise* was more than up to the task of retrieving the three treasures.

The chime rang out again, followed by Lwaxana Troi's trilling voice: "Jean-Luc! I know you're in there."

Picard rubbed his forehead.

"Just a moment," he said, steeling himself as he strode across the room. When the door slid open, Lwaxana beamed up at him, as radiant as she had been the night before, when the celebration was underway and the treasures were still safely in possession of their Keepers. She bustled inside, her gown billowing around her. "Commander Rusina just received word from the *Enterprise*," she said brightly. "The treasures have been recovered."

"Oh, that's excellent news," Picard said. "I take it the *Enterprise* is on her way back now?"

Lwaxana nodded, her gaze sweeping around the room. "I am certain Rusina will want you to attend the debriefing with Mr. Worf—who I heard did *marvelously* as captain, by the way."

"As I knew he would."

Lwaxana spun around to face Picard, the fabric of her gown twirling out dramatically. Picard felt a moment of tight-chested terror, certain she was going to fling herself on him. But she only smiled. "But as Betazoid Ambassador to the Federation, I wanted to come here and thank you personally."

Picard stiffened. "I'm afraid I had very little to do with—"

"I don't mean the retrieval of the treasures." Lwaxana gestured dismissively with her hand. "I want to thank you for the wonderful job you did of calming the guests."

Picard was unsure how to respond.

"I know you wanted to accompany the *Enterprise* when she set out to retrieve the treasures," Lwaxana continued, "but I was so grateful that you stayed to assist. We had a temple full of panicked, confused people, and you brought *such* a sense of assurance to the proceedings."

Picard hadn't felt as if he'd been of any assistance. In truth, he'd felt useless, particularly after the disrupted call from the away team on Kota. Stranded, even: moored without his ship.

"Thank you," Lwaxana said, pressing one graceful hand to her chest.

"You're welcome," Picard said, blinking through his surprise.

"*Captain Picard?*" An unfamiliar voice came through on his combadge. "*This is Lieutenant Asah with the Betazed Security team. A hail has come through for you. From Kota.*"

Lwaxana looked up at him. "Your away team! Remember what I told you—sometimes, we need to fake our telepathy."

Picard was already moving toward the hailing station in his quarters. "Ambassador, if you'll excuse me—"

"Oh, of course. I am certain you will hear only good news on the other side of that hail."

Picard nodded, impatient. As soon as Lwaxana let herself out through the door, he switched on the hail, relieved to see Will Riker's face looking back at him. Riker was outside, grass rolling out behind him, a violet sky overhead.

"Number One," he said. "Status report."

Riker grinned. "All members of the away team are safe, sir."

Picard let out a long, relieved breath.

"We're no longer in need of immediate extraction," Riker continued. "Although, as you can see, we did lose the station. But we can manage."

We all need a reminder sometimes that we can exist without those things we take for granted.

Picard couldn't help but smile.

37

Beverly Crusher stepped out from the tent the crew had erected. The station had disintegrated completely by this point. The equipment was scattered throughout the camp: the lab materials and, most crucially, the replicator.

"Are you ready, Doctor?" Data stepped out behind her, activating his combadge.

She smiled. "Maybe we'll get it this time."

Twenty-eight hours earlier, according to Data's internal clock, she had been dreaming on the beach, communicating with the Kotan life-forms. The team had successfully powered up the replicator. All of the lab equipment was working, and safety checks had been done on all the phasers. They had successfully replicated fresh, cold water, which the team gulped down. The mysterious life-forms had retreated from all their technology.

As the sun sank into the horizon, turning the light long and hazy, Crusher and Data worked on compiling a baseline for the universal translator. It was clear the entities understood technology, but they wanted to make sure the universal translator didn't collapse under the weight of the life-forms' communications. The camp was less than private, and when Commander Riker caught them, it was Data who argued to ask for forgiveness, not permission.

Eventually exhaustion overtook Crusher as it had the rest of the team. The doctor crawled into her sleeping bag and slipped into a dreamless slumber.

• • •

There was no wind the next morning, and the grass against Crusher's and Data's uniforms created a rustling sound. "It was difficult," Data said, "to determine a baseline on how to handle the Kotans' noncomprehension of *one*."

"If it doesn't work," Crusher said, "we won't be forced into a dream."

They reached the dunes. The wind picked up a little, but the waves were calm, rolling gently beneath the violet sky. The tide was out, and among the black stones, the tide pool glittered.

Crusher nodded at Data and gave him a big smile. "I'm going in," she said.

"I will be here," Data said.

The doctor went down the side of the dune. She walked over to the rocks and crouched down beside one of the tide pools. Unlike the tide pool in her dream, this one appeared empty, the water clear enough that Crusher could see there was nothing in it except for the rough walls of the stone.

She tapped her combadge twice, activating the Kota UT package. "Hello? Are you here?"

The waves answered, crashing against the shore.

"I want to be able to talk to you," she said, "in our language."

The combadge chirped. A sound rushed out of it. It was the sound of roaring winds.

Then, in the rise and fall of those winds, "*Hello, ghost-friend.*"

The combadge sputtered and then fell off her uniform, landing facedown in the sand.

She scooped it up and turned around and waved to Data. "It worked!" she shouted. "Just for a few seconds, but it worked!"

She trudged across the sand, kicking it in front of her as she did.

"I think the Kotans blew it out," she said, holding it up to Data. "I will have to work on that," he said.

For a moment, they stood side by side, watching the waves. Then through Data's combadge: *"The* Enterprise *is here,"* Riker said. *"Time to go home."*

ACKNOWLEDGMENTS

There are *so many* people who have helped me get to a place in my career where I could have the opportunity to write a *Star Trek* novel. I am certain to miss some of them, but know that I am grateful to everyone who has shown me support in my writing over the years.

A special thanks goes out to Holly Lyn Walrath, who offered feedback on my initial outline and commiseration during the revision process. As always, thank you to my beloved writing community: Amanda Cole, Chun Lee, Kevin O'Neill, Michael Glazner, David Young, Bonnie Jo Stuffleheam, Stina Leicht, Bobby Mathews, and the many others who have helped me through the years.

Thank you to Ed Schlesinger for giving me the opportunity to write for *Star Trek*, Margaret Clark for her excellent advice and feedback on the manuscript, and Stacia Decker, for being an agent extraordinaire.

Finally, thank you to my parents, for their tireless love and support.

ABOUT THE AUTHOR

Cassandra Rose Clarke's novels have been finalists for the Philip K. Dick Award, the *Romantic Times* Reviewers' Choice Award, and YALSA's Best Fiction for Young Adults. Her poetry has placed second in the Rhysling Awards, been nominated for the Pushcart Prize, and appeared in *Strange Horizons*, *Star*Line*, and elsewhere.

Cassandra graduated in 2006 from the University of St. Thomas with a B.A. in English, and two years later she completed her master's degree in creative writing at the University of Texas at Austin. In 2010, she attended the Clarion West Writer's Workshop in Seattle, where she was a recipient of the Susan C. Petrey Clarion Scholarship Fund.